Praise for

MY LAST
CONTINENT

"*My Last Continent* feels refreshingly different, vivid, and immediate. Midge Raymond has an extraordinary gift for description that puts the reader bang in the middle of the action, bang in the middle of its dangerous and endangered world. Her clean, spare prose pulls us irresistibly into the story and the wider issues it raises. She is clearly a writer in command of her craft."

—M. L. Stedman, author of
The Light Between Oceans

"A luminescent, double-layered love story: It's a love story about nature, in which a woman is drawn repeatedly to Antarctica and the vulnerable creatures who make their lives there. And it's a love story about two people who have found in the remote ice the perfect numbing refuge from their pain."

—*The Oregonian*

"[A] meditative romance . . . Raymond has shown us a continent worth visiting."

—*The New York Times Book Review*

"There is a romance about faraway, desperate places, about isolation, about ice and snow. Add penguins and you have Midge Raymond's elegant *My Last Continent*, a love story about the Antarctic and the creatures, humans included, who are at home there. Half adventure, half elegy, and wholly recommended."

— Karen Joy Fowler, author of *We Are All Completely Beside Ourselves*

"A sensitive exploration of how even the smallest action can ripple through an ecosystem — seemingly impenetrable, but as fragile as the human heart."

— *Minneapolis Star Tribune*

"You turn the pages quickly, caught up in the not-of-this-world drama of it all: Despite the heat of the central duo's connection, this is a world of ice, where warm hearts struggle to thrive. . . . Raymond shines in capturing a shivery sense of place, in taking us somewhere most of us will never go. . . . Romantic? Absolutely. Ominous? That, too."

— *The Seattle Times*

"A gripping love story . . . [A] captivating tale of love, loss, and redemption."

— Goodreads, "Debut Author Snapshot"

"At once a high-stakes romance and a cautionary tale about the precariousness of this pristine polar world, Raymond's masterful debut contemplates the ecological and emotional dangers that lurk within and without uncharted waters."

— *Booklist*

"*My Last Continent* is an original and entirely authentic love story. It is a love triangle with Antarctica as the third party, literally and metaphorically. Midge Raymond takes us, physically and emotionally, into an unfamiliar world—a world that has much to teach us. She deftly interweaves a compelling drama with a gentle and subtle love story. It's a mature novel, one that recognizes that love is seldom simple or exclusive, and that the things that bring us together can also keep us apart."

—Graeme Simsion, bestselling author of
The Rosie Project and *The Rosie Effect*

"Gorgeously written, suspenseful literary fiction."

—*Book Riot*

"An atmospheric tale of love discovered, and losses endured, in Antarctica . . . The unpredictability of the splendors and terrors of life at the southern pole creates a backdrop of foreboding entirely appropriate for the story's cinematic resolution [and] the authentic rendering of the setting distinguishes Raymond's novel from other stories of love in perilous times and places."

—*Kirkus Reviews*

"Atmospheric and adventurous . . . The story and vivid writing will keep readers glued to the pages."

—*Library Journal*

"*My Last Continent* is a complicated love story and an education in the plight of penguins in Antarctica, showcasing the beauty and terror unique to one of the world's most remote terrains. . . . Raymond skillfully captures the stunning and singular landscape and its special inhabitants."

—*Publishers Weekly*

"*My Last Continent*'s unique scenario is as refreshing as it is poignant. . . . A completely absorbing and sobering tale [that] leaves you with a far greater appreciation of a searingly beautiful world, whose fate we are squandering so casually."

—*The Independent* (UK)

"*My Last Continent* is a welcome addition to the growing catalogue of climate change fiction. It is a bold and informative investigation about the meaning and labor of love at the end of the world."

—*The Goose*

"Beautiful, vivid . . . Equal parts love story, ecological disaster, and thriller, *My Last Continent* is both atmospheric and accomplished."

—*The Summerset Review*

For Joann

MY LAST
CONTINENT

A NOVEL

MIDGE
RAYMOND

With all good wishes —

SCRIBNER
NEW YORK   LONDON   TORONTO   SYDNEY   NEW DELHI

SCRIBNER
An Imprint of Simon & Schuster, Inc.
1230 Avenue of the Americas
New York, NY 10020

First Scribner trade paperback edition June 2017

For information about special discounts for bulk purchases, please contact Simon & Schuster Special Sales at 1-866-506-1949 or business@simonandschuster.com.

The Simon & Schuster Speakers Bureau can bring authors to your live event. For more information or to book an event, contact the Simon & Schuster Speakers Bureau at 1-866-248-3049 or visit our website at www.simonspeakers.com.

Interior design by Kyle Kabel

Manufactured in the United States of America

3   5   7   9   10   8   6   4

The Library of Congress has cataloged the hardcover edition as follows:

Raymond, Midge.
My last continent : a novel / by Midge Raymond. — First Scribner hardcover edition.
pages ; cm
I. Title.
PS3618.A9855M9 2016
813'.6—dc23
2015033592

ISBN 978-1-5011-2470-9
ISBN 978-1-5011-2471-6 (pbk)
ISBN 978-1-5011-2472-3 (ebook)

For John

My Last
Continent

AFTERWARDS

As I lead tourists from the Zodiacs up rocky trails to the penguin colonies, I notice how these visitors—stuffed into oversize, puffy red parkas—walk like the penguins themselves: eyes to the snowy ground, arms out for balance. They're as determined as the penguins to get where they're going—but they're not here to ask about the birds, about these islands. They don't seem interested in the Adélies' declining populations or the gentoos' breeding habits or the chinstraps' dwindling food sources in the Antarctic.

Instead they ask about the *Australis*.

How many people drowned? they ask. *How many are still missing? How many bodies now belong eternally to the sea?*

None are questions I want to answer.

Back in 1979, a sightseeing tour, Air New Zealand Flight 901 out of Christchurch, crashed into the side of Mt. Erebus in southwestern Antarctica. More than two hundred and fifty people died that day. It was the worst disaster in the history of this continent—until five years ago. Until the *Australis*.

According to records, we know that both crafts—the plane and the ship—went down due to navigational error. Each was felled by what its crew knew existed but was unable to see, or chose not to see.

Sometimes I wonder whether some other force is at hand—something equally obscured, warning us that none of us should be in Antarctica at all.

We cross sharp-edged hills near penguin nests, the rocks covered with pinkish red guano that seeps into the snow like blood. At this time of year—late January, the middle of the austral summer—the birds are fat, their chicks tucked under their chests; they lean over to warm and protect the downy gray-and-white bodies as they watch us pass. The Adélies stare at us with their white-rimmed eyes; the chinstraps look serious in their painted helmets; the gentoos twist their heads, raising orange beaks into the air to keep us in their sights.

More than anything, the birds remind me of everything I've lost. And somehow, this only makes me more determined to save them. And so I return.

I'd prefer not to answer the tourists' questions about the *Australis*, but I do. This is my job, after all—I work not only for the penguins but for the boat that brings me here every season.

So I tell them.

I tell them I was here when the massive cruise ship found herself trapped and sinking in a windswept cove of pack ice. I tell them that the ship was too big and too fragile to be so far south, and that my ship, the *Cormorant*, was the closest one and still a full day's travel away. I tell them that, below the Antarctic Circle, the phrase *search and rescue* has little practical meaning. There is simply no one around to rescue you.

I tell them that 715 passengers and crew died that day. I don't tell them that 2 of those who died were rescuers, whose fates tragically intertwined. Most want to hear about the victims, not the rescuers. They don't yet know that we are one and the same.

ONE WEEK BEFORE SHIPWRECK

The Drake Passage
(59°39'S, 61°56'W)

From the motion of the M/S *Cormorant*, it feels as though we've hit fifteen-foot swells. This is nothing for our captain, who chugged through thirty-foot waves a little more than two weeks ago on a previous trip through the Drake Passage, where the Southern Ocean, the Pacific Ocean, and the Atlantic meet and toss boats around like toys. Though the *Cormorant* will make the voyage six times this season, it will never become routine. The Drake never gives the same experience twice.

I'm not nearly as seasick as I pretend to be, but the downtime helps me ease into my role as tour guide. Because 90 percent of the passengers are sick in their cabins and will remain sequestered for the next two days, our expedition leader, Glenn, doesn't mind if I hide out in the crew's quarters until we reach the South Shetlands.

The company's flagship vessel, the *Cormorant*, was built the same year I was born, nearly forty years ago. While I'm five foot nine and single, she is just shy of three hundred feet long and carries one hundred passengers and fifty crew members. We are both built for the ice—I've got a thick skin and a penchant for solitude; she's got stabilizers and a reinforced hull, allowing us to slip into the tiny inlets of the Antarctic peninsula and, weather permitting, to go south of the Antarctic Circle—something all visitors want to check off their lists of things to do before they die.

The promotional brochures for this cruise highlight not only the wildlife but the onboard experts like me. I'm one of six naturalists on this voyage—a group of wildlife experts and historians hired by Glenn to educate the passengers on penguins, whales, seabirds, ice, and the stories of the continent itself. While most naturalists will remain on board for the full two-week journey, several times each season two of us will disembark at one of the peninsula's uninhabited islands, make camp, and gather data for the Antarctic Penguins Project. After another two weeks, when the ship returns with a new load of passengers, we'll join them for the journey back to civilization. While I'm on the ship, I'm on call, available to answer questions, pilot Zodiacs (the small but sturdy inflatable boats that take us from ship to shore), herd tourists, spot whales, and give presentations in the lounge after dinner. This part I love—introducing the continent as it was once introduced to me. The part I dread involves the questions that venture far beyond the realms of flora and fauna.

At least once on every voyage, someone will ask me how I do it—how I can live for weeks or months at a time down here, going from ship to tent, dealing with the harsh conditions, spending so much time alone. They will ask whether

I'm married, whether I have kids—questions I rarely hear asked of a male naturalist. But because I want to keep this gig, I will bite my tongue and smile. I'll tell them I know penguin breeding habits well, but human connections are another thing entirely and are especially complicated when it comes to the Antarctic. I'll offer up a bit of the continent's history, overflowing with stories of love gone wrong: The polar scientist Jean-Baptiste Charcot returned home after wintering on the ice to find that his wife had left him. Robert Falcon Scott, who died on the continent, never even knew about the rumors that his wife had strayed while he was away. And of course I have stories of my own, from my complicated and still-evolving history of love on the ice, but these I'll never share.

The brochures also highlight the fine dining, the fitness center and sauna, the library, the business alcove with its computer terminals and satellite phone—all the things that remind our passengers that they're never far from the comforts of home. These passengers can't understand that I prefer a sleeping bag on hard icy ground to soft sheets in a heated cabin. That I'd rather eat half-frozen food than a five-course meal. That I look forward to every moment away from the ship, when I hear the voices of penguins and petrels and feel farther than ever from the world above the sixtieth parallel.

WHEN I WAKE early the next morning, the other bunk in my cabin is empty. My roommate, Amy, must be up on deck, looking for albatross and petrels. Amy Lindstrom is the ship's undersea specialist, but she's just as fascinated with the creatures hovering above the water—and the Drake offers glimpses of birds we won't see farther south.

I should drag myself out of bed, too, but instead I prop myself up on one elbow and watch a wandering albatross just outside the porthole above my bunk. I'm always mesmerized by these birds who dominate the skies over the Southern Ocean; they spend months, sometimes years, at sea, circumnavigating this part of the planet without ever touching down on land. I observe the albatross for ten minutes, and he doesn't once flap his wings. He occasionally lets the wind lift him above the ship, out of my line of vision, but most of the time he glides a few inches over the waves, just out of reach of the roiling whitecaps.

I turn my head when I hear the door creak open, but I know it won't be the person I'd expected to see by now, the one I most want to see.

"Rise and shine," Thom says.

His tousled hair is spiked with more gray than I remember. I haven't seen Thom since we last camped out amid the penguins on Petermann Island five years ago, doing APP research, and yesterday, during the madness of getting passengers boarded and settled, we'd hardly had time to exchange more than a few words. Like most of the islands we'll visit with passengers over the next week, Petermann is inhabited only by Antarctic natives—birds and seals, lichens and mosses and algae, various invertebrates. Despite the long hours we put in there, counting penguins and crunching data, it's a quiet, peaceful existence. And now I know Thom and I will fall into the same rhythms, on land and on sea, alone or surrounded by tourists. We usually work in a companionable near silence, having learned each other's moods through weeks together at the bottom of the earth.

"Let me guess," I say. "Glenn sent you."

He nods. "It's showtime."

"What's next, costumes? Batons?"

"It's as good a time as any to make an appearance," Thom says. "It's a ghost ship right now. Last chance to eat a meal in relative quiet."

I sit up slowly, realizing by the steadiness of my stomach how much the waves have lessened, and while it's not exactly Drake Lake out there, I have no excuse to keep hiding down here.

I swing my legs over the side of the bunk. Because I shower at night and sleep in my clothes, I only have to pull back my hair before I'm ready to go.

I let Thom lead the way to the dining room and observe the slight limp with which he walks, the result of a fall into a crevasse on his first trip to Antarctica, more than a decade ago. Despite the swaying of the ship, despite my own need to let my hands trace the bulkhead for balance, he does not need to hold on to anything.

We sit down at an empty table with plates of toast and fruit, our full coffee mugs sloshing. The dining room is vacant except for a steward walking through with a tray, on his way to deliver nausea-calming ginger soup to one of the bedridden passengers.

"You're right," I say to Thom. "Gotta love a ghost ship."

He nods. I look at him for a moment, then ask about his kids, his wife, how it feels to be back. We usually don't spend a lot of time talking about our personal lives. But I have a question I need to ask him, and I want to ease into it.

After Thom fills me in on his wife's new job, his kids' transitions into the first and third grades, I bring it up. "So you were called in sort of last minute?"

He nods. "I contacted Glenn last year, thinking I'd be ready to come down again now that the kids are older. He said he didn't have any openings, but then he called a couple of months ago, asked me to fill in."

"For Keller?" I ask.

"Yeah."

"Did he tell you why?"

"I didn't ask." He looks at me. "You don't know?"

I shake my head. Out of the corner of my eye I glimpse a passenger entering the room, and I feel my shoulders shrink down, an automatic reflex, the instinct to hide. But the guy sees us and comes over, his plate piled high with eggs and sausage, which would turn my stomach even if we weren't rolling through the Drake. I know from the ship's doctor that about 60 percent of the men on board take heart medication. I also know that the second most requested pill on this ship, after meclizine for seasickness, is Viagra—and that the loss of blood flow to the right places is due more to artery-clogging food than to age.

And now this middle-aged guy, who actually looks trim and healthier than most, takes a seat across from Thom and me.

"Nice binocs," Thom comments, indicating the binoculars the man has placed on the table.

"Thanks," the man says, clearly pleased that Thom noticed. "Waterproof, shock resistant, image stabilizing. They've even got night vision."

"Not that you'll need it here," Thom says.

"What do you mean?"

"It doesn't get dark," Thom says. "Just a couple hours of dusk between sunset and sunrise."

The man looks out the nearest porthole, as if he's not sure whether to believe what he's heard. "Well, for what they cost me, I'll certainly use them for other trips after this," he says at last. "I'm Richard, by the way. Richard Archer."

"Thom Carson. And this is Deb Gardner. Welcome aboard." Thom rises to get more coffee, taking my mug with him.

I nod toward the binoculars. "May I?" I ask, reaching for them.

Richard pushes them across the spotless white tablecloth. "Be my guest."

I take the binoculars over to a porthole and raise them to my face. It takes me a moment to realize they're digital, that I have to press a button before my field of vision comes into sudden, sharp focus. Their power is incredible. After a few moments, I see the barnacle-encrusted gray head of a sperm whale, barely breaking the surface of the water as it refuels with air. I should announce this over the PA, but without binoculars like these, no one else is likely to see it.

I lower the binoculars and return to the table, handing them back.

"Maybe I did spend a little too much on them," Richard says, "but this is a once-in-a-lifetime trip, right? I don't want to miss anything."

"There's a sperm whale at eleven o'clock." I point toward the horizon and watch him scan for the whale. I imagine the tiny electronic pulses that are disassembling and reassembling reality at mind-boggling speed.

Thom returns, placing fresh coffee in front of me. "What do you see?" he asks Richard.

"I'm trying to find a sperm whale."

"It probably took a deep dive," I say. "Don't worry. You'll see others."

I'm not sure he will—typically only the males feed in this region, and they prefer the deepest of waters—but I try to be encouraging, to let people believe they're going to see everything possible, that they'll get their money's worth. They don't need to know that they could visit Antarctica every year for the rest of their lives and still not see all there is.

"So," Richard says, putting the binoculars back on the table, "how long have you worked on the *Cormorant*?"

"We're actually with the APP," Thom tells him.

"Oh?"

Thom's mouth is now full of toast, so I continue. "The Antarctic Penguins Project is a nonprofit organization," I explain. "We study the three species of penguins here, tracking their progress, numbers, feeding and breeding habits. The boat transports us down here as part of the project's mission to educate people about the region."

"Nice," Richard says. "If you have to be down here, this is the way to travel, that's for sure. What's our first stop?"

Thom explains that we won't know until just before we get there—that each excursion to these tiny, remote islands depends upon ice, weather, and access, all of which change day to day, sometimes hour to hour.

My mind wanders back a few days to when I arrived in

Ushuaia, at the guesthouse where Keller and I had planned to meet. He wasn't there, and I took the opportunity to shower off the long flight and to close my eyes for a little while. When I woke up, it was morning, and I was due at the dock where the *Cormorant* was moored—with still no sign of Keller.

I sent a quick e-mail from the computer in the hotel lobby, thinking his flight had been delayed and that he'd show up that evening, just before we cast off. But when the *Cormorant*'s long blast sounded and the ship drifted into the Beagle Channel, I looked past the passengers' faces, past their champagne glasses at the waters ahead, and I wanted, irrationally, to run up to the bridge, tell the captain we had to wait.

I stare out the view windows of the dining room and try to think optimistically: Keller must've missed his flight, shifted his schedule at the last minute, made a plan to join the *Cormorant* in Ushuaia on its next voyage south, two weeks from now. I tell myself this even as I doubt all of it. I sneak a glance at Richard, who is adjusting the settings on his binoculars, and in that moment we're not so different—both of us searching for something we aren't going to find.

The last time I said good-bye to Keller Sullivan was only three months earlier, during an unexpected Stateside visit. We still live on opposite coasts, and during the eight or more months we spend away from the continent, we keep in touch via e-mail, phone, and Skype. We're like penguins that way— each of us off on our own separate journeys until we meet again, our shared nests reserved for these expeditions, for the peninsula, for the camps we build together.

It's complicated, what we share—a relationship born among the penguins, among creatures whose own breeding habits are as ever-evolving as the oceans to which they're constantly struggling to adapt. While many species mate for life, others are monogamous for only one season; still others have surprisingly high divorce rates—for all of them, survival comes first. Sometimes I think this sums up Keller and me pretty well. We have fallen in love with each other as much as with Antarctica, and we have yet to separate ourselves, and what we are, from this place. Each time I arrive at the bottom of the world, I never quite know what our nest will look like, or if it'll exist at all.

Last season, when I arrived in Ushuaia, bleary-eyed and dreading our first week on the *Cormorant* before Keller and I would be dropped off at Petermann, I didn't see him until I was on board. Until I felt my duffel being lifted out of my hand, an arm around my waist. He spun me into a bear hug before I got a chance to look at him, then set me down so we could see each other.

"Here we are," he said. *"Fin del mundo—"*

"—principio de todo," I said, finishing the sentence for him as I usually did, repeating the town's motto, lettered in blue on the white wall that borders the colorful buildings of the town and the sharp, snowcapped mountains beyond them.

The end of the world, the beginning of everything.

Starting a journey to Antarctica doesn't feel right anymore without Keller. In a sudden flurry of emotions, I don't know which to give in to: worry, anger, or simply disappointment.

AS THE WAVES continue to lose their sting, guests begin to emerge from their cabins, unsteadily navigating the passageways. They don their waterproof, insulated, bright red *Cormorant* jackets and make their way topside.

The first few guests on the deck soon grow into a crowd of dozens, and it's not long before I'm surrounded, fielding their questions. *How fast do icebergs melt? Where will that one end up? How big do they get?*

"An iceberg the size of Singapore broke off a glacier not too long ago," I tell them. "But the largest one was even bigger than that, about two hundred miles long."

"Two hundred miles?" says the guy who'd asked. "That's like the distance from New York to D.C."

I nod but don't answer, never having been to either place. But I do understand their need to put their surroundings in context—I imagine I'd need to do the same if I were in New York or Washington. I'd need to compare the Washington Monument to the tallest pinnacle iceberg I'd seen, or compare the width of Times Square to one of the crevasses I'd come across on the continent.

But the truth is, right now I'm grateful for their questions. At least when they're talking I don't have to think about anything else, like where Keller is and why I haven't heard from him, or how I can possibly reach a man who rarely answers his cell phone and tends to stay offline for weeks at a time.

"Was that a penguin?" a man asks, blinking as if he's just seen a meteor.

I'd missed it, whatever he'd seen. "Could be," I tell him. "They feed in this area. Keep your eyes up ahead, off to the side of the boat, and you'll see them. The noise of the ship scares them out of the water."

I watch as the tourists lean over the railing; I listen to

rapid-fire sounds from their cameras. How quickly they duck behind their viewfinders—in their haste to capture images of the penguins, to gather their mementos, they miss the real beauty in everything there is to see. I have to remind myself of my own first journey south, when I took more photos than I could count, hardly daring to believe I'd have the chance to see any of it again. The penguins' sleek bodies porpoising through the waves, so fast they look like miniature orcas. The way they leap and swim in formation, as if they're in the sky instead of in the water. The way they change direction in the blink of an eye.

Gradually, the cold seeps in, and everyone shuffles inside. My shoulders begin to relax as I lean against the railing. It takes a moment before I realize I'm not alone.

A woman stands about twenty feet away, where the railing curves along the bow, and while she'd been facing the other direction, she's now turning toward me.

"Hi," she says and walks over. I see her glance at my name tag, and then she holds out her hand. "So you're the penguin expert," she says. "I'm Kate Archer."

After a brief pause, I take her hand, lost inside a puffed-up Gore-Tex glove. Her smile curves a half-moon into an otherwise lonely expression, and she seems so happy to meet me that I'm guessing she's traveling alone and hasn't talked to anyone in a while.

"This is amazing," she says. "I bet you never get sick of this view."

"No, I never do."

She points toward a berg in the distance. "How tall is that iceberg?"

"I'd say sixty, eighty feet." Then I add, "About the size of an eight-story building."

"Ah," she says, then falls back into silence.

I know I should be more friendly, engage her in conversation, educate her about the Antarctic, but I already feel as though I've used up my conversation quota for the day. And then I see something ahead—a flash of reflected light, indicating the presence of something I can't possibly be seeing.

I reach into my cargo pants and retrieve my binoculars, and I see I was right: In the distance is a ship, taller than the eight-story iceberg that is nearly hiding it.

I mutter, "What the hell?" and try to adjust my binoculars, wondering if they're fogged up, or broken—or if there's something wrong with my own eyes.

Then I glance over at the woman next to me, trying to remember her name. Kate. "Sorry," I say. "It's just that I can't believe what I'm seeing."

"What *are* you seeing?" She leans over the rail, as if that'll help her vision. "I don't know what you're talking about."

"You will," I say, lowering the binoculars. "Give it a second."

"I wish I had my husband's binoculars right now. I could probably see straight *through* that iceberg."

It takes me a second to make the connection. "Is your husband's name Richard?"

"Yes," she says, looking over at me. "Why?"

"I met him this morning. At breakfast."

"Then you've seen more of him today than I have."

There's something strange in her voice, but I'm not sure what it is. I've never been comfortable with the unnatural intimacy created on these voyages—we're witnesses to crumbling marriages, sibling rivalry, love affairs. Part of the problem, I think, is that, for so many, Antarctica is the trip of a lifetime, and their expectations are so high. They come down here expecting to be changed forever, and often they are, only not in the ways they expect. They get seasick, they aren't used to the close quarters, they learn that it's because of their own bad habits that the oceans are dying. And this all seeps into not only their dream vacation but their relationships, more deeply than they're prepared for.

Just then the ship begins to emerge from behind the iceberg, her bow nosing forward, revealing as she floats onward her many oversize parts: a vast, open-air terrace; a railing encompassing a sundeck and swimming pool; some sort of playing field just beyond. The ship comes slowly into full view, along with hundreds of tiny portholes and dozens of balconies feathered across the port side.

Even Kate looks surprised. "How far away is that boat?" she asks.

"Not far enough."

"It must be gigantic."

I nod. "Ten stories high, twelve hundred passengers, four hundred crew. And it has no business being down here."

"It looks like it made a wrong turn somewhere in the Caribbean. How do you know so much about it?"

"I've been studying the effects of tourism on the penguin colonies," I say. "I keep up on these things. The *Australis* is a new ship, registered in the Bahamas but probably filled with Americans—a floating theme park, like most of them."

"You're obviously not a fan."

"I have no problem with ships like this in the Caribbean or in Europe. But down here—the last thing any of us needs, least of all the penguins, is for that behemoth to dump a small town's worth of people on these islands."

"Then why is it allowed down here?"

I sigh, staring at the ship, which is moving along the horizon like a pockmarked iceberg. "No one owns these waters. They can do whatever they want."

"Is it headed south?"

"Looks like it," I say, then shrug. "The good news is that, most of the time, ships that big just dash across the Drake to give passengers a glimpse of the icebergs and then head back up north. So we probably won't see it again. It's way too big to get into most of the places we visit."

Kate's still looking at the cruise liner, and I'm heartened to see that she appears as disgusted by it as I am. "It makes even that iceberg look small."

I let out a wry laugh. "That iceberg is nothing compared to what we're getting into," I say. "And the *Australis* doesn't have a reinforced hull like we do. That's why I'm betting it will turn around."

"What if it does come across icebergs?" she asks. "How will it navigate around them?"

"Carefully," I tell her. "Very carefully."

Petermann Island

When I notice one of our gentoo chicks is missing, I flip through our field notebook, find the colony chart, and match nest to nest. According to our records, the chick was two weeks old, but now the rocky nest is empty. I search but find no body, which means its disappearance must have been the work of a predatory skua. When skuas swoop down to snatch chicks or eggs, they leave little behind.

I move away from the colony and sit on a rock to make some notes. That's when I hear it—a distinctly human yelp, and a thick noise that I have only heard once in my life and never forgotten: the sound of bone hitting something solid.

I stand up and see a man lying on the ground, a red-jacketed tourist from the *Cormorant*, which dropped its anchor in our bay this morning. The ship, making her rounds in the Antarctic peninsula, had left Thom and me here a week earlier, and she'll pick us up in another week, during the last cruise of the season.

Petermann Island is tiny, just over a mile long, once home

to small huts serving an early-twentieth-century French Antarctic expedition. Now we create our own research base, with tents and solar-powered laptops. During the two weeks we're here, the *Cormorant* stops by, weather permitting, to show tourists the birds and our camp, offering a tour of the island and a glimpse of how we researchers live.

The man had fallen hard, landing on his back. When I see a spot of red spreading from the rock under his head into the snow, I start toward him. Fifteen other tourists are within twenty yards, yet no one else seems to notice.

Thom must have seen something; he gets to the man first. And now a woman is scrambling guardedly down the same hill, apparently taking care, despite her hurry, to avoid the same fate.

I turn my attention to the man. His blood is an unwelcome sight, bright and thin amid the ubiquitous dark-pink guano of the penguins, and replete with bacteria, which could be deadly for the birds. I repress an urge to clean it up.

"Deb," Thom says sharply, glancing up. He'd spent two years in medical school before turning to marine biology, and he looks nervous. By now, four more tourists in their matching red jackets have gathered around us.

I hold out my arms and move forward, forcing the red jackets back a couple of steps. The woman who'd hurried down the hill is trying to see past me. She looks younger than the usual middle-aged passengers who cruise down to Antarctica. "Are you with him?" I ask her. "Where's your guide?"

"No—I don't know," she stammers. Blond hair trails from under her hat into her eyes, wide with an anxiety I can't place. "He's up there, maybe." She motions toward the gentoo colony. I glance up. The hill has nearly faded away in the fog.

"Someone needs to find him," I say. "And we need the doctor from the boat. Who's he traveling with?"

"His wife, I think," someone answers.

"Get her."

I kneel next to Thom, who's examining the man's head. If we were anywhere but Antarctica, the injury might not seem as critical. But we are at the bottom of the world, days away from the nearest city, even farther from the nearest trauma center. There's a doctor along on the cruise, and basic medical facilities at Palmer Station, a forty-person U.S. base an hour away by boat—but it's not yet clear whether that will be enough.

The man hasn't moved since he fell. A deep gash on the back of his head has bled through the thick wad of gauze Thom applied. Voices approach—the guide, the wife, the doctor. The man's chest suddenly begins to heave, and Thom quickly reaches out and turns his head so he can vomit into the snow.

The man shudders and tries to sit up, then loses consciousness again. Thom presses fresh gauze to his head and looks up.

"What happened?" the wife cries.

"He slipped," I tell her.

Susan Beecham, the ship's doctor, is now right behind us, and Thom and I move aside.

"How could this happen?" the wife wails.

I place a hand on her shoulder as crew members arrive with a gurney. "We need to get him to Palmer," Susan says, her voice low.

Thom helps them load him onto the gurney, and they take him to a Zodiac. I get a plastic bag from our camp, then return to the scene and begin scooping up the blood- and vomit-covered snow. Because this is one of the last pristine environments in the world, we go to great lengths to protect the animals from anything foreign. Visitors sterilize their boots before setting foot on the island, and again when they depart. No one leaves without everything they came with.

Yet sometimes, like now, it seems pointless. Injuries like this are unusual, but I've seen tourists drop used tissues and gum wrappers on the ground. I want to chase after them, to show them our data, to tell them how much the fate of the penguins has changed as more and more tourists pass through these islands. But I must be patient with this red-jacketed species. I'm grateful for the *Cormorant*'s transportation to this remote island, and the tour company's financial support of the APP, yet I often feel we earn it more each season, that our work takes a backseat to keeping the tourists happy.

Thom returns and stands over me. "They need me to go to Palmer with them."

I look up. "Why?"

"The crew is crazed," he says, "and they need someone to stay with the victim and his wife."

He doesn't have to explain; I can picture what's happening—Susan on the radio with the dispatcher at Palmer, deckhands preparing to pull anchor, naturalists answering worried passengers' questions, and Glenn trying to coordinate with the galley about the next meal and with the captain about the next destination.

"I guess we're at their mercy." I inspect the ground to make sure there's nothing left in the snow. Thom doesn't have a choice—we're often asked to fill in for the crew when we're on the island—but I know what he is really asking me. We've worked together for three years, and I've never spent a night here alone.

I stand up. Because Thom is short and I'm tall, we look each other directly in the eye. "Go ahead. I'll be all right."

"You sure?"

"I'll keep the radio on, just in case. But yeah, I'll be fine. After all this, I'll enjoy the peace."

"I'll be back tomorrow," he says.

We go back to camp, a trio of tents a few yards off the bay. From there we can watch the ships approach and, more important, depart.

Another Zodiac is waiting to take Thom to Palmer. He grabs a few things from his tent and gives my shoulder a squeeze before he leaves. "I'll buzz you later," he says. He smiles, and I feel a sudden, sharp loneliness, like an intake of cold air.

I watch the Zodiac retreat around the outer cliffs of the bay, then turn back to our empty camp.

ON AN EVENING like this, with the air sogged with unshed rain and the penguins splashing in a pool of slush nearby, it's hard to believe that Antarctica is the biggest desert in the world, the driest place on earth. The Dry Valleys have not seen rain for millions of years, and, thanks to the cold, nothing rots or decays. Even up here, on the peninsula, I've seen hundred-year-old seal carcasses in perfect condition, and abandoned whaling stations frozen in time. Those who perish in Antarctica—penguins, seals, explorers—are immortalized, the ice preserving life in the moment of death.

But for all that remains the same, Antarctica is constantly changing. Every year, the continent doubles in size as the ocean freezes around it; the ice shelf shifts; glaciers calve off. Whales once hunted are now protected; krill once ignored are now trawled; land once desolate now sees thousands of tourists a season.

I make myself a cold supper of leftover pasta and think of our return. Back on the *Cormorant*, Thom and I will be eating well, my solitude will be replaced with lectures and slide shows, and I'll wish I were here, among the penguins.

I finish eating and clean up. At nearly ten o'clock, it's bright outside, the sun still hours away from its temporary disappearance. I take a walk, heading up toward the colony that was so heavily trafficked today, the one the man visited before he fell. The penguins are still active, bringing rocks to fortify their nests, feeding their chicks. Some are sitting on eggs; others are returning from the sea to reunite with their mates, greeting one another with a call of recognition, a high-pitched rattling squawk.

I sit down on a rock, about fifteen feet away from the nearest nest, and watch the birds amble up the trail from the water. They appear to be ignoring me, but I know that they aren't; I know that their heart rates increase when I walk past, that they move faster when I'm around. Thom and I have been studying the two largest penguin colonies here, tracking their numbers and rates of reproduction, to gauge the effects of tourism and human contact. This island is one of the most frequently visited spots in Antarctica, and our data show that the birds have noticed: They're experiencing stress, lower birth rates, fewer fledging chicks. It's a strange irony that the hands that feed our research are the same hands that guide the *Cormorant* here every season, and I've often contemplated what will happen when the results of our study are published.

Sometimes when I watch the penguins, I become so mesmerized by the sounds of their purrs and squawks, by the precision of their clumsy waddle, that I forget I have another life, somewhere else — that I rent a cottage in Eugene, that I teach marine biology at the University of Oregon, that I'm thirty-four years old and not yet on a tenure track, that I haven't had a real date in three years. I forget that my life now is only as good as my next grant, and that when the money dries up, I'm afraid I will, too.

I first came to Antarctica eight years ago, to study the emperor penguins at McMurdo Station. I've returned every season since then, most frequently to these islands on the peninsula. It'll be years before our Antarctic Penguins Project study is complete, but because Thom's kids are young, he'll be taking the next few seasons off. I'm already looking forward to coming back next year.

What I'd like is to return to the Ross Sea, thousands of miles farther south, to the emperors — the only Antarctic birds that breed in winter, right on the ice. Emperors don't build nests; they live entirely on fast ice and in the water, never setting foot on solid land. I love that, during breeding season, the female lays her egg, scoots it over to the male, and then takes off, traveling a hundred miles across the frozen ocean to open water and swimming away to forage for food. She comes back when she's fat and ready to feed her chick.

My mother, who has given up on marriage and grandkids for her only daughter, says that this is my problem, that I think like an emperor. I expect a man to sit tight and wait patiently while I disappear across the ice. I don't build nests.

When the female emperor returns, she uses a signature call to find her partner. When they're reunited, they move in close and bob their heads toward each other, shoulder to shoulder in an armless hug, raising their beaks in what we call the ecstatic cry. Penguins are romantics. Many mate for life.

IN THE SUMMER, Antarctic sunsets last forever. The sky surrenders to an overnight dusk, a grayish light that dims around midnight. As I prepare to turn in, I hear the splatter of penguins bathing in their slush, the barely perceptible pats of their webbed feet on the rocks.

Inside my tent, I extinguish my lamp and set a flashlight nearby, turning over until I find a comfortable angle. The rocks are ice-cold, the padding under my sleeping bag far too thin. When I finally put my head down, I hear a loud splash—clearly made by something much larger than a penguin.

Feeling suddenly uneasy, I turn on my lamp again. I throw on a jacket, grab my flashlight, and hurry outside, climbing my way down to the rocky beach.

I can see a figure in the water, but it's bulky and oddly shaped, not smooth and sleek, like a seal. I shine my flashlight on it and see red.

It's a man, in his cruise-issued parka, submerged in the

water up to his waist. He looks into the glare of my flashlight. I stand there, too stunned to move.

The man turns away, and he takes another step into the water. *He's crazy*, I think. *Why would he go in deeper?* Sometimes the seasick medication that tourists take causes odd and even troubling behavior, but I've never witnessed anything like this.

As I watch him anxiously from the shore, I think of Ernest Shackleton. I think of his choices, the decisions he made to save the lives of his crew. His decision to abandon the *Endurance* in the Weddell Sea, to set out across the frozen water in search of land, to separate his crew from one another, to take a twenty-two-foot rescue boat across eight hundred miles of open sea—had any of these choices backfired, history would have an entirely different memory. In Antarctica, every decision is weighty, every outcome either a tragedy or a miracle.

Now, it seems, my own moment has come. It would be unthinkable to stand here and watch this man drown, but attempting a rescue could be even more dangerous. I'm alone. I'm wearing socks and a light jacket. The water is a few degrees above freezing, and, though I'm strong, this man is big enough to pull me under if he wanted to, or if he panicked.

Perhaps Shackleton only believed he had options. Here, genuine options are few.

I call out to the man, but my words dissolve in the foggy air. I walk toward him, into the bay, and my feet numb within seconds in the icy water. The man is now in up to his chest. By the time I reach him, he's nearly delirious, and he doesn't resist when I grab his arms, pull them over my shoulders, and steer us toward the shore. The water has nearly turned him into deadweight. Our progress is slow. Once on land, he's near collapse, and I can hardly walk myself. It takes all my strength to help him up the rocks and into Thom's tent.

He crumples on the tent floor, and I strip off his parka and his boots and socks. Water spills over Thom's sleeping bag and onto his books. "Take off your clothes," I say, turning away to rummage through Thom's things. I toss the man a pair of sweats, the only thing of Thom's that will stretch to fit his tall frame, and two pairs of thick socks. I also find a couple of T-shirts and an oversize sweater, and by the time I turn back to him, the man has put on the sweats and is feebly attempting the socks. His hands are shaking so badly he can hardly control them. Impatiently, I reach over to help, yanking the socks onto his feet.

"What the hell were you thinking?" I demand. I hardly look at him as I take off his shirt and help him squeeze into Thom's sweater. I turn on a battery-powered blanket and unzip Thom's sleeping bag. "Get in," I say. "You need to warm up."

His whole body shudders. He climbs in and pulls the blanket up to cover his shoulders.

"What are you doing here?" I, too, am shaking from the cold. "What the hell happened?"

He lifts his eyes, briefly. "The boat—it left me behind."

"That's impossible." I stare at him, but he won't look at me. "The *Cormorant* always does head counts. No one's ever been left behind."

He shrugs. "Until now."

I think about the chaos of earlier that day. It's conceivable that this stranger could have slipped through the cracks. And it would be just my luck.

"I'm calling Palmer. Someone will have to come out to take you back." I rise to my knees, eager to go first to my tent for dry clothes, then to the supply tent, where we keep the radio.

I feel his hand on my arm. "Do you have to do that just yet?" He smiles, awkwardly, his teeth knocking together. "It's just that—I've been here so long already, and I'm not ready to face the ship. It's embarrassing, to be honest with you."

"Don't you have someone who knows you're missing?" I regard him for the first time as a man rather than an alien in my world. His face is pale and clammy, its lines suggesting he is older than I am, perhaps in his mid-forties. I glance down to look for a wedding band, but his fingers are bare. Following my gaze, he tucks his hands under the blanket. Then he shakes his head. "I'm traveling alone."

"Have you taken any medication? For seasickness?"

"No," he says. "I don't get seasick."

"Well," I say, "we need to get someone out here to take you back to the *Cormorant*."

He looks at me directly for the first time. "Don't," he says.

I'm still kneeling on the floor of the tent. "What do you expect to do, stay here?" I ask. "You think no one will figure out you're missing?"

He doesn't answer. "Look," I tell him, "it was an accident. No one's going to blame you for getting left behind."

"It wasn't an accident," he says. "I saw that other guy fall. I watched everything. I knew that if I stayed they wouldn't notice me missing."

So he is crazy after all.

I stand up. "I'll be right back."

He reaches up and grasps my wrist so fast I don't have time

to pull away. I'm surprised by how quickly his strength has returned. I ease back down to my knees, and he loosens his grip. He looks at me through tired, heavy eyes—a silent plea. He's not scary, I realize then, but scared.

"In another month," I tell him, as gently as I can manage, "the ocean will freeze solid, and so will everything else, including you."

"What about you?"

"In a couple weeks, I'm leaving, too. Everyone leaves."

"Even the penguins?" The question, spoken through clattering teeth, lends him an innocence that almost makes me forgive his intrusions.

"Yes," I say. "Even they go north."

He doesn't respond. I stand up and head straight to the radio in our supply tent, hardly thinking about my wet clothes. Just as I'm contacting Palmer, I realize that I don't know the man's name. I go back and poke my head inside. "Dennis Marshall," he says.

The dispatcher at Palmer tells me that they'll pick Dennis up in the morning, when they bring Thom back. "Unless it's an emergency," he says. "Everything okay?"

I want to tell him it's not okay, that this man could be crazy, dangerous, sick. Instead I pause, then say, "We're fine. Tell Thom we'll see him in the morning."

I return to the tent. Dennis has not moved.

"What were you doing in the water?" I ask.

"Thought I'd try to catch up to the boat," he says.

"Very funny. I'm serious."

He doesn't reply. A moment later, he asks, "What are *you* doing here?"

"Research, obviously."

"I know," he says. "But why come here, to the end of the earth?"

It's always been hard to explain why a place like Antarctica is perfect for me. Before you can sign on to overwinter at McMurdo, they give you psych tests to make sure you can live for months in darkness and near isolation without going crazy—and the idea of this has always amused me. It's not the isolation that threatens to drive me insane; it's civilization.

"What kind of question is that?" I ask Dennis.

"You know what I mean," he says. "You have to be a real loner to enjoy being down here." He rubs the fingers of his left hand.

I catch his hand to examine his fingers. "Where do they hurt?"

"It's not that," he says.

"Then what?"

He hesitates. "I dropped my ring," he says. "My wedding band."

"Where? In the water?"

He nods.

"For God's sake." I duck out of the tent before he can stop me. I hear his voice behind me, asking me where I'm going, and I shout back, "Stay there."

I rush toward the water's edge, shivering in my still-damp clothes. The penguins purr as I go past, and a few of them scatter. I shine my flashlight down through the calm, clear water to the rocks at the bottom. I don't know where he might have dropped the ring, so I wade in, and within minutes my feet feel like blocks of ice. I follow what I think was his path into the water, sweeping the flashlight back and forth in front of me.

I'm in up to my knees when I see it, a few feet down—a flash of gold against the slate-colored rocks. I reach in, the water up to my shoulder, so cold it feels as if my arm will snap off and sink.

I manage to grasp the ring with fingers that now barely move, then shuffle back to shore on leaden feet. I hobble back to my own tent, where I strip off my clothes and don as many dry things as I can. My skin is moist and wrinkled from being wet for so long. I hear a noise and look up to see Dennis, blanket still wrapped around his shoulders, crouched at the opening to my tent.

"What are you staring at?" I snap. Then I look down to what he sees—a thin, faded T-shirt, no bra, my nipples pressing against the fabric, my arm flushed red from the cold. I pull his ring off my thumb, where I'd put it so it wouldn't fall again, and throw it at him.

He picks it up off the floor. He holds it but doesn't put it on. "I wish you'd just left it," he says, almost to himself.

"A penguin could have choked on it," I say. "But no one ever thinks about that. We're all tourists here, you know. This is their home, not ours."

"I'm sorry," he says. "What can I do?"

I shake my head.

He comes in and sits down, then pulls the blanket off his shoulders and places it around mine. He finds a fleece pullover in a pile of clothing and wraps it around my reddened arm.

"How cold is that water, anyway?" he asks.

"About thirty degrees, give or take." I watch him carefully.

"How long can someone survive in there?"

"A matter of minutes, usually," I say, remembering an expedition guide who'd drowned. He'd been trapped under his flipped Zodiac for only a few moments but had lost consciousness, with rescuers only a hundred yards away. "Most people go into shock. It's too cold to swim, even to breathe."

He unwraps my arm. "Does it feel better?"

"A little." Pain prickles my skin from the inside, somewhere deep down, and I feel an ache stemming from my bones. "You still haven't told me what you were doing out there."

He reaches over and begins massaging my arm. I'm not sure I want him to, but I know the warmth, the circulation, is good. "Like I said, I lost my ring."

"You were out much farther than where I found your ring."

"I must have missed it." He doesn't look at me as he speaks. I watch his fingers on my arm, and I am reminded of the night before, when only Thom and I were here, and Thom had helped me wash my hair. The feel of his hands on my scalp, on my neck, had run through my entire body, tightening into a coil of desire that never fully vanished. But nothing has ever happened between Thom and me, other than unconsummated rituals: As we approach the end of our stays, we begin doing things for each other—he'll braid my long hair; I'll rub his feet—because after a while touch becomes necessary.

I pull away. I regard the stranger in my tent: his dark hair, streaked with silver; his sad, heavy eyes; his ringless hands, still outstretched.

"What's the matter?" he asks.

"Nothing."

"I was just trying to help." The tent's small lamp casts deep shadows under his eyes. "I'm sorry," he says. "I know you don't want me here."

Something in his voice softens the knot in my chest. I sigh. "I'm just not a people person, that's all."

For the first time, he smiles, barely. "I can see why you come here. Talk about getting away from it all."

"At least I leave when I'm supposed to," I say, offering a tiny smile of my own.

He glances down at Thom's clothing, pulled tight across his body. "So when do I have to leave?" he asks.

"They'll be here in the morning."

Then he says, "How's he doing? The guy who fell?"

It takes me a moment to realize what he's talking about. "I don't know," I confess. "I forgot to ask."

He leans forward, then whispers, "I know something about him."

"What's that?"

"He was messing around with that blond woman," he says. "The one who was right there when it happened. I saw you talking to her."

"How do you know?"

"I saw them. They had a rendezvous every night, on the deck, after his wife went to bed. The blonde was traveling with her sister. They even ate lunch together once, the four of them. The wife had no idea."

"Do you think they planned it?" I ask. "Or did they just meet on the boat?"

"I don't know."

I look away, disappointed. "She seemed too young. For him."

"You didn't see her hands," he says. "My wife taught me that. You always know a woman's age by her hands. She may have had the face of a thirty-five-year-old, but she had the hands of a sixty-year-old."

"If you're married, why are you traveling alone?"

He pauses. "Long story."

"Well, we've got all night," I say.

"She decided not to come," he says.

"Why?"

"She left, a month ago. She's living with someone else."

"Oh." I don't know what more to say. Dennis is quiet, and I make another trip to the supply tent, returning with a six-pack of beer. His tired eyes brighten a bit.

He drinks before speaking again. "She was seeing him for a long time," he says, "but I think it was this trip that set her off. She didn't want to spend three weeks on a boat with me. Or without him."

"I'm sorry." A moment later, I ask, "Do you have kids?"

He nods. "Twin girls, in college. They don't call home much. I don't know if she's told them or not."

"Why did you decide to come anyway?"

"This trip was for our anniversary." He turns his head and gives me a cheerless half smile. "Pathetic, isn't it?"

I roll my beer can between my hands. "How did you lose the ring?"

"The ring?" He looks startled. "It fell off during the landing, I guess."

"It was thirty degrees today. Weren't you wearing gloves?"

"I guess I wasn't."

I look at him, knowing there is more to the story and that

neither of us wants to acknowledge it. And then he lowers his gaze to my arm. "How does it feel?" he asks.

"It's okay."

"Let me work on it some more." He begins to rub my arm again. This time he slips his fingers inside the long sleeve of my shirt, and the sudden heat on my skin seems to heighten my other senses: I hear the murmur of the penguins, feel the wind rippling the tent. At the same time, it's all drowned out by the feel of his hands.

I lean back and pull him with me until his head hovers just above mine. The lines sculpting his face look deeper in the tent's shadowy light, and his lazy eyelids lift as if to see me more clearly. He blinks, slowly, languidly, as I imagine he might touch me, and in the next moment he does.

I hear a pair of gentoos reunite outside, their rattling voices rising above the night's ambient sound. Inside, Dennis and I move under and around our clothing, our own voices muted, whispered, breathless, and in the sudden humid heat of the tent we've recognized each other in the same way, by instinct, and, as with the birds, it's all we know.

DURING THE ANTARCTIC night, tens of thousands of male emperors huddle together through months of total darkness, in temperatures reaching seventy degrees below zero, as they incubate their eggs. By the time the females return to the colony, four months after they left, the males have lost half their body weight and are near starvation. Yet they wait. It's what they're programmed to do.

Dennis does not wait for me. I wake up alone in my tent, the gray light of dawn nudging my eyelids. When I look at my watch, I see that it's later than I thought.

Outside, I glance around for Dennis, but he's not in camp. I make coffee, washing Thom's cup for him to use. I drink my own coffee without waiting for him; it's the only thing to warm me this morning, with him gone and the sun so well hidden.

I sip slowly, steam rising from my cup, and take in the moonscape around me: the edgy rocks, the mirrored water, ice sculptures rising above the pack ice—I could be on another planet. Yet for the first time in years, I feel as if I've reconnected with the world in some way, as if I am not as lost as I've believed all this time.

I hear the sound of a distant motor and stand up. Then it stops. I listen, hearing agitated voices—it must be Thom, coming from Palmer, having engine trouble. He is still outside the bay, out of sight, so I wait, rinsing my coffee mug and straightening up. When the engine starts up again, I turn back toward the bay. A few minutes later, Thom comes up from the beach with one of the electricians at Palmer, a young guy named Andy. I wave them over.

They walk hesitantly, and when they get closer, I recognize the look on Thom's face, and I know, with an icy certainty, where Dennis is, even before Thom opens his mouth.

"We found a body, Deb," he says. "In the bay." He exchanges a glance with Andy. "We just pulled him in."

I stare at their questioning faces. "He was here all night," I say. "I thought he just went for a walk, or—" I stop. Then I start toward the bay.

Thom steps in front of me. He holds both of my arms. "There's no need to do this," he says.

But I have to see for myself. I pull away and run to the beach. The body lies across the rocks. I recognize Thom's sweater, stretched across Dennis's large frame.

I walk over to him; I want to take his pulse, to feel his heartbeat. But then I see his face, a bluish white, frozen in an expression I don't recognize, and I can't go any closer.

I feel Thom come up behind me. "It's him," I say. "I gave him your sweater."

He puts an arm around my shoulder. "What do you think happened?" he asks, but he knows as well as I do. There is no current here, no way to be swept off this beach and pulled out to sea. The Southern Ocean is not violent here, but it is merciless nonetheless.

ANTARCTICA IS NOT a country; it is governed by an international treaty whose rules apply almost solely to the environment. There are no police here, no firefighters, no medical examiners. We have to do everything ourselves, and I shrug Thom off when he tries to absolve me from our duties. I help them lift Dennis into the Zodiac, the weight of his body entirely different now. I keep a hand on his chest as we back out of the bay and speed away, as if he might suddenly try to sit up. When we arrive at Palmer, I finally give in, leaving him to the care of others, who will pack his body for the long journey home.

They offer me a hot shower and a meal. As Andy walks me

down the hall toward the dormitory, he tries in vain to find something to say. I'm silent, not helping him. Eventually he updates me on the injured man. "He's going to be okay," he tells me. "But you know what's strange? He doesn't remember anything about the trip. He knows his wife, knows who the president is, how to add two and two—but he doesn't know how he got here, or why he even came to Antarctica. Pretty spooky, huh?"

He won't remember the woman he was fooling around with, I think. *She will remember him, but for him, she's already gone.*

BACK AT CAMP, I watch for the gentoos who lost their chick, but they do not return. Their nest remains abandoned, and other penguins steal their rocks.

Thom makes a few attempts to ask about Dennis, and when I meet his questions with silence, he stops asking. We both know what lies ahead—an investigation, paperwork, corporate lawyers, questions from the family—and I don't want to go through it any more than I need to.

Six days later, Thom and I break camp and ready ourselves for the weeklong journey back. Once we are on the boat, the distractions are plenty, and the hours and days fly past in seminars and lectures. The next thing I know, we are a day away from the Drake Passage.

I wander around the ship, walking the passageways Dennis walked, sitting where he must have sat, standing where he may have stood. I'm with a new group of passengers now, none of whom would have crossed his path. A sleety rain begins to fall, and I go out to the uppermost deck, the small one reserved for crew. As we float through a labyrinth of icebergs, I play with Dennis's wedding ring, which he'd left on the floor of my tent. I wear it on my thumb, as I did when I'd first found it, because that's where it fits.

It's probably because of this vantage point that I see her — an emperor penguin in the distance, standing alone atop an enormous tabular iceberg. It's uncommon to see an emperor this far north, and a good field guide would announce the sighting on the PA — the passengers aren't likely to get another chance to see an emperor.

But I don't move. I watch her as she preens her feathers, as she senses the sounds and vibrations of our ship and raises her head — an elegant, gentle pirouette in our direction. It feels as though she's looking directly at me, and in that moment we are mirror images of each other, lone figures above the vastness of all this sea and ice. She's so far from her breeding grounds that for a moment I wonder whether she's lost, but when she looks away and turns back to her feathers, I sense instead that she is feeling leisurely, safe, enjoying a rare moment of peace before returning home.

The Drake Passage
(59°39'S, 61°56'W)

Thom and I stand together on the rear deck, watching the *Australis* moving in the distance like a time-lapse image of a drifting iceberg: slow, massive, inevitable. In one of the articles I'd read about the ship, a spokesman for the parent cruise company had bragged about how the *Australis* would cruise to every last inch of the planet, that no place was off-limits to a ship this invincible. It reminded me of what people once said about the *Titanic*.

The last disaster down here happened a few years ago, when a small tourist ship sank fourteen hours after colliding with an iceberg. That ship was lucky enough to be within an hour of another boat, and small enough that all her passengers could be rescued—but of course thousands of gallons of fuel were spilled, coating the penguins, destroying their waterproof feathers.

I tighten my grip on the railing. "It just drives me insane to see that ship down here. Maybe Glenn can nail them on some IAATO violation or something."

"I doubt it," Thom says.

I sigh. "What good is an association that's supposed to protect this place from cruise ships if membership is voluntary?"

Thom doesn't answer; this conundrum frustrates us all. Back in the early nineties, when the International Association of Antarctica Tour Operators was founded, only six thousand travelers a year visited Antarctica—now it's closer to forty thousand. That alone makes our instincts to protect the continent seem futile—not to mention the fact that there's no such thing as an Antarctic coast guard.

And nothing yet has prevented the cruise-bys: the ships that come down just so their passengers can say they've been. I'd complained about it to Keller the last time I saw him, which wasn't long after I'd read yet another story about the fancy new *Australis*. He'd tried to make the point that our *Cormorant* passengers are no different—they are simply able to pay more for the luxury of a small expedition with scientists and Antarctic experts on board, and all passengers sign liability waivers no matter what ship they're on. We'd argued about it, but in a way, of course, he's right. We're all at risk down here because every day we venture into the unknown.

Thom pushes away from the railing. "I'll go up to the bridge," he says. "See what I can find out."

I nod. A nausea spreads through me that is far worse than seasickness, far worse than the guilt of taking our own hundred tourists to shore. Down here, ships look after one another—but how do you look after a ship that's more than ten times the size of your own?

Thom doesn't return, and after a while I assume he's been detained by a tourist or given a task. I step inside, to the lounge, where small groups of passengers gather around tables drinking coffee; a few sit alone in chairs, reading or gazing out the view windows. My roommate, Amy, is setting up the afternoon slide show. As a full-time employee of the tour company, Amy travels from Antarctica to Alaska, from Mexico to the Galápagos, and she's often with the *Cormorant* during the entire Antarctic season, late November through early February. This is her fifth year in Antarctica, and we always bunk together when we can.

"What're you showing later?" I ask.

"Just some footage from the ROV," she says.

The ship's remotely operated vehicle reaches depths of up to a thousand feet, far deeper than Amy herself can dive—and her video of the ocean floor is alive with colorful and intricate corals, ghostly icefish, pale sea sponges, graceful brittle stars.

"Any footage of the yeti crab yet?" The existence of a blind, hairy Antarctic yeti crab is a new discovery, first seen in the Southern Ocean just a few years ago, and I'm always teasing Amy because it drives her crazy that she hasn't captured it on film yet. Last season, Keller helped me Photoshop images of the elusive crab into places on board the *Cormorant*— on a table in the dining room, next to a glass of beer in the lounge—and throughout the voyage we'd e-mail them to Amy, writing, *Did you see the yeti crab?*

"Piss off," Amy says cheerfully as she taps at her laptop's keyboard. She leans over to attach the laptop to the projector, then accidentally tangles the cord around her arm and pulls the projector off the table. She catches it just before it hits the floor.

Amy is small, with a soft, pale beauty, as if she herself had emerged from the unblemished depths of the sea, and when she puts on a dry suit and scuba gear and descends into the water, she disappears below the surface seamlessly, as if she belongs there. When she's not under the water or on board a cruise vessel, she writes picture books for kids.

A blast of cold air comes through the lounge, and I turn to see Kate and Richard Archer walk in. I let my eyes linger on them, curious. Kate's hair is windblown, curling into ringlets from the moist air outside, and her skin is flushed with cold. She stands close to Richard; he's more than a head taller, with wheat-colored hair and a thin build. As they walk toward a table, I realize from his slower gait that he's at least ten years older than she is. After they sit down, he looks at Kate, then reaches out and tucks a lock of hair behind her ear. Her round face breaks into a smile as the curl bounces loose, back into her face, and then she leans forward and gives him a kiss.

"So where's Keller?"

I turn back to Amy and shrug.

"I thought he'd be here," she says.

"So did I."

"So what happened?"

"Wish I knew."

Amy is looking over my shoulder. "Well, there's Glenn," she says. "Ask him."

Glenn is talking to the bartender, and I walk over, standing a bit behind him until they finish.

"Hey, Glenn," I say as he turns around. "Do you have a second?"

Glenn looks at me, waiting. He has a smooth, unblemished face partially hidden by a perfectly trimmed goatee. His physical youthfulness is belied by a consistently somber expression and dark, serious eyes. I try to remember the last time I saw him smile, and I can't.

"I wanted to ask you about Keller."

"What about him?"

"Why isn't he on board?"

"He didn't tell you?"

I feel my face redden. "If I knew, I wouldn't be asking you."

"Deb, I'm not sure I should be talking about this. It's technically a human resources issue."

"Really?" I say. "You're going to hide behind human resources?"

Glenn sighs. "You remember that last voyage," he says. "It shouldn't come as any surprise that Keller is no longer welcome on this ship."

I shouldn't be surprised—but I am. While I knew Keller had pushed Glenn's limits, neither of them had given me any indication that Keller wouldn't be here when the season began.

"Why didn't you talk to me?" I say. "I would have vouched for him. Kept an eye on him."

"This isn't child care, Deb. And clearly he didn't want you to know." I sense that Glenn is censoring a snide remark. "He came to see me in Seattle. He lobbied hard to come back, I'll give him that."

I'd nearly forgotten about Keller's quick trip from Eugene to Seattle. About a job, he'd said. But he'd never mentioned Glenn.

"I did consider it," Glenn continues, "for the sake of the APP and the fact that he's a good worker. But I can't take any more drama."

"He was only telling the truth."

"People come on this trip to be entertained," Glenn says, "not accused."

"They also come to be educated. What about awareness? Isn't that part of it?"

"You know as well as I do that you can't raise awareness if you don't have any passengers," Glenn says. "And those who do come here—well, they deserve better."

"It was that one guy who started it," I say. "I remember—"

"That passenger," Glenn interrupts, "demanded a full refund, or he threatened to sue. I can't afford to employ Keller. Simple as that."

I try to process what this means.

"So I take it he didn't tell you where he is now?" Glenn says.

I look at him, waiting.

"He's on the *Australis*."

"What? That's impossible."

"He asked me for a reference," Glenn says. "Wisely, it was for a position with minimal passenger interaction. I just spoke to the HR manager last week."

"But he would never—" I stop, the nausea I'd felt earlier suddenly surging back.

"Are you okay?"

"I'm fine."

Glenn looks as though he's about to say something more, but the nausea overtakes me, and I push past him to the nearest lavatory. I lean over the toilet, and even as I tell myself it's just seasickness, maybe a minor stomach bug, I can't help but remember the last time I'd felt this way, years ago, after Dennis—the caustic feeling of having been left out, left behind.

McMurdo Station

McMurdo Station is a U.S. base on Ross Island, on the south side of the Antarctic continent and in the shadow of Mt. Erebus. The planes used to transport scientists and staff from Christchurch, New Zealand, are like large tin cans with rows of military-grade seating, cramped and cold. At this time of year, during the austral summer, when McMurdo is the Grand Central Station of Antarctica, with its maximum capacity of twelve hundred residents, the planes are as packed as commercial jets during the holidays.

I secure my bag in the middle of the fuselage, take a seat, and close my eyes for the eight-hour flight. I'm heading to McMurdo on a National Science Foundation grant to do a census of the emperor colony nearest the base. During the station's busiest period, the LC-130 cargo planes arrive regularly to bring people and supplies. Eventually the flights will taper off, and from February to October, except for the very rare fly-in, planes won't land at McMurdo at all.

I hear a voice above me. "Seat taken?"

I open my eyes and say, "Suit yourself." A guy about my age is pulling down the metal bar of the jump seat next to mine. He's tall and thin, with overgrown dark hair that falls into his eyes and a red bandanna loose around his neck.

The guy leans his head back against the red nylon webbing that constitutes our seats, his head angled toward mine. "It's my first time here," he says.

"Mmm."

"And you? You look like an old-timer."

I look over at him.

"I don't mean *old*," he says. "Just—experienced. Like you know the drill."

"Yeah, I get it. You here to do research?"

"To do dishes, actually," he says. "I'm with maintenance. Just something to get me down here. What about you?"

"I'm studying the emperors at Garrard."

He regards me with new interest. "Really? Is that the colony that was wrecked by that iceberg?"

I'm surprised, and pleased, that he knows of the colony; so many who come to McMurdo for the manual labor and maintenance jobs seem to know about the wildlife only on a superficial level.

"I'm Keller," he offers. "Keller Sullivan."

"I'm Deb."

"Good to meet you," he says.

"Likewise."

"I'd love to hear more about the colony," he says.

He's turned his head and is looking at me almost sideways. In the dim industrial lighting, the dark of his eyes deepens against his pale face.

"Maybe later? I'm a little tired," I say. "Didn't sleep at all on the flight to Christchurch."

"Me, neither," he says.

I let my eyes fall shut again. It's not often anymore that my mind wanders toward Dennis, but right now, it goes straight back. I'm always surprised by how, even after all this time, it can feel like only days ago.

There'd been an investigation, of course, an autopsy, more questions than I knew how to handle. The worst was the media. News of the investigation had leaked out—everything from the fact that Dennis and I had spent the night together to details on his drowning. I think the family hoped, and I certainly did, that Dennis's death would've been kept as private as possible—but when something happens in Antarctica, it's newsworthy by default. Everyone knew, from my colleagues at the university to the tourists on the new season's trips south. The investigation ruled Dennis's death a suicide; the tour company and everyone involved, including me, were officially off the hook.

I still have his ring, the wedding band he'd tried so hard to lose. I've kept it hidden away in a small box at the top of my closet with a few other valuables. No one had ever asked about it. When I saw pictures of his wife in the news, I convinced myself that, by being there with him during his last hours, I had more right to keep it than she ever would, since she'd been off with someone else when he died.

I drift away to sleep, and the next thing I know, I'm awakened by an announcement from the pilot. I open my eyes and see Keller's confused face. When I hear the sighs and groans of everyone in the cabin, I know what the news is—the plane is turning around.

"What's a boomerang?" Keller asks.

"Bad weather at the station," I explain. "If the plane can't land at McMurdo, the pilot has to turn around."

He nods. We don't speak again, and we go our separate ways when we land back in Christchurch. When I arrive at the Antarctic Program passenger terminal the next day, I don't see him. But then, soon after I board, I feel someone sink into the seat next to mine, and there he is.

"We meet again," he says.

All around us, passengers are pulling their parka hoods over their heads and faces, preparing to sleep, and I offer Keller a brief smile and then do the same, closing my eyes quickly so I don't have to look at him, so he won't keep talking to me.

The only problem is, I can see his face even with my eyes closed.

I remain awake, aware of Keller beside me, of his arm lightly brushing mine as he reaches into one of his bags, as he opens a book to read. I don't know how much time passes until I feel movement next to me again, what I think is the motion of Keller leaning his head back against the netting behind us.

Finally I succumb to sleep—there is little else to do on these flights—and wake to a dull pain in my neck. I've slouched over in my seat, my head resting on Keller's shoulder.

I straighten up, mumbling an apology. Then I notice that he looks very pale. The LC-130 is heaving and pitching in the sky. "I don't remember it being this bad the last time," he says.

"We didn't make it this far last time. It's often like this when we get close."

I watch his face, just a hint of tension under the stubble of his jaw, and when he gives me a sheepish grin, I notice that his brown eyes are streaked through with a color that reminds me of the algae veining the snow on the peninsula islands—a muted, cloudy green.

There are no armrests on an LC-130, nowhere to put your hands during a stressful landing. Keller is gripping his knees, his knuckles white. Biting back a smile, I reach over to pat his hand in a *there, there* sort of gesture, and I'm surprised when he turns his palm upward to clasp mine.

There's not really any such thing as a routine landing at McMurdo, and by the time we approach the ice-hardened runway, the storm has whipped up whiteout conditions. The pilot circles several times in an attempt to wait out the weather, but eventually he must descend. When the plane touches its skis down on the ice, a sudden gust of wind seems to take hold of its tail, spinning it across the runway and nose-first into a fresh bank of snow.

But the plane holds together, as do Keller and I, our hands still clasped. After the plane stops moving, we let go at the same time. I try to ignore the fact that I hadn't been ready to let go. That a man's hand in mine, after so long, had felt good.

With Keller behind me, I step through the hatch, down the half dozen steps to the ice. The air hitting my face is so cold it stings, the whirling snow a blinding white. As I put my hand up to shield my eyes, I see the Terra Bus that will transport us to the station from the runway. The bus is even more cramped than the plane, and after boarding I don't see Keller among the parkas, hats, and luggage stuffed inside. Fifteen minutes later, the station comes into view through the bus's small, square windows.

With its bare industrial buildings, McMurdo looks like an ugly desert town whose landscape is drab and brown at the height of the austral summer and so white in the winter that you don't know which way is up. On clear days, Mt. Erebus is visible in the distance, steam rising from its volcanic top, and later in the season, when the sun finally begins to set, the mountain looks as if it's on fire.

I'm stretching my legs, taking it all in, when I notice Keller watching me.

"I was thinking," he says. "Maybe I could shadow you out there one day? See the colony firsthand."

I tell him, "Maybe," both charmed by his interest and a bit wary of it.

We've been assigned to different dorms and say quick good-byes before going our separate ways. We don't make plans to see each other, but I know I'll eventually bump into him around the station, in the cafeteria. At McMurdo, during the busy season, you can't avoid people even if you want to.

Yet I don't see him again until two days later, when I'm heading out for my fieldwork and find him standing outside the Mechanical Equipment Center, wearing a jacket that looks too light for the temperature and that same red bandanna tied around his neck like a scarf.

"Hey," Keller says in greeting as I approach the building. "Are you heading to the Garrard colony?"

"That's right."

"Is this a good time for me to tag along?" he asks.

I look at him, wondering how serious he really is about learning about the penguins. "Don't you have dishes to wash?"

"Not until tonight," he says.

"Why don't you spend some time getting the lay of the land?" I suggest. "You could visit Scott's hut—it's a nice walk from here."

"Already tried," he says. "It's closed for renovations. Indefinitely, they told me. What are they doing in there, anyway? Adding indoor plumbing? Central heating?"

I can't help but smile.

"I promise I won't get in your way," he says.

I glance toward the MEC building, then back at Keller. "Have you been trained on the snowmobiles?"

He shakes his head. "Not yet."

Which means if he comes along, he'll need to ride with me. There's just enough room for two on the Ski-Doo, and I don't carry many supplies for day trips: a counter, field notebook, water, pee bottle and plastic bags, and a survival kit, all tucked into a compartment of the snowmobile.

"I'm not on a schedule," I warn him. "I can't drive you all the way back here so you can be on time for your shift."

He grins. "You scientists. No respect for the workingman."

I give him a look, but he's still smiling. "What're they going to do, fire me?"

"Probably."

He only shrugs. "Look, I may not know a lot about penguins yet," he says, "but I could be a great assistant."

I'm not sure I need an assistant, but I consider it anyway. There's a lot of data to collect, and he could be helpful—as long as I don't have to spend my time picking up after him or fixing his mistakes. At least he knows about the colony, which is something. A decade earlier, a gigantic iceberg calved off the Ross Ice Shelf and blocked the penguins' access to the ocean, their only source of food. They had to find a new path, which was more than twice as long. None of the chicks survived that season, and most of the adults starved. Once a fairly healthy colony, with thousands of breeding pairs, it had to start over—but it's been recovering, growing slowly, and thanks to our five-year grant from the NSF, someone from the Antarctic Penguins Project travels down here to do the annual census. This year, it's me.

"I guess I could use an extra hand," I say. Keller's smile is so genuine I can't resist smiling back.

It's a clear day, with lucent vanilla ice sandwiched between blue ocean and bluer sky. When we arrive at the colony, I set about my work, instructing Keller to either stay put and watch or follow my footsteps exactly so as not to disturb the molting birds.

"It's called a catastrophic molt for a reason," I tell him. Unlike most other birds, penguins molt their feathers all at once, rather than shed them gradually. The emperors' molt happens over a month, a physically exhausting feat that uses up all their energy. The penguins, fattened up in preparation, look as though they've gotten bad haircuts, their brownish feathers sloughing off in a patchwork of fluff, the beautiful, sleek new feathers coming in underneath.

"Don't do anything to cause them to move," I say. "They need every bit of energy they've got."

Keller nods and follows me, just as slowly and carefully as I've instructed. In addition to counting the birds—a job made easier by the fact that they're molting and standing still—I slip quietly among them to inspect carcasses on the ground. The dead are mostly chicks, killed by starvation or skuas—the mean-beaked predators that feed off penguin eggs and dead chicks — but this means that at least the adults are making it back out to the ocean to feed.

It isn't until later that afternoon, when I press my hand into an ache in my back, that Keller suggests we take a break. "You haven't stopped once," he says.

I look at my watch — it's been five hours since we left the station. And it occurs to me that Keller hasn't stopped either; he hasn't gotten cold or tired or hungry.

"I always lose track of time out here," I say, almost to myself.

He swings his slim backpack off his shoulder. "I brought lunch."

"You go ahead," I say.

"You forgot to bring food, didn't you?"

"I don't usually eat when I'm in the field."

"I have enough for both of us," he says. "Sit down."

He shakes out a small, waterproof blanket, and we settle down about thirty yards away from the birds. I don't bother looking at Keller's food — vegans become accustomed to not sharing meals. It can be rare even to meet garden-variety vegetarians down here.

But Keller's pack is filled with fruit and bread, with containers of leftover rice and beans and salad. "Seriously?" I ask.

"Rabbit food, I know," he says, as if he's had to defend his food a hundred times before. "It's all I've got. Take it or leave it."

I almost laugh with the sudden pleasure of this strange, simple thing — sitting with Keller on the ice, sharing a meal among the molting emperors, on a blindingly bright Antarctic day. It's been so long since I've made a connection with someone else. I haven't been with anyone since Dennis, and even after a year, it hasn't been difficult; in fact, life's been a lot simpler. Or maybe I've just managed to convince myself of that.

In science, in the natural world, things make sense. Animals act on instinct—of course, they have emotions, personalities; they can be cheeky or manipulative or surprising—but, unlike humans, they don't cause intentional harm. Humans are a whole different story, and I learned at a young age that, in most people, meanness is more instinctual than kindness. I'd been a boyish kid—tall for my age, with cropped blond hair, a science geek. After being physically kicked out of the girls' restroom in junior high by girls who were convinced I was a boy, I grew my hair halfway down my back. I wore it that long, usually braided, until just last year, when I chopped it to right below my chin—long enough to look like a female, since I never wear makeup, and to still be able to pull it back and out of the way.

"What is it?" Keller asks. "What're you thinking about?"

"Nothing," I say, and he hands me a fork.

"How long have you been with the APP?" he asks.

"About eight, nine years." I take a bite of salad and rice. "And what about you? What did you do before entering the world of janitorial services?"

He shrugs. "Something a lot less interesting."

There's something closed off about the way he speaks, and I don't ask him anything else. We finish eating, and I get back to work. Despite my earlier vow not to cater to Keller's schedule, I get everything loaded back into the snowmobile in time to return to the base for his shift.

That night, I lie awake in bed for a long time, despite the exhaustion that sears the space behind my eyes. A lot of people have trouble sleeping at this time of year, thanks to nearly twenty-four-hour daylight, but I know this isn't the reason.

The next day, Keller's waiting for me at the MEC again, and he asks if he can help me count the birds.

"Did you bring me lunch?"

He nods.

"All right, then."

At the colony, I spend more time observing Keller than counting the birds. I watch how carefully he moves among the penguins, clicking their numbers on my counter. I watch his eyes inspect every inch of the carcasses we kneel beside, as I explain how to identify the cause of death. "Only an autopsy can determine if their stomachs are empty," I tell him, pointing at a thin, hollowed-out body, "but you can see here that this one was in really poor condition. Hardly any body fat at all."

I become so absorbed in the work that I fail to notice the wind whipping up around us. It isn't until I feel icy snow pelting my face that I look up and see that there's no longer a delineation between ice and sky, that the world has gone white.

"Shit," I say under my breath, and I radio the station. They've already restricted travel, and the winds are over fifty knots. We need to get back now.

I call out to Keller, and immediately he's at my side, helping me load the snowmobile. Within a few minutes we're ready to go—but the engine won't start.

I try again, the engine grinding slowly but refusing to turn over.

"Dead battery?" Keller asks. He's sitting right behind me, his mouth next to my ear, but I can hardly hear him over the wind.

"Could be," I shout back. "But if it was, I probably wouldn't get any juice at all."

We dismount, and it's then I realize that we don't have time to troubleshoot, let alone to fix the vehicle. The wind is bracing, my hands so cold I can barely move them, even inside my gloves. When I glance back at Keller, only a few feet away, he's a blur, his hat and parka coated with snow.

"We need to take shelter," I say.

"Let me check the battery."

"Forget it, Keller." The driving snow is pricking my eyes. "Even if we fix it now, we're not going to make it back."

While Antarctic weather is notoriously capricious, I'm annoyed; I can't believe I let the storm creep up on us this way. Keller is still going on about fixing the Ski-Doo as I pull our survival pack out of its hutch, and I turn and shove it into his chest. "You have no idea what this weather can do," I shout over the wind. "Get the tent out. Now."

There's no time to dig ourselves a trench, which would be the best way to wait out the storm. As it is, we're barely able to pitch the emergency tent and scurry inside. We've got just one extreme-weather sleeping bag and a fleece liner, and I spread them both out over us. Even if the tent weren't so cramped, the freezing air instinctively draws our bodies close, and without speaking we wrap ourselves up, pulling the fleece to cover us completely, including most of our faces. Despite the protection from the wind and our body heat, it's probably no more than thirty degrees inside the tent.

"I bet this isn't what you had in mind when you came to Antarctica," I say, my voice muffled by the fleece.

"On the contrary," he says. "This is exactly what I had in mind."

I turn slightly toward him in the dim light.

"For God's sake," I say. "You're not worried at all, are you?"

He moves his head slightly, and when he speaks I hear a smile in his voice. "I'm impervious to ice."

This feeling he has—insane, illogical though it is—is one I understand. I'd felt similarly invincible once—at times, my life down here on the continent seemed surreal, a dreamworld in which whatever happened remained separate, protected from real life. It's a notion that many who come here can relate to, but it lasts only for a brief time.

"You've read about the continent's history, I take it?" I say. "You know how many bad things have happened here."

"Plenty of miracles, too."

"Is that what you're hoping for?"

"Not really," he says. He pauses, then adds, "Maybe."

"What do you mean?"

"I know I'm not the first one who's come here for a change of scenery. Midlife crisis sort of stuff."

"Definitely not."

"You wouldn't have recognized me three years ago," he says. "I was a lawyer. Married. Nice house outside of Boston. Everything most people want."

"Everything my mother wanted for me, that's for sure," I say. "So what happened?"

A pause, and then he says, "The unthinkable happened."

He goes quiet. I listen to the rhythm of our breathing,

barely audible over the keening of the wind outside. I can tell he is still awake, and I ask, "You okay?"

"Yeah," he says. "You?"

I nod, and we're close enough that my head nudges against his. We fall silent again, snuggled together like puppies for warmth. As time drifts, I think back on the day's work, and then I sit up with a start.

"What is it?"

"My notebook," I say, patting my parka, trying to recall whether I'd stashed it in one of the oversize pockets. "I don't remember where I put it."

"It's in the hutch."

"Are you sure?"

"I saw you put it away."

I stare at the opening of the tent, though I know it would be foolish to venture outside. "I hope it hasn't blown away."

"It won't. You secured it tight."

I wonder then if he's been watching me as closely as I've watched him.

"Relax," he says. I feel his hand on my back, and when I lie down, his arm remains around my shoulders. I feel the day's exertion, finally, take over, draining my body and mind of what little energy is left. I turn toward Keller, and my icy nose meets the warmth of his neck.

I let my breathing slow, but my eyes remain open wide, fixed on the stubble on Keller's face, on the spot where his earlobe joins the skin of his jaw. I never imagined I'd find myself in a situation like this again—in a tent with another civilian, another amateur—and a part of me is afraid to sleep, afraid to risk waking up alone.

I don't remember closing my eyes, but I wake hours later to a bright gold glow. For a long moment, I don't move, savoring the heat of Keller's body next to mine. When I sit up, he stirs and opens his eyes. The look on his face is one I haven't seen in a while—sleepy, not quite sure where he is, a hint of a smile as he remembers.

But it's not me he's smiling about; he's looking past me, at the shadow hovering over my shoulder against the backlit tent.

"The snow," he says. "Look how high those drifts are."

Outside the tent, the sun is a halo behind thin clouds, and a light wind lifts the snow, surrounding us with sparkling dust.

We have to kick the snow away to step out of the tent, and I'm glad I'd remembered, at the last minute, to bury a flagged pole in the snow near the Ski-Doo, which is now hidden under several feet of snow. I radio the station to check in, let them know we'll be on our way soon. By the time I turn back, Keller's uncovered the snowmobile and is bent over the engine.

"I think the spark plugs got iced over when the temps dropped yesterday," he says, straightening up. "Clean and dry now. Give it a try."

The engine starts right up. I let it run while I pack our tent. As we head toward the base, with Keller sitting behind me, his arm around my waist, I wish we weren't on our way back. The cold, exhaustion, and hunger don't compare to my sudden desire to remain with Keller, away from the busyness of the station.

As we return the snowmobile to the MEC and set off for our dorms, I try not to delude myself into thinking he's more interested in me than in the birds. In fact, when I see him later and he suggests we meet at the Southern Exposure, one of McMurdo's bars, he asks if I can bring my notes, if I'd mind sharing them.

And so, over the next couple of weeks, we continue our routine—days counting birds together, nights in the bar after his cafeteria shift. We get to know each other slowly, drink by drink. Once we're a few beers into the night, the conversation becomes personal. Keller doesn't like to talk about himself, and I have to fit together his pre-Antarctic life in puzzle pieces. It's an image that remains with me when I see him each morning—a faded cardboard picture with the seams still visible, the cracks still open.

But I want to put the puzzle together; I want to understand who he is. He's unlike most men I've known, men whose experience here is more academic. Keller seems to go about discovering Antarctica like one of the early-twentieth-century explorers, part fearlessness, part eagerness, and part ambition, as if he's got something to prove. I'm intrigued, as if I've unearthed a new species, one I'm eager to study, bit by bit.

One night I'm gazing at him, trying to picture it—the buttoned-down life he said he'd once lived—this man I've never seen in anything but denim, flannel, and Gore-Tex, whose hands are chapped from nights working in the galley and days counting penguins.

"So you were a lawyer, married, house in the suburbs," I say, wanting the rest of his story. "Kids?"

He says nothing, and something in his face makes me wish I could withdraw the question. I stand up and wobble my way over to the bar to get us another round of drinks. When

I return to the table, he's staring at the wall, at a photo of an emperor colony. Our beers slosh as I put them down on the table, and I tumble into my seat.

Finally he turns to me. "Remember the other day—you told me how penguins that fail to breed will sometimes choose new partners."

For a long moment, I can't comprehend what he's telling me. "It was our first child," he says. "Only child."

He takes a long drink, and I try to remember how many rounds we've had. "She died," he says. "Car accident."

I don't know what to say. He is very drunk, and he's talking far more than he ever has, yet his body remains still, lean and almost statuesque in the chair. "I thought we might try to have another baby," he says. "But she decided to try another husband."

"Just like that?" As I look at Keller through the bar's haze of cigarette smoke, I'm finding it impossible to imagine anyone walking away from him so easily.

"Just like the birds," he says with a harsh laugh. "I can't blame her."

I want to touch him then, but I don't move.

He shifts in his seat and pushes his hair off his forehead in a slow, tired motion. "It was my fault," he says. "Ally was nineteen months old. Britt, my wife—she went back to work after Ally's first birthday, and we took turns dropping her off at day care, picking her up. I was supposed to pick her up that afternoon, but a meeting got rescheduled. I called our babysitter, Emily—a grad student who took care of Ally from time to time. Ally loved her. I even bought an extra car seat so Emily could take her places. She used to joke we were killing her love life, with a baby seat in her car. It was this crappy old subcompact. If only I'd bought her a new car instead."

He reaches for his beer, but he doesn't pick it up, doesn't drink. "I had my phone off during the meeting. I went home and no one was there—no Ally, no babysitter, no Britt. Then I turned on my phone."

His hand tightens around the glass. "I went to Children's," he says, "but she was gone. A driver on a cell phone had run a red light and slammed into the back, on Ally's side. Emily survived. Britt blamed me more than anyone. I was the one who should've been there."

I reach over and touch his hand, still wrapped around the glass, his skin rough and wind-chapped, and I think of how Antarctica toughens you up, how maybe this was what he wanted—maybe this is what we all want—to build calluses over old wounds.

He turns slightly in his chair, leaning almost impercepti-bly closer to me. "It didn't fall apart all at once," he says. "It's strange, how people disappear. No one likes to talk about it— as if it might be catching. Our friends, Britt's and mine, didn't know what to do—I mean, all of a sudden, we didn't have kids who played together anymore. My sister was the only one who would listen, really listen. She's the only one who calls me on Ally's birthday. The only one who invited us over for dinner on the first anniversary of her death, so we wouldn't have to be alone. She's good that way, like my mom was. Everyone else—they seemed to want to pretend it never happened."

He lifts his shoulders in a shrug. "Britt and I tried to make the marriage work. She couldn't move on—or didn't want to. We didn't last much more than a year. After she left, I tried to immerse myself in work." He looks down into his beer. "When we were together, when Ally was alive, the days always seemed too short—there was never enough time to fit it all in. Then, all of a sudden, every day was endless. Nothing seemed to matter anymore. I wanted to escape—like Britt had, I guess. But she only went as far as Vermont."

He takes in a breath. "I started reading about the explorers, you know, wondering whether there was any uncharted territory left. Even by the time I decided to leave the country, I didn't really know where I would go. I didn't have a plan." He pauses, and a small, sad smile emerges on his face. "Looking back, I guess I did know. I remember the day I went into my boss's office and handed over my resignation," he says. "I told him, 'I am just going outside and may be some time.'"

I know, of course, that these were the last words of Captain Lawrence Oates, who died along with Robert Scott and the rest of the expedition team on their return from the South Pole. Knowing he was near death anyhow and a liability to his party, Oates walked out of his tent and onto the ice. No one ever saw him again.

Eventually I tell Keller about Dennis, and he's not surprised; he'd known all along. "I remember reading about it," he says, "and seeing your picture. I thought about how alike we were, even though I'd never met you before."

"Alike how?"

"Abandoned," he says.

Antarctica gets her icy claws into a certain type of person, I've realized over the years, and I can see now that Keller is one of them. Now that he's caught, he'll return again and again, and he'll learn that no one back home can quite understand what brings him here—the impulse to return to the ice; to these waddling, tuxedo-feathered creatures; to the hours-long fiery sunsets; to the soothing wild peace of this place—and he'll eventually build his life around Antarctica because he'll feel unfit to live anywhere else.

That night, we leave the bar as usual, and my heartbeat stutters as we're about to part because I notice the way his eyes are latched to mine. But though his gaze lingers for a moment, he offers only his usual good-bye: a quick wave and a quicker smile.

The next afternoon, we hike up to a ridge overlooking the Ross Ice Shelf—a massive, flat blanket of ice stretching out into the ocean. Though it's the size of France and hundreds of feet thick, it looks as thin as a wafer from high up, and about as fragile. From here we have a good view of a large Adélie colony. I watch a smile spread across Keller's face as he studies them through the binoculars. "I love their faces," he says. "Those eyes."

Adélies have completely black heads, and the tiny white feathers surrounding their glossy black eyes give them a wide-eyed, startled look. Compared to the emperors, the Adélies are tiny; making little huffing noises, they walk with their wings sticking out, feet wide, heads high, looking almost comical, whereas the emperors always look so serious, their wings down at their sides, their heads lowered.

"They might be my favorite species," I admit, "if I had to choose."

He lowers his binoculars, then reaches out to touch my sunburned cheek, and that's when he kisses me. It happens quickly—his hand at the back of my neck, the spontaneous meeting of lips—and then time slows and nearly stops, and suddenly my body feels as wet and limpid as melting ice.

Sex at McMurdo happens in stolen moments; it's furtive and quiet, thanks to too-close living quarters, roommates, thin walls. I don't know how many days blur together between that first kiss and the first night we spend in my dorm, but finally, after an aeon of helpless and constantly rising desire, we sneak out of an all-staff party and crowd into the narrow bunk in my room, ravishing each other like sex-starved teenagers, which is also typical of McMurdo residents.

Afterwards, as the bass traveling on the wind from a distant building echoes the thumping of our hearts, in the arid heat of the room, sweat evaporating from our skin, it seems we could be anywhere—but at the same time, I realize this is the only place where our sudden relationship could feel as familiar to me as the icy, moonlike terrain surrounding us outside the room's tiny windows.

In the weeks that follow, we steal time whenever we can—when my roommate is in the field, when Keller's is at work; it becomes difficult, at other times, to think of anything else. When we come in from the field, we have to peel off so many layers I think we'll never find skin, until there it is, burning under our hands, dry and hot, two deserts finding water.

Under the days' perpetual sunlight, we compile data, we eat and talk, we pack up and hurry back for his shift in the galley. Late one afternoon, when he has the day off, we stretch out in the blinding light, hands folded together, my head on his shoulder, and we listen to the whistling of the wind across the ice and the cries of the birds. I savor the utter silence under those sounds; there is nothing else to hear—none of the usual white noise of life on other continents, no human sounds at all—and Keller and I, too, are silent. It feels as if our own humanness has dissolved, as if we have no need to communicate other than by breath and touch. And I feel the chill that has always seemed a constant and necessary part of me finally begin to thaw.

AS I DRESS in the dark, what seemed like a good idea earlier now seems silly, impractical. I fumble to find my sunglasses and hear my roommate turn over in her bunk, and I'm thinking about taking off my cold-weather gear and getting back into bed myself.

I tiptoe to the door and, in the ray of light from the hall, I glance back at my roommate—still asleep, thick orange earplugs filling her ears, a slumber mask over her eyes—and slip out of the room.

At Keller's dorm, I knock quietly, hoping his roommate doesn't answer. I wait, then knock again, wondering if I've overestimated us, to be so certain he'll welcome a middle-of-the-night surprise wake-up call, that he'll be willing to sacrifice one of the more precious resources of McMurdo summers: sleep.

Finally the door cracks open, and he stands there blinking as the hall's fluorescent lights hit his eyes.

"Get your coat," I whisper.

He shuts the door and a few moments later opens it again, fully dressed. We slink through the dorm. Outside, we shade our eyes from the nighttime sun, still high in the sky and obscured by a veil of wispy clouds. It's about twenty degrees out, maybe colder.

I love that Keller hasn't asked a single question about where we're going, why he's out in the broad daylight of three in the morning. He's just letting me lead the way.

We walk toward Hut Point, a little more than three hundred yards away. The land under our boots is black and white, volcanic earth and frost. The ice-snagged waters of McMurdo Sound stretch out in front of us—and before that: a plain, weathered square building.

The hut that Keller has been so eager to see was built in 1902 for Scott's *Discovery* expedition. For months it's been closed and locked to all but the conservation team that's finishing its restoration—except for tonight.

I dig into my jacket and pull out a key. I let it dangle between us.

His still-sleepy face breaks into a smile. "How'd you get that?"

"I'm well connected."

He grins, and I hand him the key.

Under the awning Keller pulls off his hat, pushing his sunglasses up over his head. He unlocks the door, and we step inside, standing still as we wait for our eyes to adjust to the dim light coming in through the building's small, high windows.

I watch as Keller walks carefully through the hut. I follow his eyes around the soot-blackened room: boxes and tins of oatmeal and cocoa, biscuits and herring; rusted frying pans on the brick stove; shelves scattered with cups and plates, bottles and bowls; oil-smudged trousers hanging on a line, a dog harness from a beam. A pile of dark, oozing seal blubber drips with oil; seal carcasses hang, well preserved, on one of the walls. A large box labeled LAMP OIL reads, SCOTT'S ANTARCTIC EXPEDITION 1910 — one of several other parties that once inhabited this place.

It's eerily noiseless — the hum of the station gone, no penguins outside, no petrels above. Instead of the diesel fumes of the station, we breathe in the thick, musty flavors of hundred-year-old burnt blubber and the dusty artifacts of men whose time here was both celebratory and desperate.

Keller knows not to touch anything, and he moves as little as possible, taking in everything he can. I hadn't thought to bring a camera with me — but then I realize, in all our time together, I've never once seen him take a photograph.

"Remember the lost men?" Keller asks.

"You'll have to be more specific."

"The Ross Sea Party," he says. "They were right here — in this room — never knowing they'd devoted their lives to a lost cause."

"They knew the risks." In 1915, ten men from the Ross Sea Party, the group Shackleton had tasked with laying supply depots for his *Endurance* expedition, had gotten stranded when their ship lost its moorings and drifted. Not knowing that Shackleton's crew had been forced to abandon their own ship, the men kept going, completing their mission, but three of them didn't survive.

"That's exactly what I appreciate about being down here," Keller says. "You know the risks — the hazards are tangible." He takes another look around, as if what he's trying to say is written on the time-scarred walls. "Back in Boston, I was living this so-called normal life, blissfully ignorant of the dangers all around us. That's so much worse. Because when something does happen, you're not prepared for it."

I move closer, and he pulls me into a long hug, so long I feel as if maybe he's afraid to let go—as if by clinging to me, in this hut, in this faraway place, he can preserve his memories and leave them behind at the same time. I want to assure him that he'll find a balance, that it's the same fine line as going from here to home and back again, but I know he'll learn this soon enough, in his own time.

At last he pulls away, kisses my forehead. "Thank you for this," he says.

We go back out into the summer night and walk around the other side of the hut, facing the sound. Clean, cold air freezes through my nostrils, carrying the faint scent of ocean and iced rock.

In the water, flat fragments of ice float around like puzzle pieces; in the distance beyond, thin layers of silver glisten over the light blue of large bergs. As a breeze begins to stir, I lean into Keller, a chill biting through my clothes.

He pulls me closer, staring over the top of my head. "Sea leopard," he whispers, using the explorers' term for the leopard seal that is passing within fifty feet of us, on its way to open water. We watch the seal, a full-grown male, as he propels his sleek gray body forward, focused on the sea ahead.

Then the seal stops and turns his head toward us, sniffing the air, revealing his lighter-gray, speckled underside. He gazes at us, his face like that of a hungry puppy with its wide, whiskered nostrils and huge wet eyes. We're downwind, but

I feel Keller's breath stop halfway through his chest. After a few long moments, the seal turns his head and continues on his way, slipping silently into the water.

Keller exhales, slowly, and I feel his weight settle against me as he relaxes. Though a leopard seal had once hunted a member of Shackleton's *Endurance* party—first on land, then from under the ice—and while they can be highly dangerous, attacks on humans are rare.

I look at Keller, thinking he'd been worried about the seal—and I see he's smiling.

"I could get used to this," he says.

"To what, exactly? Close encounters with deadly predators? The subzero temperatures? The six-day workweeks?"

"You," he says. "I could get used to you."

WITH CONSTANT DAYLIGHT, time loses its urgency, and it's easy for me to believe we'll be here forever. Yet eventually the sun sets for an hour a day, and then a few more—and soon conversations on the base begin to eddy around the transition from summer to winter season. As our time at McMurdo grows shorter, I can't stop myself from thinking ahead. Real life begins to intrude into every moment. Lying in Keller's bed one afternoon, I tuck my head under his chin. "Where do you live now? Back home, I mean?"

We still don't know some of the very basic facts about each other. Here, none of it matters.

"After the divorce, I got an apartment in Boston," he says. "When I came here, I put everything in storage." With my face against his neck, I feel the vibration of his voice almost more than I hear it.

"I have a cottage in Eugene." I curl an arm around his chest, wrap a leg around his. "Plenty of room for two, if you wanted to visit. Or stay."

The moment the words are in the air, I feel myself shrink away from them, anticipating his reaction. I pull the sheet over my bare shoulder, as if this could shield me from hearing anything but yes.

Yet he lifts my chin to look at me, intrigued. "Really?"

"Sure."

A pensive look crosses his face, and I think of his life before, how rich and full it must've been — and now this: a dorm room with frayed sheets and scratchy, industrial woolen blankets, and ahead only the promise of a storage unit in Boston, or a tiny cottage and a wet Oregon spring.

Then he smiles. "Remind me," he says, "how long have you lived alone?"

"We're practically living together here. I've spent more time with you than with any non-penguin in years."

He pulls me up and over until I'm on top of him, looking down at his face. Our weeks here, with long workdays and rationed water, have left him windburned and suntanned, long-haired and scruffy. I lean in close, and he says, "What are we waiting for?"

WE DON'T TALK much about it after that day. I don't think about what Keller might do for work in Oregon, about the fact that he'd only recently begun a whole new life. All I can think about is him coming back with me—the first time I've been able to bring home something I needed, a part of the place that always seems to make me whole.

The last days in Antarctica before heading Stateside usually make me jittery, but this time it's Keller who's on edge during our final week at the station.

"It's always hard to leave," I assure him. "But we'll be back."

"I know *you* will," he says. "You've got a career. I'm just a dishwasher. And everyone wants to be a dishwasher in Antarctica."

He's right; the competition for the most menial jobs at McMurdo is astounding. "But you got here," I say. "You've proven yourself. They'll want you back."

Our last days are busy—I'm gathering my final bits of data and wrapping up the project; Keller, as well as working in the galley, has been filling in for Harry Donovan, one of the maintenance guys, who's been sick. We're spending less and less time together, which doesn't concern me because soon we'll have nothing but time. We're among the last of the summer staff still here—already the base is shrinking down, getting closer to its winter size of two hundred. In six more weeks, the sun will set and not rise again for four months.

When I see Keller at Bag Drag, at the Movement Control Center from where we'll load our bags onto the Terra Bus headed for the airfield, the place is overstuffed with people, cold-weather gear, and luggage—amid all this, Keller looks strangely empty-handed. It's not unusual for flights to be delayed or canceled, but I have a sinking feeling that's not the case. I lower my bags and look around. "Where's your stuff?"

He hasn't spoken, hasn't moved; he's just watching me.

"Deb," he says.

His tone, low and cautious, causes my chest to tighten, and I don't want him to say anything more. With my foot, I slide my duffel toward him. "Help me with my bag."

But he doesn't move. "I don't know how to tell you this," he says, "so I'm just going to say it. I'm staying. For the winter."

I sling my laptop bag over my shoulder, keeping my eyes on the floor. I'm afraid to look up at him, as if seeing his face will make what he's telling me real. For the moment, it's all just words in the air.

"Harry's got bronchitis," he goes on, "and he's going home. I'm here, I'm vetted—so they offered me his job." A pause. "It's a step up from dishwashing, at least."

I'm silent, still staring downward.

"I'm not sure if I'll ever make it back here otherwise, you know?" I hear a pleading note in his voice. "Come on, Deb, say something."

I look up at him finally. "What's there to say?"

"Tell me you understand."

"I don't."

"I need this, Deb. I've tried to start over—with Britt, with my job—nothing worked. But here"—he raises his hands as if to take in not just the building but the whole continent—"I feel as though it's possible here."

He steps forward, gathers my hands. "You'll be back before you know it. Next season. Or even sooner—for Winfly, maybe," he says, referring to the six-week fly-in period between winter and the main season. "Or I'll see you in Oregon. Like we planned."

When I don't answer, he squeezes my hands. "I'm doing this for my future here. For ours."

When I look at him, I know that he's fallen head over heels—not for me but for this continent. I can't blame him. I myself had overwintered after my first visit to McMurdo. Much like Keller, after I'd gotten a taste of Antarctica, I didn't want to leave. Because there'd been no research for me over the winter—the wildlife disappears when the sea ice encompasses the island—I'd taken a job as a firehouse dispatcher. I'd have done anything to stay.

And I want to tell him so many things. That it's exhilarating—the way the sun dips below the horizon for longer and longer each day, a glowing orange yolk that leaves behind a reddish black sky. That it's lonely—that he will hear the waning sound of the season's last plane echoing in the sky for a long, long time. That it's dangerous—that the storms here are unlike anything he's ever seen, with winds at a hundred knots, temperatures at eighty degrees below zero, snow blasting through the air like violent ghosts and seeping into buildings through the smallest cracks imaginable. That in the six months of total isolation, with no supply deliveries, no company other than two hundred other wintering souls, he will long for things like city streets, oranges, the leaves of trees.

Yet he's made up his mind. While overwintering isn't for the faint of heart, I know Keller believes it will be easier for him to be here than at home. And he's probably right.

I drop his hands and pick up my duffel. I can't speak, so I nudge past him toward the door.

"That's it?" He's speaking to my back as I approach the exit, the sunlight from the open door blindingly bright.

I stop and turn around. "Come with me, Keller. If you stay here . . ."

He comes close, puts a cool hand on my cheek. "It'll be fine," he says. "It's just a few months."

"Six months," I remind him.

"That's nothing, in Antarctic time," he insists.

It's forever, but I don't tell him that. I'm still holding my duffel, which is heavy, and I feel the painful stretching of muscles in my arm as I stand there, waiting for Keller to change his mind, knowing he won't. When he reaches for my bag, I let him take it. We don't talk as I get weighed with my bags, have my passport checked. We share a brief wisp of a kiss, nothing more. Keller waits on the ice as I board the bus, as it rumbles toward the airfield on its massive tires.

As I watch Keller through the bus's small windows, I think of the look on his face when he'd watched the Adélies that day on the ice, the first time he kissed me. I remember telling him that the Adélies will sometimes mate for life, but they are loyal first and foremost to their nesting sites—and now it seems that Keller and I are no different, loyal first and always to the continent.

At McMurdo in the depth of winter, people come together for many reasons—loneliness and boredom even more than attraction and compatibility—and I wonder if Keller will emerge from the dark with another woman in his life, just as at the end of each winter, an Adélie will return to its nest, but if its partner doesn't show, it will choose a new one and move on.

Aitcho Islands, South Shetland Islands
(62°24'S, 59°47'W)

It's early in the morning when I go up to the ship's "business center," a tiny space with a short row of computer terminals and a satellite phone. On the *Cormorant*, the emphasis is on seeing the sights, not on staying connected, but there's just enough here for the die-hard workaholics to plug in if they need to. From what I've heard about the *Australis*, all the passengers' and crew's quarters have in-room phones, so it should be easy enough to reach Keller.

After an operator connects me, I listen to the ringing of the phone—a strange sound to hear as I look out at nothing but sea and ice. I've never had to reach anyone from the Southern Hemisphere before—everyone back home knows when I'm away and when to expect me back—and this need to connect fills me with an unfamiliar anxiety, as though I've learned a new language and am fumbling to find the right words. As the ringing continues, I wonder: Do these in-room phones have voice mail? And if so, what will I say?

After another moment of static, I hear his voice—clear and familiar.

"Keller, it's me."

"Deb?" He sounds concerned. "What's the matter? Are you all right?"

"You're asking *me* what's the matter?" The worry, the skip in my heart upon hearing his voice, unexpectedly translates to anger, and I can't mask my irritation.

He sighs but says nothing.

"Why didn't you tell me?"

"I thought Glenn might change his—"

"I know, I talked to Glenn," I interrupted.

"I was hoping to see you in Ushuaia, but we set off earlier, and since then it's been so busy I haven't had a moment to think. I've been trying to figure out how to contact you."

"Why the *Australis*? That ship is a bull in a china shop. You know that."

"I needed a job; they needed extra crew. And it gets me closer to you."

I picture his face, in an expression of the innocent, misguided hope that we might actually see each other, and this softens me a bit. "But what are you planning to do, jump ship and steal a Zodiac? I want to see you, too, but how in the world is that going to happen?"

"I'm still working on that part. We're in the same hemisphere, at least."

"I just wish you'd told me," I say. "Back in Eugene. Maybe we both should've stayed home."

"That's exactly why I didn't tell you. You need to be here, just like I do. I'll patch things up with Glenn eventually. I actually think he would've taken me back, if he hadn't been able to find anyone."

"Thom. He found Thom."

"I know."

"Why didn't you just keep your mouth shut?" I'm thinking back to last season, the moment that got him on Glenn's blacklist—our shipboard lecture, the defiant passenger, Keller's short temper—and I wish I could go back and seize the mic from Keller's hands.

"Like you wouldn't have said the same things?" he says.

"But I *didn't*. That's the difference."

"Well, I can't do anything about it now. I'm here. That's what matters."

"Why does it matter so much if we can't be together?"

"You'll see."

"What does that mean?"

"It means you'll know when I see you."

Thoughts sweep through my mind—whether we might actually see each other, whether Keller does have a future with this program—and a moment later he says, "Look, we'll figure it out. Let's talk later, all right?"

I'm not ready to let him go; I want to ask, *When? How?* But before I can get the words out, the line goes dead. I'm not sure whether we've been disconnected or Keller has simply hung up.

AS I HEAD toward the dining room to pick up a quick bite before our scheduled landing, I'm still arguing with Keller in my head, changing words and sentences, hoping for a different outcome. Our voices rising. The line going silent.

Then I stop—the voices are real, and they're apparently coming from a couple just inside one of the hatches to the outer decks. I don't want to listen, but I can't pass without interrupting, so I wait, hoping they'll move on, or at least reconcile quickly.

After a moment, I recognize the voices—Kate and Richard Archer.

"If you don't want to do the landing, why on earth did we come down here?" she's saying. "Why come all this way if you don't even care?"

"For you," he says. "You wanted this trip."

"I wanted something for us. To get reacquainted, Richard. Not just to be on a boat with a hundred other people. To go for a walk, to see the penguins, to see their chicks, to—I don't know, share a moment together."

"Do you remember how we met?" he asks.

"What are you talking about?" She sounds exasperated. "Of course I do."

"That day in the café, when your computer crashed. You had a memory leak."

"Richard, can we talk about this later?"

"Let me finish," he says, his voice louder.

"Okay, okay." She speaks in a whisper, as if she might be able to quiet him by example.

"The software was eating up your laptop's memory," he continues. "That's why it crashed. It was an easy fix, but you didn't know that. I wanted you to think I was a hero."

"What are you saying? You don't think I value you enough?"

"No, I'm saying that this trip, this sudden obsession with the penguins and the melting ice, it's like a memory leak," he says. "It's consuming your mind, our plans—"

"Richard—"

"To retire early. To start a family."

"No," she says. "*You* wanted to retire, not me. And you've earned it. About the baby—I never said never. I just wanted to talk about it some more, that's all."

There's a pause, and then Richard says, "I thought we'd already made the decision."

"We aren't like your computers, Richard. Our life is not a software program. We're allowed to change our minds, to change our plans."

"Except that you're the only one changing," he says. "I've held up my end of the bargain. What about you?"

"What *about* me? You're bargaining with yourself, Richard. You've left me completely out of it. And that's not my fault."

He doesn't answer, and I hear the slamming of the hatch, which means that at least one of them has gone out to the deck. I wait a little longer, until I'm certain they both must be gone, and then I continue on to the dining room. Breakfast is in full swing, but I don't see either one of them.

LANDINGS ARE METICULOUSLY organized in order to appear efficient and seamless. Glenn and Captain Wylander find a spot to anchor, a place to land the Zodiacs. Glenn gives us a timetable, since he has to coordinate everything with the galley as well; due to the ever-changing weather, the chance to go ashore takes precedence over scheduled mealtimes. A few naturalists set off to scout trails for hiking, to make sure there are no leopard seals napping nearby. We find the best place to bring passengers ashore—preferably a shallow beach where we can haul the Zodiacs as close to dry land as possible.

The passengers, meanwhile, line up in the B Deck passageway leading to the mudroom, where they'll sterilize their boots and move magnetic tags with their names and cabin numbers from an ON SHIP to an OFF SHIP position. It's low tech, unlike the *Australis*-style ships that have electronic swipe cards for everything, but it helps us make sure every passenger who leaves the ship eventually gets back on.

The Aitcho Islands are an ideal place to land—plenty of penguins, fairly even terrain. As I lead a group of tourists away from the landing site, the chinstraps roam all around, their webbed feet leaving watery prints in the thick mud near the shore. I issue a strict warning not to go near the birds—but I can see how tempting it might be to pet them, to feel their silky black heads and snowy white faces, to trace the thin black lines encircling the undersides of their chins. The adult penguins, with no predators on land, will often pass close by; sometimes they'll even walk right up to you. We constantly need to remind passengers that this is not a marine park, that we're actually in the wild. Sometimes Keller will show them his ragged penguin-bite scars, which works pretty well as a deterrent.

When it comes to the tourists, our patience can wear thin, Keller's especially—but I'm always reminding him that while we've grown used to this environment, for everyone else it's like a cold, faraway planet that probably doesn't feel quite real.

And, more important, what people learn here might actually make a difference if they go home thinking about how much their actions up north affect the creatures down here.

I point to the guano that covers the nests and rocks, and now covers our boots as well—its sharp, overwhelming stench is the reason many of the passengers have covered their noses with scarves or the tops of their sweaters. "You'll see how the guano is a reddish pink over there, where the chinstraps are," I say. "That means they're eating krill. Over here, the color's more whitish pink, which shows the gentoos are eating fish as well as krill. What we don't like to see is guano that's a greenish color, which indicates a bird is starving."

We continue our hike. The hills are studded with nests of rocks and pebbles, and penguins with fat, gray-and-white chicks are nestled up against them. Kate is in my group—Richard is not—and I can't help thinking of what I'd overheard earlier. I feel sorry for her, for both of them, and, for once, I can relate to such relationship issues: to one person wanting something the other doesn't, to missed connections. I'd finally begun to feel that Keller and I were past all that, yet here we are, with him in one place and me in another, not knowing whether we'll be able to find our way back.

I feel a sudden lurch of nausea and pause midstep. Perplexed, I take a breath and try to steady myself. Despite the jet lag, despite the Drake, despite all the passengers and crew crowded together on these trips, I never get sick. And I don't like the thought that I'm getting myself this worked up over Keller.

One of the tourists asks if I'm all right, and I shake it off and keep walking.

At the crest of the hill, we stop and look out over the bay. Beyond lies a sea of rich blue, the water broken by ice and lava flats, the skyline broken by the sharp, ice-blanched peaks of the rugged island chain. I direct the tourists' attention below, to where gentoos and elephant seals share a beach of thick, volcanic sand and fist-size rocks.

I watch Kate, who stares ahead as if she hasn't heard me, as if she's not aware of the giant, belching, molting seals, their smooth, shiny coats emerging underneath a thick, peeling brown layer that's more pungent than the penguin guano. The seals, under the sun's steady glow, use their flippers to fling sand over their bodies, grunting with every move. The humans are wearing hats, gloves, boots, and several layers under thick parkas, but for the animals, it's too warm. The white-bellied gentoo chicks, still fluffy without their insulating adult feathers, are panting in the heat.

The birds are especially active today, and we proceed back to the beach, more slowly than I'd usually walk because my stomach is still threatening to rebel. Once the shoreline is in sight, I let the group go ahead to the landing site and hang back to radio Glenn.

"I need to come back," I tell him. "I'm not feeling well."

"What's the matter?"

It's the first time I have ever called in sick. "I'm sure it's nothing," I say, but I can't explain further than that.

"I'll send someone out to take your place," Glenn says. "I want you to see Susan when you get back to the ship."

I know I don't need a doctor, but I also know better than to argue with Glenn.

As I make my way to the Zodiacs, I watch the chinstraps

continue their shuffle from their colony down to the shoreline, where they wade in, then dive under and vanish in swirls of water. Other birds emerge, shaking the water off their backs, and head back up to the colony. The cycle continues, over and over, and all of a sudden something feels familiar in their consistent path, in their methodical gait. I see my own life in theirs: a constant back-and-forth motion, always ending up where I started, and circling back again—focused and simple—and perhaps this is why I chose this life, for the straightforward beauty I'm witnessing right now. Maybe I thought that life down here would remain uncomplicated, and that I could keep the same pace, the same arm's-length existence from the world, forever.

Ushuaia, Argentina

I arrive in Ushuaia late, and by the time I reach the docks I'm a full day behind everyone else and horribly jet-lagged. I'm still on the gangway, holding my duffel bag, as Glenn begins to introduce me to a new crew member. I don't recognize the tall, dark-haired man Glenn calls over until he turns around.

The red bandanna around his neck. The mossy brown eyes.

"Keller Sullivan," Glenn says, "Deb Gardner."

"We've already met," Keller says, extending a hand.

I take it. Keller's hand, ungloved, is warm and rough. I let my eyes hover on his.

"Briefly," I say, withdrawing my hand. "A while back."

I haven't seen Keller since the day I left him at McMurdo, two years ago. He looks at once the same and different—still beautiful, his skin a little more weathered, his stubble a little scruffier. Most noticeable of all, he exudes a confidence he hadn't had before. He looks as though he belongs here.

Keller had e-mailed me faithfully from the station during

his austral winter, and over my own long, humid summer in Eugene, I tried to understand his decision, to put myself in his shoes. I even envisioned him on that bus instead of me, pictured myself staying behind for months of lightless cold while he left for home alone. Yet I wasn't sure I'd have been able to make that decision as effortlessly as he had.

We had only talked once; phone calls were expensive and hard to coordinate; with limited bandwidth, Skype wasn't allowed. After that first call, after I could no longer see Keller's face or hear his voice, as he wrote about overwintering—the biting chill, the inky dark, the supernatural green light of the aurora australis—he only seemed farther and farther away.

His choosing to stay made sense to me—he'd suffered losses that would never fully heal, and perhaps he thought the austral winter in Antarctica would help because, with the onset of darkness, the notion of time disappears along with the sun. That he could trade our plans so easily for an overwinter at McMurdo proved that he was ready to build a new life for himself, but it was one that didn't include me.

I had worked hard to let him go, and I'm wholly unprepared to see him again, here on the *Cormorant*, though I should've known it would happen. Antarctica is a small world.

After introducing us, Glenn leaves us standing there.

"What are you doing here?" I ask.

"I have a job, same as you."

"You could've told me, at least."

"How?" Keller says. "You stopped writing me back. You didn't return my calls."

I look down at my hands, red from the chill in the air, and try to settle the thoughts swarming through my head, to articulate what I want to say. "It seemed pretty clear that was what you wanted, by staying at the base, then going back to Boston—"

"I only went back to Boston because I hadn't heard from you. Where was I supposed to go?"

"It's fine; I get it," I say. "You did what you had to do. So did I."

A crackle through Keller's radio startles us both, and he pulls it from his waist—it's Glenn, calling with a chore.

"Can we talk later?" Keller asks, and I shrug.

Despite my casual gesture, the knowledge that Keller is on board stays with me every second. The day is chaotic, with my attention pulled in myriad directions—helping the expedition team sketch out a rough itinerary, gathering data and photos for the presentations I'll give during the journey, pitching in wherever I'm needed—and I see Keller only in passing, within groups of crew members or other naturalists. Yet my heart rate quickens at the sight of him—and even when he's not around, I feel his proximity like an electric current, a frayed wire, loose and dangerous.

Finally, after the ship is prepped and everything quiets down, I go out to the uppermost deck, the one reserved for crew. In the evening dusk, I look at Tierra del Fuego as thick clouds hover over the mountains and creep down amid the sunset-hued buildings of Ushuaia. Opposite are the calm waters of the Beagle Channel, from where we'll begin our journey tomorrow evening.

I hear the creak of a hatch opening, then the sound of footsteps on the deck. It's Keller approaching, smiling just as I remember—a quick, easy smile with a hint of sadness underneath. He carries a worn paperback in his gloved hands. Seeing him, I feel a familiar cool hollowness, like an ice fog settling into a valley—the way I'd felt long after leaving him at McMurdo.

I'd kept busy the spring after I left, working on my data and writing a paper on my findings at the Garrard colony; when the days in Oregon grew long and bright, I taught a summer school class and then got a last-minute gig in the Galápagos on another ship from the *Cormorant's* tour company. I'd returned to Antarctica as usual last season, and being on the peninsula felt far enough from Ross Island that I managed not to think too much about Keller. By then, I didn't know where he was; I'd let our correspondence go months earlier.

Now, as I look at him on the deck, with the breeze in his hair and his eyes fixed on mine, it seems as if time has frozen, as if I'm back in the same moment at the Movement Control Center at McMurdo, when he told me he was staying behind.

He holds up his book, its pages fluttering in the night's breeze. *Alone* by Richard Byrd. I'd read the book years ago, a memoir by the first person who'd wintered by himself on the continent.

"The first time I read this," Keller says, "it was about two years after Ally died, after Britt and I split up. I came across Byrd's home address—it's right there in the book—and I knew exactly where it was. He lived on Brimmer Street, in Beacon Hill, not even a mile away from me."

He palms the book between his hands. "I was still at my old job, so the next morning, I worked a half day from home, then headed over to Beacon Hill on my way to the office. It wasn't hard to find the address, but I began to doubt it was Byrd's real house because there wasn't a plaque or anything setting it apart—and this was the home of a man who had three ticker-tape parades in his honor during his lifetime, and a state funeral after he died, a man who's buried in Arlington National Cemetery. So I was about to keep walking when a woman emerged from the house with a bag of garbage. I said hello and blurted out that I was admiring her house. Without missing a beat, she said, 'So you've read the book.' I said yes, and then she invited me in for a tour."

Keller's lips turn up in a half smile. "She showed me the paneled library on the first floor with a carved oak fireplace mantel, where Byrd planned his journeys. She showed me the little backyard where Byrd tried to keep penguins after one of his trips. It was unbelievable that she did that—she didn't know me; I could've been any kind of lunatic. But I knew why when I told her she should put a plaque up on the building. She shrugged and said, 'Nobody remembers Byrd anyway.'" Keller looks up, his eyes meeting mine. "That was the day I quit my job. I wanted to do something worth remembering."

"And so you became a dishwasher at McMurdo."

He smiles. "I thought of it as a temporary distraction—the part where I got away from it all and discovered what I wanted to do. I had no idea this would be what I really wanted. Which meant I had to start over, catch up to you."

"You thought leaving me was the best way?"

"For the record, I never planned to stay on," he says. "I never wanted to separate, but that was my chance—to learn as much as I could, to become something new. I tried to explain it. If only you'd picked up the phone."

He steps closer, leaning his body next to mine against the railing. "I wasn't ready to go home. Not then."

"But you weren't planning to go home," I say. The cry of a petrel in the distance adds a background whining note to my voice. "You were planning to come to Oregon with me."

"And wash dishes in Eugene?"

"There were other options. Other ways to come back down here."

"Like what? By staying, I could put the hours in, learn how things worked. Whenever I wasn't working, I was out helping anyone who needed it."

"So why'd you leave McMurdo at all?"

"Because that was only the beginning of the journey." He takes my cold hands, and I don't resist. "You were the destination."

I shake my head, my mind trying to return to the way it was between us, wanting to get it all back.

"What is it?" Keller asks.

"Just trying to remember the last time you kissed me."

Keller puts a hand on one side of my face, and as he slips his hand to the back of my neck, he pulls me forward and kisses me, a long slow deep kiss that in an instant melts away the icy edges that had frozen since I left McMurdo.

Finally he steps back and looks at me. "So," he says, with that grin of his. "Does that jog your memory?"

I try to look nonchalant, though my hands are shaking. "Vaguely."

He kisses me again, and we stay out on the deck for a long time, huddled together, trying to fit the past two years into the next two hours as night settles over Ushuaia.

It doesn't take us long to pick up where we'd left off—and, as at McMurdo, our time together is so unpredictable, so divided among shipboard duties, that every moment feels tenuous, as if we might easily lose each other again.

Over late nights on the crew deck, Keller fills me in on what he's been up to the past two years: He'd done legal consulting as he went back to school full-time, earning a master's in ecology, behavior, and evolution in only two semesters. He wrote his thesis on the impact of rising global temperatures on Adélies, and he impressed the APP enough for them to recommend him to Glenn as a naturalist this season so that he could gather data on Petermann Island.

I'd known that, with Thom taking time off, I'd have a new research partner on Petermann, but I'd assumed it would be one of the long-timers from the APP. And then, after six whirlwind days on board the *Cormorant*, one of the other naturalists escorts Keller and me to the island by Zodiac, with two weeks' worth of supplies.

As soon as the *Cormorant* recedes into the Penola Strait, Keller and I work quickly to establish our small camp, pitching all three tents though we know one will remain empty. After a week of pent-up sexual energy on board, we're both eager to take advantage of being alone, at last. As I lie naked in the tent, my body awakening in the cool air, under Keller's hands, I realize the extent to which I'd let myself grow numb, forgetting the pleasures to be found in my own skin. The tent is tight and cramped, not unlike our individual sleeping quarters on the *Cormorant*—but now, rather than the hum of the ship, we hear the sounds of the penguins and waves lapping the bay; rather than dry heated air, the night is alive with a gelid summer mist. It's effortless, being together again, as if it were days later rather than years, and the emotional scrim that had begun to envelop me falls away again. Keller, too, seems more at peace, as though he has shed the very last of his former self, traces of which I'd seen when we first met. Now he's only muscle and bone, as if distilled down to his very essence—the part of him I still feel may be just out of my reach.

In the morning, we rise early; it's a balmy forty degrees, and we work in light jackets, forgoing hats and gloves. Our tasks for the next two weeks include counting birds, eggs, and chicks, as well as weighing a sampling of chicks to contribute to one of our ongoing studies on the connections among penguin populations and factors like climate change, food sources, the fishing industry, local weather, oil spills.

We've continued to examine the effects of tourism on the birds. Two hundred years ago, the penguins had the continent all to themselves; now they come into contact with bacteria they have no defenses for. Four years ago, Thom and I tested tourists' boots as they boarded after a landing and found almost two dozen contaminants. Glenn wasn't at all happy about our stopping guests from the Zodiacs on their way to lunch, so that was our first and last experiment. And in truth, we can't blame only tourism; migrating birds bring new toxins, too—we've found salmonella and *E. coli*, West Nile and avian pox. Still, whether it's climate change or tourism, the only thing not changing is the penguins' vulnerability. So we keep studying, and I keep wondering what impact our data might have.

Seeing Keller working nearby throughout the long days, sharing our meals, retreating to our tent as dusk settles over the island—all this has given me a sense of optimism I haven't felt since my early years here. For so long I've identified with the continent in its icy despair, the ephemeral nature of its wildness—but I feel newly energized, as if what we accomplish here may make a difference after all.

The weather holds up for nearly our entire stay—it isn't until the last day that an icy rain begins to fall midafternoon, while we're still in the midst of the day's work. The adult penguins are unfazed, going about their business as the raindrops roll off their feathered backs—but the chicks, still covered with dark-gray fluff, can't shake out the water that sinks into their down, and many of them will freeze to death this year.

Keller and I are both as waterlogged as the chicks when he convinces me it's time to give in; the temperature is dropping, the rain turning to sleet. We scurry into our tight two-person tent, where Keller takes off his boots and helps me with mine. We toss our dripping jackets into the corner, on top of the boots, as we shiver in the frigid air.

"Lie back," Keller says. He pushes my shirt up over my shoulders, and I close my eyes, trying to stop my body's shaking as I feel his mouth on my belly, my breasts, my neck, then holding my breath as he travels downward. With his tongue he limns the angles and curves of my body, filling the hollow places he'd left behind, until new tremors flood through me, washing away all but the two of us, our bodies damp and drying in the wind-rattled tent.

Later, when the rain stops, we hang our clothes to dry outside. I'm quiet, thinking about what comes next. After our return voyage, when the *Cormorant* docks in Ushuaia, we'll watch the passengers crowd onto a coach bus bound for the airport, and we'll have one more night together before Keller himself heads to the airport. Because this is Keller's first trip with the *Cormorant*, he'd only been offered one voyage, one assignment at Petermann. He'll travel from Ushuaia to Santiago to Miami to Boston while I prepare for the next group of passengers to embark. I'll spend another week on board and two more weeks on Petermann with another naturalist from the APP before heading back to the States myself.

"Don't worry," he says, as if reading my mind, as we begin a walk along the edge of the gentoo colony near our camp. "It won't be like before. We'll figure things out."

He stops, looking out over the colony, then raises his hands, as if framing the scene for a photograph. "All this—it reminds me of a word I learned from my grandmother, a long time ago," he says. "Her parents were German immigrants, and this was back when there was a lot of anti-German feeling in the States, so they distanced themselves from their heritage. My grandmother had always wanted to visit Germany, but she never did—she taught me this German word, *fernweh*, which doesn't have an equivalent word in English. It means something like being homesick for a place you've never been. She said that was how she felt about Germany, her whole life." He motions toward the hills, peppered with nesting gentoos. "I finally understand what she meant."

A looming intuition seeps from below my consciousness, like the weighty, hidden part of an iceberg—the unwelcome awareness that for Keller, this is still about Antarctica, not about me. The continent has given him the unexpected liberty of beginning again—and while I know I can never understand the depth of his loss, I'm not sure he can truly begin again, even if he doesn't fully realize it. He'd let me go once already, by staying at McMurdo, and, though I'd managed to let him go, too, I won't be able to do it twice.

"So is there a word in English—in any language—for what we're doing?" I ask. "For thinking we can make it work this time?"

"Insanity?" he says.

I laugh. "The ecstatic display," I say, thinking of penguin mating rituals. "The flipper dance."

"Normal people," he says, "just call it love."

WE MEET UP late in the day, at the edge of one of the island's largest gentoo colonies, each of us clutching a hand counter. We settle on a large, flat rock about twenty feet from the colony to rest for a few minutes before heading back to camp.

We watch a crèche of juveniles waddle eagerly forward as adult penguins return from the sea, ready to feed their still-dependent offspring. A few penguins sit on eggs, and others are feeding very young chicks, taking turns to forage for food. One gentoo tries to steal rocks from another's nest, evoking a shrieking match among several of the birds. A skua lands dangerously close to a nest, stepping toward one of the tiny chicks, and five nearby gentoos turn on the skua, who lets out a rubbery caw and flaps away. Moments later, the gentoos are squawking at one another again.

"I'm still getting used to not intervening," Keller says.

One of the challenges of being a naturalist is letting nature take its course, no matter what. "I'm not sure that feeling ever leaves you."

He lifts his eyes from the penguins to the ocean beyond. "One day at McMurdo," he says, "a Weddell seal wandered onto the base—I have no idea how he got there, so far away from the water. He was all alone, just sort of limping along. He was small—a juvenile."

I listen, remembering when we met, when Keller couldn't tell a crabeater seal from a Weddell. How he'd called the leopard seal a sea leopard.

"I followed him, wanting to help. There was no way I could get him back to the water, but I could tell he was dying, and I wished I could put him out of his misery, at least. I stayed back, waiting, as he slinked along. I don't know if he was aware of me or not. Finally he stopped moving. I watched him die." Keller turns his head toward me. "Is that crazy?"

"I'd have done the same." I stretch out my legs until one of my thick-soled boots touches his. Those who winter over at McMurdo occasionally see animals heading away from the sea when they should be going toward it—some are confused, lost; others are steady and determined, as if they are on some strange suicidal mission. Of all the challenges of overwintering, this is the most disconcerting.

"I'm sorry I didn't stay in touch," I say. "I was trying to protect myself, I guess."

"I shouldn't have given you a reason to."

I nudge his boot. "Only one more week until we're back in Ushuaia."

"I wish I could stay down here," he says.

"I can give you the key to my cottage," I suggest. "You can

make yourself at home. The place does need a good cleaning, though, and you'll have to feed my landlord's cat."

He smiles. "Can I take a rain check?"

"Why?"

"I'll be teaching at Boston University, believe it or not—just summer term, a freshman bio course. When they offered it to me a month ago, I didn't know whether I'd see you. After we lost touch, I thought—" He stops. "It's a different sort of complicated, this life, isn't it?"

I think of two volcanologists I know from McMurdo, an "ice couple," meaning they are together whenever they're at the station but then happily return home to their families, thousands of miles apart, after their research time ends—an arrangement not at all uncommon among Antarctic research-ers and staff.

"Couldn't you get out of it?" I ask. "I mean, if you really want to come to Oregon instead."

"I don't know. I guess a part of me needs to see this through."

"Teaching? You could do that in Eugene."

"It's not that. It's about"—he pauses—"not disappearing."

"What do you mean?"

"It's been almost five years," he says, "but still I go home and think of how things used to be. Wiping up Ally's dinner from the kitchen floor while Britt gave her a bath, or vice versa. We traded off these things, but usually we both read her a story. Sometimes it was the only time we all were together in a day, but we always had that." A smile lights his face, and I feel as though he's talking more to himself than to me. Then it fades. "Britt donated all of Ally's books to Children's Hospi-tal before I had a chance to go through them. I'd have liked to keep just one. Her favorite was *Make Way for Ducklings*. Since we lived in Boston and we'd taken her to see the bronze ducks in the Public Garden, she thought it was a true story."

He leans back slightly on the rock, propping himself up with his hands. "After she was gone, after Britt left, I'd be at the office until nine, ten, eleven. Until I was tired enough to know I could get to sleep in an empty apartment. Before I could register how quiet the place was, and how neat—no food on the floor, no toys in the bathtub, no picture books." He angles his head toward mine, though his focus is on a pair of gentoos walking past a few feet away. "Just before I went to McMurdo, I called Britt. A week before Ally would've turned four. Britt had met her new husband by then, but they weren't married yet. I told her I was thinking about her because of Ally's birthday—but the truth was, a part of me was worried that she'd forget. She'd been trying so hard to move on, to erase both of us from her life—it was as if we'd both disappeared." He raises his eyes to mine. "And then I did disappear. I came down here."

There's nothing I can say, and I suddenly feel selfish for wanting all that I want for us, for even attempting to weigh my own desire against the depth of his pain.

I move one of my gloved hands over to touch his and lean against him. We watch a penguin raise her head, calling to her chicks, and they emerge from the crèche, wobbling toward her, ready to eat.

The weather has turned, the wind blasting tiny frozen chips of rain into our faces, our hats and jackets. We sit and watch the penguins for a few more minutes before packing up our supplies and heading back to camp.

THE NEXT MORNING, we're packed and ready by the time Glenn radios with the *Cormorant*'s ETA. Keller and I are windblown and grubby; I feel the sweet, worn-out exhilaration that comes from the end of a research trip, as well as the nagging anxiety about what our data will ultimately reveal.

Keller has already taken a load of supplies to the landing site, and as I follow, approaching the bay where a Zodiac will appear for us at any moment, I feel the same irresistible pull toward Keller I always have, taut as ever. I slow as I get nearer, and the few feet left between us feels vast, wide open; in this space I see our entire relationship, or whatever this actually is — both clear and opaque, entirely comfortable, and completely whole.

An hour later, after a hot shower on board, I glimpse my face in the tiny mirror above the sink. I hardly recognize myself, and it's not the sun- and wind-reddened skin or the dark circles under my eyes or the deepening of a few wrinkles. With a jolt I recall learning, in a long-ago biology class, about a section of the cerebral cortex that, when damaged, causes a condition known as face blindness. If you damage this part of the brain, you can no longer recognize friends, family members, or even your own face in the mirror — and this is how I feel, as though I'm looking at a stranger — someone with features just like mine, only relaxed, softened: someone in love, someone loved back, someone happy.

IN THE MUDROOM after the morning's landing at Cuverville Island, I hang up the extra life preservers and get ready to signal the crew to bring up the remaining Zodiac. Then I notice there's still one tag in the OFF SHIP position. I don't recognize the name, but who it is doesn't matter as much as the fact that we've left someone on shore.

"Shit," I mutter and radio Glenn to tell him to wait up.

I turn the Zodiac back toward the landing, my shoulders tensing. It's extremely rare for tourists to get left behind, and my mind flashes to Dennis. When I round the coast to the landing spot, the sight of a lone passenger standing there nearly stops me short.

"Hello?" I call out, but he doesn't seem to hear me.

I bring the Zodiac closer and call out again. "Sir, I'm here to take you back to—"

Then the red-jacketed figure turns around, taking off his hat. It's Keller.

Often during the last week of this voyage, I've felt my chest constrict at odd times—when I see Keller across the dining room during meals, when we pass each other en route to some task, when I watch him take off across the water in a Zodiac full of passengers—tense with the knowledge that, while he's here now, he'll be gone soon enough. And now, as he heads toward me, I take a long, full breath.

He wades into the water. "Permission to come aboard?" he asks.

"What exactly are you doing?" I ask, glancing backward. We're just out of sight of the ship.

"I knew you were on mudroom duty," he says, "so I made up a fake tag to lure you out here."

I shake my head, trying to look disapproving, yet I have to laugh at the sight of him bundled up in a red tourist's jacket.

"Are you *trying* to get fired during your first season? Stealing passenger clothing and going AWOL? Glenn's going to have a fit."

Keller steps into the boat. "Borrowed, not stolen. And as far as Glenn knows, you're just picking up a wayward tourist."

He puts an arm around my waist and holds me to him as he takes the helm and steers the boat out of the bay—heading not toward the ship but in the opposite direction, toward a maze of icebergs. Moments later, we're surrounded by towers and turrets of ice.

Keller loosens his hold but keeps his arm around me. "I just wanted a few minutes," he says.

He cuts the engine, and we drift.

After days of tourist chatter, of Glenn's voice on the PA, of the steady rumbling of the ship, the silence fills my mind like water in a jar—the world goes smooth and clear, with nothing but the whisk of wind around the ice, the splash of a penguin entering the water, the gurgle of waves against the ice.

We float along the edge of an iced city, the bergs rising out of the water like skyscrapers. The sea has arched door-ways into the sides; the wind has chipped out windows. In the distance, several conical formations tower over the bay, with deep crevasses in their sides, as if enormous claws have slashed through them, drawing blue light instead of blood.

Keller turns his body in to mine, looking over my head at the drifting icelands beyond. Within days, even hours, these icebergs will be unrecognizable—the water will turn them around, flip them over, wash away a little more from below. The icescape we're viewing now no one's ever seen before, and no one will ever see again.

"What do you love most?" he asks.

"About you?"

He grins. "About the icebergs."

I rest my head against his shoulder for a moment before answering. "I love the way some of them look like houses. How they seem to have doors and windows and awnings and porches. It makes me want to climb inside and live in them."

"I wish we could."

He runs his hands up my arms, over my elbows to my shoulders. I want to shed my naturalist's jacket, and strip him of his tourist's coat, as he pulls me forward and kisses me, finding a slip of bare skin at the back of my neck. In the near silence, the lick of the water against the Zodiac fills my ears, and I feel as though I, too, am floating, buoyed by his hands.

Moments later, the boat lurches us back to where we are—we've drifted into view of the *Cormorant*, a dark shadow behind a thickening layer of mist, and the wind is increasing, blowing snow off the tops of the bergs.

I murmur into his neck, "We should get back."

"Not yet," he murmurs back, and as we stand in the gliding boat I sense what he's thinking: We are like the ever-shifting, ever-changing ice—and whatever happens next, wherever we end up, we'll never be quite the same again.

FIVE DAYS LATER, after disembarkation, Keller and I spend the night in an Ushuaia guesthouse, not knowing when we'll see each other next. We speak very little, even during our last moments together, when, in the sharp, bittersweet morning air, I stand with him on Calle Hernando de Magallanes as he puts his bag into the cab that will take him to the airport. He turns to me, and I press into the heat of his body, his arms around me, his fingers on my back. I want to feel the roughness of his hands one more time, his tall lean body against mine, skin to skin. I slide my hands under his pullover, landing somewhere between cotton and fleece, knowing as I do that I won't be able to reach any further, that this is as far as I can go.

FOUR DAYS BEFORE SHIPWRECK

Bransfield Strait
(62°57'S, 59°38'W)

There are no portholes in the exam room of the medical suite, and though I can feel that the sea is calm, my nausea is getting worse. I've managed to put off Glenn's insistence on a doctor's visit until today, and now I'm hoping my queasiness is only because I can't see the horizon. I know Susan has something stronger than meclizine for seasickness—she doesn't prescribe it except in extreme cases, but I'm getting to the point where I think I qualify.

I always feel a little out of sorts when I can't see the ocean—which is strange for someone who grew up in the Midwest and spends most of the year landlocked in Oregon. Growing up, I loved the water and would often swim in Shaw Park's public pool in Clayton, Missouri. I'd dive off the ten-meter platform, pretending it was a seaside cliff. I'd put on my mask and snorkel and imagine that people's limbs, in their myriad shapes and sizes, were sea creatures. I'd see their colorful swimsuits as brightly hued fish.

My other favorite place had been the geodesic dome at the botanical garden. My father used to take me there when he was in town, which wasn't often, and the rainforest inside, with its tropical humidity and mist, with waterfalls and wildly exotic plants, made me want to explore the world. By the time I was in junior high, my neighborhood had gotten one of the first outdoor-gear stores in greater St. Louis—it was a small store, but just walking through its narrow aisles felt like adventure. I'd try on the extreme-weather clothing and imagine myself at one of the poles.

I didn't know back then that I would, in fact, end up spending much of my life in one of the polar regions, and, over the years, I've come to think of the continent not only as a place but as a living, breathing thing—to me, Antarctica has always been as alive as the creatures it houses: Every winter, the entire continent fattens up with ice, then shrinks again in the summer. When I'm here on the peninsula, looking out at the green and white of young ice and the deep, ancient blue of multiyear ice, I feel as though the bergs, too, are alive, sent forth by thousands of miles of glaciers to protect the continent from such predators as the *Endurance* and the *Erebus*, the *Cormorant* and the *Australis*.

And this is what worries me.

Keller knows as well as anyone that the *Australis* isn't equipped to take on these icy sentinels. He knows what an iceberg looks like underwater, that beneath the exquisite beauty above the surface is a sharp, jagged, nasty thing that will destroy ships if they attempt to pass too close. Even for an experienced captain, miscalculating the distance is not difficult to do, with the constantly shifting winds and waters, the continual calving of new icebergs. Charts of this heavily traveled area have regions not properly surveyed, and every captain knows there is nothing more dangerous than unseen ice.

Sometimes I wonder how long this alien invasion—the ships, the humans—can continue before the continent strikes back.

Susan opens the door, returning to the closet-size examining room where I've been waiting. Earlier, she'd had me pee in a cup, had taken my vital signs and done a quick exam, asked me a dozen questions. I'm starting to feel a bit better, and I stand up as she enters the room, ready to forgo medication and be on my way.

"Have a seat," she says.

"I'm good to go, actually. Shouldn't have wasted your time."

"Please," she says, motioning me back down. Her face is serious, too serious for something like the flu.

I sit.

"Deb," she says, "I don't know if this will be good news or bad news, but"—she pauses—"you're pregnant."

"What?" I can barely choke out the word. Feebly, I lean back in the chair.

"You're pregnant."

"That's not possible."

"You mentioned that you had sex—"

"I know what I said." I can hardly think straight. "What I mean is, I was careful. Very careful. Can you run the test again?"

"Already have." Susan looks at me. I've known her for years; like so many, we see each other down here and nowhere else.

"You're going to have to take extra care on the landings. You're about eight weeks along."

She doesn't bring up options, as most doctors would, because down here there are no options for something like this.

"This can't be right," I say.

"I'm sorry," she says. She begins talking about what foods I should avoid, what activities I should let other crew members handle, but I'm barely listening. When I leave her office a few minutes later, promising I'll return, I can't remember anything she'd said.

"There you are." It's Glenn, jogging behind me in the passageway to catch up. "You all right?" he asks. "What did Susan say?"

"Don't worry," I say. "It's not food poisoning. The ship's not contaminated with norovirus. I'm fine."

"You sure about that?" He studies my face. "You don't seem yourself."

"Residual jet lag, probably. I just need a bit of rest, that's all."

He nods. "Take the rest of the day off. We don't have another landing until tomorrow. You'll probably feel better then."

I nod back, then make my way to the sanctuary of my bunk. I lie down and lay my hands across my belly, which feels the same as always. I think again of icebergs, of how much is hidden away under the surface of the water. How appearances can be so deceiving. I can conceal this pregnancy for the duration of the voyage, but then what? My mind can't move beyond this concept of ice, how everything you have to fear is what lies beneath, what's unseen and unknown.

THREE MONTHS BEFORE SHIPWRECK

Eugene, Oregon

I cross the garden from my cottage to the main house, a light rain dampening my hair. As the austral summer begins in the Southern Hemisphere, October in Oregon is much the same: gray, rainy, a chill that sinks into your bones. A few strands of hair stick to my forehead, and I pause on the back porch, securing the bottle of wine I've brought between my knees as I release my ponytail and shake out my hair, slipping the band around my wrist.

I hear the sounds of raised voices and laughter, and before I reach the door, it bursts open. "Sorry!" a woman says. The guy beside her is laughing, his arm around her waist, and they stumble out into the garden.

As usual, I'm late to the party and a bit too sober.

For the last five years, I've rented the little cottage behind this restored Craftsman where my landlord-now-friend Nick Atwood lives with a fluffy white cat named Gatsby. Nick and I basically share custody of Gatsby—Nick's an entomologist at the university, and his house is so often filled with col-

115

leagues and friends that Gatsby frequently comes to my place for some peace and quiet.

Nick's kitchen is warm and smells of his famous Brazilian risotto cakes. I put the wine on the counter. Gatsby comes over, tail in the air, and lets me scratch him behind the ears. "What're you still doing here?" I ask him. "I expected you at my place hours ago." He flicks his tail and stalks into the laundry room.

I head toward the living room and immediately bump into Nick, who's on his way to the kitchen. He gives me a big hug, and a kiss somewhere around my ear. "I was about to give up on you."

"Sorry. Traffic was brutal."

"Right."

Nick draws me into a circle of colleagues and their plus-ones; he slips a brimming wineglass into my hand, makes introductions, and leaves me with the group. I wish for a few familiar faces, like my friend Jill, a fellow bio lecturer who's away visiting her boyfriend in San Francisco. It's much more fun when she and I can be each other's date for the evening amid all the couples.

"So *you're* Deb," says a professor from Nick's department.

I turn to look at her—a dark-haired woman named Sydney, sharp-featured but soft-eyed, her slender body standing very straight. "Have we met before?" I ask.

"No," Sydney says. "But I've heard a lot about you."

Before I can ask what she's talking about, she introduces me to her boyfriend, a construction manager who draws us into a discussion about LEED-certified building and local politics. I listen, trying not to think about how I'm neglecting the lesson plans for my biology course. Eventually I ease my way out of the conversation and wander across the room.

The house is neat and clean, with Nick's love of invertebrates on full display; the walls in the living room are covered with photographs and illustrations of bees and butterflies. As much as I dislike parties, I do like the white noise of them, and I always enjoy being in Nick's house. I love seeing the way he's merged science with art, and I like the semisocial aspect of being around people, even if not fully engaged with them.

Soon I feel the draft of Nick's front door opening and closing, the noise level in the room fading slowly as the party winds down. As I turn the corner into the empty hallway, the ambient sounds of people talking and laughing and saying good night are almost like a lullaby.

The first time Nick invited me over, soon after I'd moved into the cottage, I demurred—as I did the second and third times. Finally, to be polite, I went, feeling the whole time as though I were in a dollhouse, as if I were back home, where my mother's eagle eye would catch every fingerprint I left, every speck of dirt my shoes deposited on the floor. Then one of his friends toppled a glass of wine onto the couch, staining its beige cushion with a large, deep-crimson moon—and Nick simply poured her a fresh glass and tossed a pillow over the stain. *Trust me, Gatsby's done a lot worse to that couch*, he said.

That's when I began to relax—once I noticed the claw marks on the coffee table, the shredded arm of the sofa, the tiny nose prints on the inside of the kitchen window. And over the years, as we've grown closer, Nick has become one of the few constants in my life, someone who's always here when I come home after months away.

Now I wander back into the kitchen, where Nick's talking to Sydney. Her boyfriend isn't around, and they don't see me, and I feel, as I often do in these situations, that I'm not really a part of what's happening but observing it from a distant place; I'm on the periphery, like something in the background of a photograph that never catches the untrained eye.

When the boyfriend returns, we say our good nights. Nick walks them both to the front door, his hand brushing against my back as he passes by.

I open the dishwasher and begin to run water over the glasses in the sink. A few minutes later, Nick is back, depositing empty beer bottles into the recycle bin in the corner.

"Leave it for the maid!" he says, pouring himself another glass of wine.

"I would, if you actually had a maid."

He leans over to shut off the water, gently hip-butting me out of the way. I see that he's used a rubber band to tie his hair—a thick, light-brown mop he never seems to know what to do with—into a little bob at the nape of his neck.

"Come here a second," I say.

I stand behind him and begin to untangle the dirty rubber band from his hair, as gently as I can. He tilts his head back to help, and I feel the waver of his inebriated body trying hard to stand still. I pull my ponytail holder from my wrist and put it between my teeth, running my hands through his hair, smoothing it out. It's a little damp from the rain outside, and it smells green, like a forest. I pull the hair back and tie it behind his head again. Then I turn him around to face me. "No more rubber bands," I tell him. "They tear the shit out of your hair."

"I'm thinking of cutting it, actually," Nick says, running his hand along the back of his head.

"Don't," I say. "It looks good long."

"Really?"

"Sure." His hair, especially when it's tousled, reminds me of Keller's.

He looks as if he's about to ask me something, but he doesn't. Nick has a sweet face, like a Saint Bernard's: calm, competent, a little somber. He's tall and solidly built, and with his year-round suntan, from studying insects up and down the West Coast, he looks more like a rugby player than an entomologist.

As I sneak a couple of glasses into the dishwasher, I say, "That professor friend of yours, Sydney—what have you told her about me?"

"Nothing."

"She said she's heard a lot about me."

"That's what friends do," he says. "We talk from time to time."

"About what?"

"Why you never come to my parties. Despite the fact that I'm an excellent cook and you have nothing but dehydrated camping food in your house."

"I'm here. Fashionably late, but here."

"You know what I mean," he says. "When would I ever see you, if I didn't drag you over here for food and booze?"

"I'd bring the rent check by eventually."

"Funny," he says.

"Oh, you know I'm kidding."

"Right. Because you pay by direct deposit."

"It's not that."

"It is, though, isn't it?" He props himself against the counter. "Don't you ever go out?"

"Sure I do," I say. "Just the other night, Jill and I went out to Sam Bond's to grade quizzes."

"Doing work at the local pub is still working," he says.

"We had beer."

"Unless you woke up in someone else's bed with a raging hangover, it doesn't count."

"For the record," I say, "I *do* have a social life. He just doesn't live here. In Oregon, I mean."

Nick raises his eyebrows. "I'm familiar with the concept of long-distance relationships," he says, "but don't you think that's a little extreme?"

"You're one to talk, Professor Kettle. I don't recall seeing any single women at this party."

"I thought you counted penguins for a living."

"Your point?"

"You counted wrong." He steps closer. "But then, she was the last one to arrive."

I reach for a nearby wine bottle and refill my glass because I don't know what to say.

"Remember what Freud said?" he asks. "You need two things in life—love and work. You know, as in a balance of the two?"

"Maybe I like being off-balance."

He takes a step backward, still slouched against the counter, as if holding himself up. "I'm serious. When are you going to settle down? Join the real world?"

"Come on, Nick—you're a scientist. Reality's depressing."

"I'm not talking about bugs and birds," he says. "I'm *trying* to talk about the birds and bees."

I smile and take a long drink of wine.

He leans forward. "Don't you think you could ever be involved in a relationship that's not quite so long distance?"

"Define *long*."

"The same county? Zip code. Street, maybe."

He's close again, his face next to mine, and I look down at his mouth, at his full, wine-stained lips, and then I back up and turn to the fridge, where he keeps the aspirin. I shake two pills into my hand and pour him a glass of water.

"Take these," I say. "And drink the whole glass. Every drop."

He takes the water and aspirin but doesn't say anything. I give his hair a quick tug and say, "See you tomorrow."

As I open the door, I look back and watch his expression change—a furrowed brow, a quick smile, something wistful—and then I shut the door behind me and walk across the garden.

LATE THE NEXT afternoon, as twilight falls, I'm trying to focus on my lesson plans when Gatsby's yowl at my back door gives me an excuse to get up from the kitchen table.

I let him in and step away as he shakes the water from his long fur. He stretches, then jumps up onto one of the kitchen chairs and starts a bath. "You hungry, Gatsby?" I ask, scratching the top of his head. He pauses and looks at me, then resumes bathing. He's sometimes hungry, sometimes not—such is life between two households—and I keep cans of cat food among the beans and soups in my cupboard for the days that he is.

I glance out the window, across the garden, and am surprised to see the windows mostly dark, the house quiet. I picture Nick inside alone, hungover, and I feel a little guilty for having invited Gatsby in when he should be keeping his real owner company.

I sit back down at the table and return to work, but it's not long before I hear a knock. It's Nick, blinking rain out of his eyes, holding a stack of mail and a bottle of wine. I open the door to let him in.

"Isn't that the bottle I brought last night?"

"It's probably the only thing I didn't drink," he says.

He puts the wine down on the table and leafs through the mail. "Thanks for coming by," he says, lifting his eyes briefly as he hands me my mail—a couple of bills and *Conservation* magazine. "You didn't need to clean up, though."

"You barely let me anyway."

He motions toward the wine. "Where's your corkscrew?"

I get the corkscrew from the drawer next to the stove, and, while he opens the bottle, I plunk down two wineglasses on the table.

Nick tilts his head toward my laptop and says, "What're you working on?"

As I sit down again, I shove the laptop and my folders across the table, out of the way. "Class stuff."

He fills our glasses and sits down across from me, in the chair next to Gatsby's. "I want to apologize for last night," he says.

I've been half-hoping he didn't remember. "No need."

"It wasn't fair," he says. "Your life is your business. Your love life especially."

"Don't be like that. I want you to be a part of my life."

"But only a few months out of the year, right?" He looks at me and shakes his head. "Will you ever get that place out of your system?"

"Why, so I can settle down here in Eugene? Build a picket fence and have a few kids?"

"What's so wrong with that?"

"You're lucky, Nick. Your work is right here in our back-yard—*Bombus vosnesenskii, Bombus vandykei*. The *Pygoscelis* penguins are in short supply around here, in case you haven't noticed."

"Right," he says with a laugh. "Like you didn't choose penguins for the very reason that they take you to the other end of the planet."

I don't answer.

"It has cost me, you know," he says. "Staying here."

"What do you mean?"

"I was supposed to get married," he says. "Years ago, before you moved in. This cottage was going to be her art studio. She got a job with a magazine in New York and decided to take it."

"And?"

"We told ourselves we could make a commuter marriage work," he says. "But the truth was, we were both stubborn. Selfish. I thought she'd move back here, and she assumed I'd join her in New York. Neither of us got what we wanted."

"You did what you had to do. Why's that so wrong?"

"Because I regret it. Because I couldn't see past the present moment—that I might want something different one day. Do you think I wouldn't take off to the other side of the globe if I could? That I wouldn't be in Antarctica myself, if it had bumblebees?" He meets my eyes, studying me. "Don't you worry you'll have regrets?"

The sound of a fist on the front door is so jarring in the following silence that we both jump. Nick's leg bumps against the table, rattling our wineglasses. He follows me as I walk through the living room.

I open the door to see Keller, his rain jacket soaked, water dripping off the brim of his Antarctic Penguins Project baseball hat. He's close enough to touch, but I stand there, stunned, the rain breezing in, my heart beating in my ears. I haven't seen him since we parted ways in Ushuaia almost eight months ago. I try to speak, taking in the glitter of the porch light in his eyes, his breath in the cool evening air, and I only get as far as parting my lips.

"Hope it's not a bad time," he says.

AS KELLER CHANGES into dry clothes, I walk Nick to the back door, handing him the wine. The introductions had been quick and awkward.

"At least now I know he exists," Nick says. He attempts a smile and reaches down to pick up Gatsby from his spot on the chair. I watch Nick walk across the yard and into his house; Gatsby looks back at me from over Nick's shoulder. I'm still staring out the window when I hear Keller's voice.

"Did I interrupt something?" he asks.

Keller's tone holds no jealousy, no reproach, as if he knows there couldn't be anyone else for me but him. Still, I almost can't believe the sight of Keller in my living room, a vision I've imagined for so long but have given up on ever seeing.

He's looking around, as if scanning a penguin rookery, searching for clues about its welfare, its status, its future. He glimpses the emperor skull I keep on one of my bookshelves, and steps over for a closer look.

I'd salvaged the skull from the lab when a professor heading to another university was planning to toss it out. It's one of the few possessions I treasure, as morbid as that might seem. While a penguin's bones are solid, and the skull is heavier than you'd expect, there's something graceful and delicate about it: the narrow, three-inch-long beak, the wide eye sockets, the gentle curve of the head.

Keller picks it up, running a finger along the fine bones of the penguin's head. He seems lost in thought, and I'm silent until I can't take it anymore.

"I'd given up hope of ever seeing you on my doorstep," I say.

He puts the penguin skull down and comes over to me. He gives me a tentative kiss, then pulls me close, holding me far longer than he ever does, and he whispers in my ear, "Sorry I didn't warn you. I didn't know I was coming myself until I went to the airport and got on standby."

"What's going on? I thought you'd be teaching."

He rests his chin on the top of my head. "Summer term was it. My contract didn't get renewed."

I pull back and look at him. "Antarctica's only a couple months away. Just stay here until then."

He releases me and says, "I'm going to Seattle, actually. See a friend who teaches at UW."

He doesn't look me in the eye when he says this, and I think back to what I'd said during our last voyage, after he got into trouble with Glenn. We'd never really talked about it, but it had only been Keller's second season on board the *Cormorant*, and I worried it would hurt his chances of having a third.

"Keller, about last season—" I begin.

"Let's forget about that," he says, meeting my eyes. "More important, I hope Glenn can."

"So do I."

He gives a half laugh and shakes his head. "I'm having bad luck all around. Soon I'll be back to dishwashing at McMurdo, if I'm lucky."

"Don't worry," I say. "You'll have a spot on the boat. Glenn needs you."

"I hope so," he says.

Suddenly I have an uneasy feeling in the pit of my stomach. While we don't usually know when or where we'll see each other next, it's been understood that we'll meet in the Southern Hemisphere if nowhere else. Filling a cruise with knowledgeable and reliable naturalists, with a diversity of skills and expertise, can be a challenge—some, like Thom, have families; others have tenure-track jobs and teaching commitments. I'm assuming that people like Keller and me, for whom Antarctica comes first, will be guaranteed spots on the *Cormorant*. Perhaps I've assumed too much.

I try to put my thoughts aside as I toss Keller's wet clothes into the dryer. We order Thai food, and as we wait for it to arrive, I watch him open a bottle of wine, thinking that I've seen his hands do many things before, but never this. Never something so ordinary and domestic.

I think about Nick—*Don't you worry you'll have regrets?*—and try to imagine Antarctica without Keller, or both of us here instead. How much I'd be willing to sacrifice if I needed to.

Keller twists the cork from the corkscrew and lays it on the kitchen table. He fills our glasses. We talk about the APP staff, the other researchers we know. We talk about the next phase of our study, which we'll begin during this upcoming trip, after the *Cormorant* drops us off at Petermann. As usual, we don't talk about us.

But later, when I lead him to the bedroom, he follows as if he's glad to leave everything else behind. It's the first time we've been together so far north of the equator, so far away from what first brought us together, and even as I feel his hands on my body, as I become immersed in the full presence of his skin, I also feel an absence, as though he is not entirely here, as I suppose he's never entirely anywhere anymore—as maybe I'm not either.

OVER THE NEXT few days it surprises me every time I see Keller sitting on my couch, one hand balancing a glass on his knee, the other hand scratching the ears of Gatsby, who usually settles down between us when he's here. I can't help but envision Keller's past life—the chaos of dinner with a toddler, bath time, story time. This vision bears less resemblance to the man in front of me than to Nick, or who Nick might've been if he'd ever settled down, perhaps who he still is, deep down.

I wonder who the real Keller is—whether he has become who he was always meant to be, or whether he's simply adapted, like the penguins, out of necessity. And I wonder whether he'd return to the way things used to be if he could, and where that would leave me if he did.

We coexist much the way we do down south, each doing our own work, coming together now and then by day and always at night. Instead of the crew lounge, it's my kitchen table; instead of sleeping bags on the rocks of Petermann, it's the lumpy mattress on my queen-size bed. It takes me a while to get used to another presence; I'll glimpse Keller's toothbrush and do a double take; I'll hear a door shut and remember that it's not just me in the cottage anymore. If I go to bed while Keller is still awake, reading or working on his laptop, I like knowing that, sometime in the night, he'll slip into bed next to me, and I won't wake up alone.

One day, he meets me after my afternoon bio lecture, and we walk through the university's verdant campus, red brick and ivy all around. It had rained while I was in class; water drips off orange- and red-hued leaves, and cyclists spray up mist as they bike past us on the walkways.

I tell Keller about my class, how I'm certain that half the students slept through it.

"No way," he says. "You're a natural teacher."

"One on one, maybe," I say. "Like with you—that was easy. Not so much in front of a class full of restless freshmen."

We move aside as a student, walking backward as she gives a tour, heads in our direction. "What was your class like in Boston? Did you enjoy teaching?"

"I did," he says. "It felt a little like being in a courtroom, only I was talking about things I'm actually excited about."

"You weren't passionate about your cases?"

"Yes and no," he says. "I've always been fascinated with the law itself—building an argument, making it sound, thinking about opposing counsel's next move. It's like chess. But the corporate cases our firm handled . . ." He trails off. "It was a relief to quit, actually."

It's starting to rain—fat, heavy drops that splash up from the shallow puddles on the blacktop. I pull the hood of my rain jacket over my head.

"Where to?" Keller asks.

I think for a moment, the rain splatting against my hood. We're not far from a pub where I often meet Jill, other colleagues, and grad students from the biology department—but when I think about showing up with Keller, I hesitate. While there are plenty of people on the periphery of my everyday life—the ones who know me as an underpaid adjunct professor who's constantly flying south to be with penguins—those who know me best are usually the ones I'm with for those few weeks a year. And I'm not quite ready to merge these two worlds.

Keller's still waiting.

"I know a place," I say, and we head west on Eleventh Avenue. The restaurant is farther away than I'd remembered, and half an hour later we leave our dripping jackets on a coatrack near the door as we slide into a booth whose vinyl seats are patched with duct tape.

I know it was worth the long, wet walk as Keller looks around, smiling at the brightly colored walls, the long bar with its teal-green barstools, the black-and-white checkered floor. "I love a real diner," he says when a heavily tattooed server comes by with menus—vegan comfort food—and jelly-jar glasses of water.

We order plates of southern-fried tofu with crinkly fries, coleslaw, vegan mac-and-cheese, and corn bread. I use my napkin to pat dry the ends of my hair, dribbling rain onto the table.

As I reach for another napkin, I notice, next to the ketchup, a little box filled with Trivial Pursuit–style cards. I shuffle through the cards, pulling one out to ask Keller a question from the nature category: *The diet of which bird creates its pink plumage?*

"Flamingo," he says. "Too easy."

I draw another few cards, yet these are different, posing what-if types of questions. I hold up the first one. "New game. Here we go. 'Would you rather lose the conveniences of e-mail and cell phones, or lose one of your limbs?' "

He laughs. "Really?"

"Right. No moral quandary for you there." I move on to the next card.

"Wait," he says. "What about you?"

I think for a second. "I do like e-mail as an alternative to talking on the phone. But I'd give it all up. Especially since you hardly use either anyway." I read from the next card. " 'If you were to get amnesia, would you want to lose your long-term memory or your ability to form new memories?' " I catch Keller's eyes and wish I'd read the question to myself before reading it aloud.

"That's a tough one." He looks out the window, the rain on the glass turning the cars in the parking lot into wavy lines of color. "You'd think it would be easy for me," he says. "Forget the past, live in the moment, enjoy the new memories. But forgetting would change everything."

"How's that?"

"I wouldn't understand my own life," he says. "How I got here. Why I'm here with you. Where we'll be in a few months, why it all matters." He looks back to me. "Which would you choose?"

"Easy. Erase the past. Focus on the here and now."

"Just like that?"

"Just like that."

"What if part of what you erase is McMurdo, four years ago?" he says. "What if it meant looking at me and asking yourself, 'Who the hell is this guy?'"

"But I'd still have the ability to create new memories, so I'd just fall in love with you all over again."

"Even if we met here, in Eugene, instead of in Antarctica?" he asks. "Would that have changed anything?"

"Not a chance."

Our food arrives, and as our conversation turns to the article Keller is writing for *Outside* magazine, to a documentary we might see over the weekend, in the back of my mind I'm still thinking of his question, of how things might've been different if we'd met anywhere but Antarctica. Even now, his being here in Eugene is an adjustment, and I feel myself taking a mental step backward, looking at this scene from a pace away—Keller and me, sitting in a diner, talking about the weekend like any normal couple—and yet to me it's as strangely exotic as crossing the Antarctic Circle is for the rest of the world. As we eat, I feel time shift and stall while I try to preserve these moments, to commit them to permanent storage in my brain—Keller holding a crinkly fry to my lips, the clink of his fork as it slips from the edge of his plate, the skin of his hand in the diner's yellowish light as he slides the check across the table and picks it up.

AFTER I TAKE Keller to the airport for his flight to Seattle, I return home, and the vacancy of my cottage, which would usually feel normal, suddenly seems too quiet. Even Gatsby's disappeared on me—through my kitchen window I can see him across the yard, in the window of Nick's house, looking back at me. I wonder if Nick has called him home as a way to call me there, too.

I find myself looking over at the house all afternoon, and as evening falls I finally cross the yard. As I step up onto the porch, through the window Gatsby sees me first; his mouth opens in a silent pink meow, and then Nick looks up and sees me, too. He opens the door, motioning me in, then looks past me. "Is he gone already?"

"Just for a couple days," I say. I pick Gatsby up off the kitchen counter, and he digs both paws into my shoulder before resting his chin on them, as if I'm a place to nap. I lean my ear against his rib cage, feeling the comforting vibrations of his purr. "I wasn't expecting him here."

"I could tell," Nick says. "So how's it going?"

"Fine," I say. "Weird," I add. "Different. Being together here instead of there. But it's good."

Nick smiles. "Who knew? This is starting to sound almost like a real relationship."

I laugh. "Maybe."

He looks at me for a moment. "Love suits you," he says

at last. "Just promise not to elope to Argentina or anything. Gatsby and I would miss you."

"Don't be ridiculous," I say, though I feel my heart catch at the thought.

Nick looks over at the clock on the stove. "What're you doing tonight?" he asks.

"Not much."

"There's an exhibit opening at the museum," he says. "A bunch of us are going out afterwards. You should come along."

"Oh," I say, taken aback. "Well, I—"

"It's okay," he says. "You've got work, I know."

I hold Gatsby in front of me for a second, then kiss the top of his head and hand him to Nick. "Have fun," I say. "I'll see you soon?"

"Sure," he says.

Back in my empty cottage, I pour myself a glass of bourbon and think about Dennis, about that lone emperor penguin I'd seen shortly after he died, on my way back north. How alone she was, how at peace. It's something I'd always tried to believe—that I'm at home with myself, at peace with my solitude. Maybe this is what separates us from other animals— the inability to live simply by our instincts, the need to talk ourselves into who we wish we could be.

WHEN KELLER RETURNS, I ask him how it went with his friend at the university. I'm driving us home, so I can't see his face when he says, "It was all right. We had a good chat."

"Does he know of any teaching gigs?"

"Nothing in Seattle."

"Well, I'll check in with my department head before we leave. Maybe she'll find something for you in the spring."

"You don't have to do that," Keller says. I feel his hand on my knee. "I've got a good lead on something, actually. It'll all work out." Yet his voice sounds odd, strained.

Later that night, as we sit in the living room, drinks in hand, I watch Gatsby stroll over to inspect Keller's duffel, still on the floor where he'd left it earlier, its contents beginning to pour out. "How about you unpack this time?"

"I'd like that." Yet the tension in his tone is still there.

"But . . . ?" I ask.

"I got a call this afternoon. About a job." He glances over at his bag, and when he speaks it looks as if he's talking to it, or Gatsby, instead of me. "A colleague fell off a ladder at home and broke his back. He's all right but can't get back to the classroom. They've asked me to finish the semester. I told them yes."

"You're going back to Boston? When?"

"Tomorrow."

"Tomorrow? But you'll be ready in time for—"

"Yes." He looks at me. "I'll be there."

I rattle the ice in my glass. "I guess this is our fate, isn't it?"

"What do you mean?"

"Being apart more than together."

"If I had another offer—"

"I know, I know, you need to do this. Just let me be disappointed."

"At least I'm here now."

"Yes, but you're leaving again. Why didn't you just fly straight to Seattle if you're not going to stick around?"

Gatsby, who has settled on a chair across the room, looks up, as if to object to the high pitch in my voice. And I, too, hate this needy timbre, an echo of the powerless feeling of watching our lives unfold this way.

"I thought you loved this life," Keller says.

"I do—but it's different now. Everything changed when you showed up." I sigh. "I'd just like to see you for more than a few days at a time, that's all."

His eyes meet mine in that way I love, almost like the sidelong glance of a penguin: intent, curious, unwavering. "This is what we've got. We'll make it work. I promise."

"I know. It's just so hard sometimes."

"Of your many virtues," he says, smiling, "patience is not among them."

"Nor is trust," I say. "Or faith. Or optimism. What *are* my virtues, anyway?"

He laughs. "You're resilient. Passionate. Stubborn. Whenever you have doubts, just trust *me*. I'm not worried about us."

I reach for his hand, and he folds it into mine. "Do you ever think about having stayed?" I ask. "Back in Boston, with your wife, I mean."

Keller takes another drink. "Not anymore," he says. "I don't think we'd have made it. I think we both realized, after Ally died, that she was the thing keeping us together. Maybe if we'd had another baby. That's the one thing I used to wonder about."

I don't say anything. For a long moment, I wait for him to go on.

"I really wanted that, years ago," he says, "and I don't know—maybe a part of me still does. Children are so hopeful.

Ally was all future because she had no past. And after she died, the notion that I might be able to see the world through innocent eyes again was pretty tempting."

I lean close and kiss him. Then I say, "I want to give you something."

I return a moment later with a penguin tag from my early days of graduate school in Argentina. I hand it to him—a thick piece of metal about the size of his thumb, shaped like a melting triangle. Six numbers are on one side, and the other side has the address of the research station where I used to work.

Keller turns it over in his hands as if it were as priceless as a Fabergé egg. "Punta Tombo," he reads from its back.

"I've had this tag for fifteen years," I say. "It's from the Magellanic colony in Argentina, in Chubut Province. Where I met my first penguin."

"Do you know the one this belonged to?"

I nod.

"I'm sorry," he says. When you have a tag without the penguin, it's never a good story.

"I saw dozens of tags when I was down there, but I've kept this one as a reminder. That the birds aren't just numbers."

I take a deep breath. I hope he's listening between the lines, hearing what I'm saying as an apology, of sorts—for what happened on our last voyage, for my wanting more than he can give. "Anyway," I continue, "you're the only person I know who can understand."

He lifts my face toward his and kisses me. "Thank you." He looks back at the tag between his fingers. "I'd love to hear about the bird who wore this."

I rest my head on his shoulder. "I'll tell you about her over a beer on the *Cormorant*."

He holds the tag up toward the light, and we look at all its scars—its numbers and letters, its scuffs and scratches—and I sense he's thinking, as I am, of these tags and their long and mysterious journeys, from the hands of researchers to the left flipper of a penguin, to the hundreds of miles of seas where they forage for food, and, finally, to the sloppy wet deck of a fishing boat, before they make their way back to where they came from, completing a full and tragic circle.

THREE DAYS BEFORE SHIPWRECK

Whalers Bay, Deception Island
(62°59'S, 60°34'W)

The first time I saw Deception Island, I thought I'd been struck color-blind. Under a steel-hued sky, the landscape is all gray, black, and white, with streaks of snow melted into the sharp, serrated black hills that form a horseshoe around Whalers Bay. As the *Cormorant* passes though Neptune's Bellows—a passage so narrow that most early seafarers missed it, giving Deception Island its name—her white-and-blue reflection bounces off the dark mirror of greenish black water. The island is awash in varying shades of light and dark, the only color coming from human sources: the ship, the bright red parkas crowding the main deck.

As we prepare for our landing, thoughts of what to do with the news I received from Susan run through my head. Of how to tell Keller. It now feels stranger than ever that he's not here with me, and I'm counting the days in my head, my thoughts skipping ahead to when there's a possibility, however remote, that I'll see him again.

I certainly can't e-mail news like this, but I dread another awkward ship-to-ship phone call, afraid of what I'll hear in his voice when I tell him—that this news may be not welcome but instead a painful memory of all that he's lost.

I think of the emperors, the devoted males who guard the eggs—this is Keller. The depth of his devotion would equal that of the birds, while I've avoided motherhood. But nature has a way of surprising us, of overpowering us, of reminding us that, no matter what we believe and no matter how hard we try, we're not in control after all.

Thom and I direct passengers into a Zodiac, which I then maneuver across the expansive, colorless bay toward the island, easing through the sunken, watery caldera of the peninsula's most active volcano. The penguins don't build nests here, on the unstable black volcanic sand, and their absence gives me a lonely feeling as I pilot the Zodiac toward the beach. When we're close, I hop out and drag the boat onto dry sand.

It occurs to me, for a split second, that maybe I shouldn't be doing this, that Susan had told me to take it easy. But I can't slack off on work without drawing attention to myself. I haven't confided in anyone—not even Amy or Thom—and I'm not about to tell Glenn.

Steam rises from the sand as I help passengers from the Zodiac. Behind them is the dark, glimmering jewel of the bay; in front, yards of black sand stretch out before the zebra-striped hills. With no penguin colonies on this side of the island, we let passengers wander on their own, and I watch them make their way from the beach toward a shantytown of enormous oil containers and abandoned buildings—relics of the Antarctic whaling industry—so old and suffused with rust that they blend into the lava-blackened cliffs behind them. This reminder of whaling's gruesome past makes me shudder: the whalers removing the blubber on the ships, then bringing the remainder of the bodies to shore, where they'd boil them down to get every last bit of oil. And the whaling industry isn't even history—though the International Whaling Commission banned whaling in 1986, the Japanese have continued hunting in the Southern Ocean, killing minke and fin and even endangered sei whales under the guise of "research," even though they haven't published a paper in years and continue to sell the whale meat commercially.

Thom arrives in a second Zodiac with more tourists and our ship's historian, an older British guy named Nigel Dawson. As if sensing my mood, Thom asks Nigel to begin a tour, then hands me a shovel and offers to ferry the tourists back and forth as I get to work. I walk down the beach, away from our landing spot, and start to dig. The water under the rocky sand is hot-tub temperature, and one of the highlights for our passengers is taking a dip in Antarctica, even though our reservoir will be large enough for only three or four bodies at a time.

The sand is wet and heavy; it's like shoveling deep snow, and I pause to catch my breath. The water pooling in the shallow basin is somewhere around 110 degrees, and though we won't dig more than two feet deep, my arms are already beginning to ache. When Thom returns to the beach and offers to trade places, I don't hesitate to hand over the shovel.

As I walk along the shoreline, taking advantage of a few moments to myself, I notice that couple, Kate and Richard.

They're standing several yards away, near one of the abandoned oil containers, and it looks as though they're arguing again. Then Kate stalks off toward the water, and Richard turns and heads the opposite way. I study them as I would a pair of birds—not because I've never seen an unhappy couple on a cruise but because I assume they're continuing the same conversation as before, about starting a family. Penguins cannot successfully raise a chick alone; they need each other, or the chick will perish. With humans, child rearing is infinitely more complex and yet still so black and white. There's no such thing as compromise, as having half a child—it's all or nothing.

Turning back toward the bay, I glimpse the round black back of a penguin as it swims by, revealing its white belly when it streaks out of the water. I keep my eyes on it as it porpoises along, and I don't notice that Kate is next to me until she speaks.

"So there are no penguins on this island?" she asks.

I turn toward her. "Not right here. There's a big chinstrap colony on Baily Head, over on the eastern side."

"It's probably for the best," she says with a sheepish smile. "I assume Thom told you."

"Told me what?"

"During the tour the other day, I wandered off," she says. "I sat down near the beach, and a penguin came up to me. It seemed really friendly, so—I reached out to pet it."

I shake my head. "You could've gotten a nasty bite."

"I know. Thom read me the riot act."

"Maybe you should stick with the group next time."

"I know," she says, then adds, "It just felt so nice to get away."

"Get away? You don't get any farther away than here."

"I meant, from all the people," she says. "It's ironic—you're down here in the middle of nowhere, but you're still surrounded by people."

"That's the nature of a cruise."

"How do you deal with it?" she asks.

"I drink," I say, only half-joking. Keller and I always used to share a drink at the end of a long day, but without him here I haven't had a drop. Then it hits me, as it keeps hitting me—I can't drink. I'm pregnant.

Kate smiles. "That seems to be Richard's solution, too, these days. At home, he usually doesn't drink at all. It's fun to see him get tipsy. Loosen up a bit."

"That's what vacation's for, right?" I say.

"I guess."

I look at her. "Aren't you having a good time?"

"Sure I am," she says. "We both are. It's just—it would be nice to have a little space sometimes."

"Any particular reason?" Normally, I wouldn't engage her like this, but she clearly wants to talk. And I'm curious about how a couple deals with the fact that one person wants a baby and the other doesn't.

"We're so fortunate, it's embarrassing to even hear myself complain. My husband sold his business, and now that he's retired, he wants to start a family. Simple, right?"

"Not necessarily," I say.

"I'm not sure he should've retired so young," Kate continues. "He's a workaholic, which isn't really so bad—I admire his work ethic, all that he's accomplished. But when it came to getting away, taking a break, I always had to drag him out of the office. And now he faces a *lifetime* vacation. I've never seen him so restless."

"Why'd he retire if he likes to work?"

"It's more like he can't stand still," she says. "The ink had hardly dried on the deal before he signed up for rock climbing, surfing lessons—all these things I don't have time for, since I'm still working. So he says, 'I know what we can do together. Let's make a baby.'"

"Is that what you want, too?"

"I just wish I had more time," she says. "I would never tell him this, but part of me wishes his business hadn't sold. He worked so hard for it—we both did—but I have a feeling it all happened too soon. That we're just not ready."

"What do you do for work?"

She waves her hand as if to brush off a pesky gnat. "Oh, I'm in marketing. For a beverage company in San Diego. They make organic kombucha, juices with chia, stuff like that."

"Do you like it?"

"It's okay," she says. "I don't know, maybe having a ridiculously successful husband makes a girl feel inadequate. I've bounced around a lot, work-wise, mostly because I love to travel. Maybe it's because I have no idea what else I'd do if I ever had to get serious about just one thing." She looks down at the sand, digging into it with the toe of her rubber boot. "Maybe what bothers me most about Richard's rush to have a baby is that I feel like we're not enough anymore—you know, just the two of us. Like *I'm* not enough anymore."

She turns to watch a few passengers walk past. "I'm the only woman I know without kids. Some of my friends have kept working, some haven't—but I'm just not a part of their lives anymore. It's not their fault—they probably don't think to invite me to every toddler's birthday party, but those are the only times they get together, which means I never see them. And to them it's so normal, so I feel like I must be the crazy one. You know? Because even though I feel left out most of the time, I still can't picture my life like that."

She stops then and turns to me. "I'm so sorry," she says. "I should've asked. Do you have children?"

"Me? No." I feel my face flush with heat.

"I guess you can't exactly put them in a stroller and take them on the landings, can you?"

"No. You can't."

"So how did you get interested in penguins?" She suddenly seems eager to change the subject.

"I've always loved animals."

Kate smiles. "Don't we all. Even Richard, who claims not to like our cat, secretly does. I always catch him scratching her under the chin when he thinks I'm not looking. But pets are different from penguins."

"I suppose I gravitated toward penguins because they're so dapper and good-looking—what's not to like? And then, in junior high, I learned about this Japanese company that wanted to harvest penguins in Argentina for gloves. This'll tell you how naïve I was, but I couldn't believe people could do such a thing to penguins. To any animal. It was actually the first time I'd made the connection between the animals I loved and where my shoes came from."

"They actually make shoes from penguins?" Kate looks stricken.

"No," I say. "But really, how's that different from using snakes or alligators? Just because they're not as cute?"

"Definitely," she says with a laugh.

"What about calfskin, or sheepskin?"

"I see your point. I guess I haven't really thought about it." Then she asks, almost tentatively, "So what happened to that colony in Argentina?"

"Fortunately, enough people fought to save the penguins, and now the colony is part of a research station and tourist center. I worked there when I was in grad school."

"So how'd you end up in Antarctica?"

"I wanted to learn more about other species," I say, "and I suppose I also wanted to keep going south."

"You like to travel?"

"It's not that, really. My family—we didn't do much traveling. Not together, at least. The first time I got on a plane, I was on my way out west for graduate school. I was twenty-two years old."

Kate's eyes widen. "And look at you now."

"I'm not that well traveled. I just go where the birds are." I've surprised myself by talking so much, and I gesture toward the long, shallow hole in the sand near the water. "So are you going to take a dip?"

"I guess I should," she says. "It's what I'm here for, isn't it?"

We part ways, and I amble along the beach in the opposite direction. After gaining some distance, I turn back toward the hot tub, where Kate is stripping off her winter clothes, down to a bikini and a pair of sneakers, which we recommend swimmers wear for comfort on the hot sand.

Kate lowers herself into the pool, which is just deep enough to cover her as she stretches out horizontally, her hands propping her up from behind, her legs extended in front of her. She begins chatting with another passenger, and I wonder whether she's telling her new companion all the same things she was just telling me. But she's acting different than she had with me; her sentences are short, her smiles brief. She's closed off again, and I consider what it was that made her open up to me, of all people. Maybe we're more alike than I realize; maybe, like me, she's always been the type who's had more books in her life than friends.

To say I wasn't popular in school is an understatement as vast as the Ross Ice Shelf. Even my home life was quiet— my father, the one I was closest to as a child, traveled for work, or so I'd thought at the time; my older brother, Mark, kept busy with sports and friends when he wasn't trying to fill my father's shoes. My mother was in her own world—lost in prayer, or obsessively cleaning the house. Whenever Mark or I were home, she admonished us for leaving water spots in the bathroom sink, or footprints on the newly vacuumed carpet. Mark wasn't around as often, but I spent my time skimming around the edges of rooms, ghostlike, hoping to remain unseen. When the weather was warm enough, I stole away to the tree house my father had built years earlier for Mark, who'd since abandoned it. It was my favorite place to read, and the bird feeders I hung on nearby branches fed the cardinals and sparrows as well as the fox squirrels.

I did enjoy school, in a nerdy sort of way—I embraced Science Club and the library's book club rather than sports or social events. And it wasn't until my junior year in high school that I finally made a good friend, Alec. It happened after he'd been seen kissing a guy in a car somewhere in the Central West End; back then, Clayton, Missouri, wasn't ready for that sort of scandal. His conservative parents almost sent him to one of those so-called reform schools for him to be "cured," but the guidance counselor at school managed to talk them out of it.

I saw Alec sitting alone in the cafeteria a few days later, and I sat down next to him. He gave me a weary look and said, "What do you want?"

"Fuck 'em," I said. "One day you'll leave here and none of this will matter. We both will."

On weekends Alec and I would park over by the airport to watch the planes take off and land. When his popularity rebounded after everyone mellowed out, Alec enveloped me into his circle of friends, and he made my last two years of high school more bearable—weekends at Cardinals games, nights at the Steak 'n Shake, jogging in Shaw Park. After graduation he moved to New York. We're still close, though we rarely have an opportunity to see each other. I've always admired Alec for living the life he'd dreamed of having. He married his partner of four years, a poet he'd met through the publishing house where he worked, and eventually moved to the suburbs with his husband and their two adopted daughters.

About thirty feet away, I notice a Zodiac heading toward the shore, piloted by an orange-jacketed crew member I don't recognize. I think of the *Australis* and reach for my radio—no more than one tourist vessel is allowed to come ashore at a time, and whoever this is will have to back off—but as I'm about to call Glenn, I stop. There's something familiar about the driver, and I start walking toward the landing, holding my breath.

I see the red bandanna as he swings himself over the side of the inflatable and begins to pull it up on the sand, not far from the makeshift hot tub where Thom looks up from taking photos of the wading passengers. As soon as Keller's feet hit the ground, Thom's face breaks into a smile, and I watch the two of them shake hands and slap each other's backs. And by the time Keller turns around, I'm right there, my arms around his neck even before he has a chance to speak.

"This is an illegal landing, you know," I whisper into his ear. His shaggy hair whips against my face in the wind, carrying the scent of the sea.

"You going to report me?"

"Maybe." I pull back to look at him, at the spreading grin creasing his face, which is thinner than when I last saw him, but also, somehow, more relaxed.

"What are you doing here?" I ask. "You can't land all those passengers, can you?"

He shakes his head. "We've got a few VIPs who paid big bucks for a special landing," he says. "Group of ten. We'll bring them over later tonight. But when I heard the *Cormorant* was here, I couldn't miss the chance to see you."

"You're crazy, you know that?" I say. "You'll get fired. Again."

He kisses me. "It'll be worth it."

I look around—a few yards away, Kate is still in the hot tub with two other passengers, and Thom is stowing equipment in a Zodiac. The beach is otherwise empty; for the moment, I'm free.

I grab Keller's hand, and we make our way inland, toward relative privacy behind a large rusted oilcan where, about twenty feet away, a chinstrap penguin stands alone. We're not exactly out of sight here, but we're out of earshot, and the penguin is the only one watching us.

"I'm sorry I—" I begin.

He puts a chilly finger to my lips. "I don't have much time here," he says, "so let's not waste it."

He pulls something from his pocket, then reaches for my hand. He turns my palm upward and lays the object down in my beat-up glove.

At first I can't tell what it is, exactly—it looks like a thick, tarnished, silvery ring with some kind of engraving—but when I hold it up and look closely, I recognize it. The penguin tag I'd given him, completely transformed.

On the outside of the narrowed band are six numbers and the word *Argentina*. On the top is a raised setting into which is nestled a ruddy stone, barely larger than the face of a pencil eraser; the white streaks veining the layers of pink resemble the wave of a mountain range.

"It's Argentina's national stone," Keller says, "*rodocrosita*. Nothing fancy," he adds, "but somehow I didn't think you'd want a big diamond from Tiffany's."

I look from the ring to Keller's face.

"I love you," he says. He takes the ring and pulls off my glove. "I figured if we make it legal, you'll finally believe we can find a way to be together." He slips on the ring.

I hold my hand up so I can get a better look. The tag-turned-ring is both elegant and sturdy against my red, chapped skin—the only piece of jewelry I've ever been given. "I always wanted to wear a penguin tag. It seems only fair, given how many I've doled out."

He smiles. "I have a jeweler friend in Boston who's a wizard." He takes my hand. "By the way, you haven't said anything."

"About your tagging me, you mean? What do you need for your field report? I'm a known-age bird—"

"—who still hasn't chosen a mate."

I laugh. "Is there a question on the horizon, Mr. Sullivan?"

"Will you marry me, Ms. Gardner?"

I look down at the ring again, then back up at Keller. I press my body against his, my gloveless hand against his neck. "Yes."

"I came so close to asking you over the phone because I didn't think I'd get a chance to see you," he says. "I know the timing isn't the best—"

Then I lean back in his arms so I can see his face again. "It couldn't be better," I say. "There's something I need to tell you."

Right then, loud voices bark from my radio, and I reach toward my hip so I can turn off the volume. Just for a few more minutes.

But from the corner of my eye I see Thom bursting into a sprint, running toward a gathering crowd near the base of a cliff. Keller sees him, too. "Something's happened," he says. "We better go."

"Wait—" But Keller's already racing after Thom, so I follow, pulling my glove back on as I jog over the rough sand. We reach the crowd, and I touch my stomach briefly before looking up at the cliff, which ascends sharply above the black sand.

Nigel, who was supposed to be giving a tour, is near the

top, around what would be the fourth floor of this five-story mountain, and down below, around the second floor, clinging to the rocky surface like a gecko, is Richard.

"What the hell," I mutter, and, next to me, Thom is shaking his head. Nigel should have known better than to rock-climb with tourists around.

Nigel's not unlike me—here as a historian because it's a way to get to Antarctica. At seventy years old, he's hardy but decidedly old-school, and he's never quite learned that, on these trips, he's no longer an explorer or a researcher but a tour guide, and he needs to set a good example. *He's an old dog,* Keller said once, as an excuse, and he was right. Nigel's cracked, leathered face bears the marks of four decades of frostbite and sunburn; his nose is a permanent, unnatural shade of red, and his beard is white with age and sun—I'd once been astonished to see a photo of a young Nigel, black-haired and smooth-faced. When he'd worked for the British Antarctic Survey, he helped restore the survey's research huts across the continent and, later, helped dismantle them. Last winter, he told me how he'd helped dismantle the Station J hut at Prospect Point, clearly conflicted about the orders to take it down. "Tough choice," he said, "preserving history or preserving the continent." We've become comrades in conflict as we guide heavy-footed tourists across the ice.

Still, Nigel tends to forget that he is not here on his own, that when he is on the staff of the *Cormorant*, he is being watched at all times—not just by Glenn but by the tourists. And apparently, when he decided to climb up the sheer side of a bluff in plain view of a tour group, he had a copycat, who is now stuck. Richard had made it about twenty feet up, but now he isn't moving, too high to jump down, and too unstable to keep going up.

Thom is on his radio, telling Glenn what's going on, and in the meantime Keller moves closer to the cliff, shouting up at Richard as Nigel shouts down. Through the grayish haze, a light snow is falling, slickening the rocks that Richard is trying to hold on to with his bare hands and rubber boots. As I get closer, I can see him searching for a better hold, his whole body quivering with the exertion of trying to stay put. The ground twenty feet below him is rocky and rough, and I hope he hasn't looked down.

Nigel's gaze is locked on Richard, and even though Nigel's snow-flecked beard covers most of his face, I can see he is serious, focused.

"Stay where you are," Keller calls out to Richard. "Don't move."

But at the sound of Keller's voice, Richard turns, and as he does his balance shifts, and rocks crumble beneath his boots, the stones tumbling down toward us.

"Hang on!" Nigel shouts.

Richard has managed to find a solid piece of rock, and he hugs the cliff, stable for the moment, shoulders ticking upward with each short breath. He's not going to last long, and my own breath begins to shorten as I realize what might happen here. A tourist, dead on our watch. His own fault—but that won't matter. He shouldn't have come here; he doesn't belong. Really, none of us do. As I watch the trembling of his body, his arms and legs straining to keep a hold, it feels suddenly as if it's the ridge itself that's quaking, the island shuddering underneath us—as if this long-dormant volcano is awakening, ready to reclaim the island, the entire continent, all of us who are doing our part, bit by tiny bit, to destroy it. I feel as if we're poised for disaster, as if the cliffs might break apart at any moment, as if the seas might start to boil, as if we might all be buried in another layer of carcasses, bones over bones—the goddess Gaia's final revenge for all her grievances.

Nigel has climbed up about ten feet, to a small plateau, and he's now on his stomach, lowering a rope toward Richard. Meanwhile, Keller has begun climbing up the side of the cliff toward Richard and is about halfway between him and the ground.

From below, Keller snatches the rope, looping it around his hand. Richard's grip loosens, and his body begins to peel away from the face of the cliff—but Keller reaches out, catching his wrist.

Both men drop, falling fast—and then the rope grows taut, jerking them hard against the side of the cliff. Nigel slides forward on his stomach, his arms bracing against the rocks at the edge as he struggles to keep himself from going over.

Keller is holding on to Richard's wrist with his bare hand, his other hand clinging to the rope, which has to be cutting painfully into his skin.

Nigel lowers the rope at a rapid, almost free-fall pace. Richard scrapes against the jagged wall on the way down. Keller is holding tightly on to Richard, but then his other hand begins to slip. When they are about six feet off the ground, the rope finally, inevitably, rips through Keller's grasp, and the two of them tumble onto the rock- and snow-strewn sand.

"Oh my God."

I haven't even noticed that Kate has been watching right beside me; she rushes toward Richard, her winter clothes having been quickly donned again, ski pants stuck above her boots, her coat unzipped.

She helps Richard stand up. "Are you okay?" she asks. She sounds more vexed than concerned.

"I think so."

I kneel next to Keller as he gets to his feet, his hand bloodied and torn. "Oh, no."

"It's fine," he says. He takes off his bandanna and wraps it around his hand, blood darkening the fabric.

With Thom now at his side, Richard takes a tentative step, then another. As he looks down at his own body, as if to make sure it's still intact, I see a round beige disk behind his ear—a seasickness patch. He keeps his head lowered for a few moments, looking embarrassed. Finally he turns to look at Keller, and then up at Nigel, who is gingerly making his way down the face of the cliff. He doesn't look at his wife.

"Thanks," he says in Keller's direction, still not making eye contact. "It didn't look that difficult from the ground." Then he starts walking toward the boat landing. His shoulders slump, and his gait is hesitant and awkward.

Kate stares after him, her expression incredulous. As Thom hands her Richard's jacket, she glances toward Keller's wrapped-up hand. "I'm so sorry," she says.

But Keller's eyes are looking past her, and I turn to see Glenn approaching, walking in that rapid, no-nonsense way that means he's pissed off. Nigel is now on the ground, collecting the rope. His hands, too, are scraped and bleeding.

Glenn plants his feet and glares at Keller. "I should have

known. Can you go anywhere on this planet without causing trouble?"

"It's not his fault, Glenn," Thom says. "Keller and Nigel saved the guy's life."

"That passenger never should've been up there in the first place."

"What're we supposed to do, chain them to the beach?" I can't help but come to Nigel's defense. "He snuck up there before Nigel could stop him. We can't control the crazy ones."

"This doesn't concern you." Glenn turns his glare on me, then Keller. "I'd like to speak with Nigel," he says coldly, nodding pointedly at Kate, who I hadn't realized is still standing there, taking in every word.

Thom takes her arm, and Keller and I join them as they begin walking back toward the landing site.

"Is your husband always such a daredevil?" Thom asks Kate.

She shakes her head, visibly upset. "No. Not at all."

"You might tell him to lose the seasick patch," I tell her. "Those things have some weird side effects."

She looks alarmed. "Like what?"

On a voyage about six years ago, a man came up to me during a landing asking where he was—he had no idea he was in Antarctica. He wore a medicated seasickness patch, and once it was removed, he recovered completely within twelve hours. Not everyone suffers side effects, but when they occur, they can be serious.

"All sorts of things," I say to Kate. "Blurred vision, confusion—in rare cases, hallucinations. I'm just saying, if this isn't like him—you never know, it could be the meds. At any rate, you should take him to the ship's doctor. Make sure he's really okay."

She nods, and she looks so overwhelmed that I feel bad for not speaking to her more gently. "I'm sorry about your hand," she says to Keller.

"Don't worry about it."

Richard is waiting at the landing site, eyes on the ground, and Thom helps them both into a Zodiac. I feel Keller's hand on my back.

"I better go," he says. "I've stayed too long already."

I don't want him to go—there's too much more to say— but when I look over my shoulder and see Glenn and Nigel approaching, I know we don't have time.

Keller hauls the Zodiac into the water, and, with one foot in the boat, he leans over to kiss me one more time. I feel the icy water through my rubber boots as I move as close as I can. His mouth feels different now, and it's not just the wind-chapped lips, the prickle of his beard; he's looser, and there's a give in his touch that I've never felt before, a lack of the old intensity, as if it had dropped away like the life he'd been planning to leave behind in Boston. Maybe he finally had.

After he spins the boat away from shore, I pull off my glove again and look at the ring. It's nothing I can imagine any woman wanting, a recycled piece of metal with a chunk of marbled stone in its center. It's beautiful. It's perfect.

JUST AFTER THE announcement that dinner is being served, I wander into the ship's library to waste a few minutes; we naturalists always go into the dining room last so we can sit where the empty seats are. I scan the bookshelves, looking for something to distract me.

I glimpse a book on a table and pick it up. *Alone*, Byrd's book. I wonder for a moment who had plucked it off the shelves this afternoon, who might've sat here reading it, perhaps leaving it to return to later.

I think of Keller, who embraced aloneness after his marriage fell apart. At least he'd been married once and wants to try it again. My whole life has been stats and inventories and censuses and hypotheses. People like Kate think I'm worldly because they've met me at the end of the earth, but in reality my world is very small.

Most of the time, I keep myself preoccupied with the birds; I've rarely let myself succumb to the charms of the males of my own species. There was Dennis. There was Chad, in college, who never knew the extent to which he'd altered my life. There was a professor in graduate school, an ornithologist twice my age. And, in the years after that, my love life consisted of little more than the occasional blind date set up by Jill and other university colleagues who worried I didn't get out enough. I'd eventually give in, unravel my hair, wear something other than cargo pants and fleece—but nothing ever lasted more than a few weeks, a couple of months; I'd eventually break it off, or the guy would save me from having to do it by bowing out first.

Traveling, of course, makes relationships a challenge, though perhaps it's only an excuse. I often thought my eagerness to see the world stemmed from my father's long absences; his work kept him in cities across the country more often than at home, and it was rare to see him even on holidays. I came to believe that whatever was out there had to be far better than what was at home in Missouri.

He was also the one who'd fostered my curiosity. When he was home, he'd take me "fossil hunting," which in St. Louis meant amateur geological digs at the sides of highways. My father would pull off the road, and, along an I-170 road cut, we'd find the shells of crinoids and corals, unearthed by construction crews that had dug into the limestone hills. "All this was underwater once," my father would say, waving his arm around the flat, suburban landscape. "Right where we're standing—this used to be the bottom of the ocean."

I was vaguely aware of my mother's dislike of these outings, the fact that my father would arrive home after a week or two away and set right out again, with me, on what she called "silly scavenger hunts." Yet we didn't talk about any of this—denial was, for us, as natural as breathing—and her unhappiness remained veiled in offhand comments rather than actual conversations.

I, too, learned to keep quiet, having discovered early the perils of being curious, of speaking one's mind, of asking the wrong questions. Early one summer, when I was about eight years old and poking around in the briefcase my father had left on the bed while he packed for yet another business trip, I'd caught a glimpse of something colorful—a flash of red and pink—and automatically reached for it. I pulled out a greeting card with a watercolor heart on the front, and as I opened it my father snatched it from my hand. I'd caught only the word *love*.

"Deborah," he snapped. "You know better than to mess with my things."

He never spoke sharply to me. And he never called me Deborah.

"Is this for Mom?" I asked.

A pause. "Yes. Of course."

"But her birthday isn't until November."

"It's a surprise," he said. "So don't say anything to her, okay? It's going to be a very special birthday."

By late November, I'd forgotten all about it. My father was home for Thanksgiving that year, and he was still in town for my mother's birthday a week later. We had a snowstorm that week, and I went outside to help him shovel the driveway. When it was too cold and icy for fossil hunting, this was one of the few chances we had to be together. As he shoveled the snow to the side of our long driveway, I packed it together to make a short, thick snow wall. When he was finished, he helped me decorate it with turrets and a few guard snowmen. I remember the way he smiled at me—his eyes, usually set somewhere in the distance, looking this time directly into mine.

Later, we took my mother out to dinner at Pasta House— which had my favorite food, toasted ravioli—and later, back home, we seated my mother at the dining room table, where my dad presented her with a birthday cake. It was from Schnucks, but even a supermarket cake was more of an effort than he'd made in years. While Mark and I stood next to her, Mom looked like a child herself as she blew out the single candle on top, then moved on to open the card and the long, slender, gift-wrapped box on the table.

After my father helped my mother try on the delicate gold bracelet he'd given her, she opened the card—and that's when I remembered. "That's not the card with the heart on it," I said.

My dad pursed his lips together and didn't answer. The knife Mark was using to cut the cake stopped deep inside and stayed there, and my mother's face seemed to shrink into itself, like a deflated balloon. I don't even remember how our little party ended; I only remember the silence that followed and eventually became the norm.

I didn't know my mother had once been different until I found an old photograph of her and my father, tucked away in a drawer of the dining room sideboard. It looked like summer, and they were sitting together on a balcony, leaning against the railing, my father behind my mother, his arms around her waist. They were both laughing, looking at something happening to the left of the photographer. My dad held a cigarette and my mom a glass of wine; they wore their hair and clothes long and loose. I hardly recognized them when I saw it—they were so rarely together now, and so rarely smiling—and for a long time afterwards I studied them closely, trying to see my dad's once-thin frame, to imagine my mother's face round and happy.

As we grew up, Mark did his best to take my father's place during his long absences. He covered all my dad's chores; he was the last one to bed, after walking around the house turning off the lights, making sure the front and back doors were locked. On summer nights, he'd stand over the grill, my mother handing him a plate of pork chops and foil-wrapped corn, while she and I made deviled eggs and salad and opened cans of fruit.

Why my mother didn't leave my father, I don't know—

maybe she wanted to, and maybe she'd even tried. She spent a lot of time praying. When I was twelve and got my first period—she'd never sat me down for "the talk," so even armed with sex ed and biology, it took me half the day to realize what was happening—she waved me out of the room, as usual, without opening her eyes or lifting her head. I rummaged in the cupboard under her bathroom sink and helped myself to her supply of tampons. Another two months went by before she noticed.

Back then, my favorite companion was nonhuman. That year, when my father was home for my birthday, he took me to the shelter to adopt a cat—an orange tabby I named Ginger. He'd done this without my mother's knowledge, and when we got home, she refused to let Ginger inside. "I don't want dirt and fleas in my house," she told us. I was allowed to set up a bed in the garage for Ginger, who spent her days outside, and my father installed a cat door. But I left my bedroom window open at night, and when I called her, she would walk along the roof's gutter and climb in; eventually I'd find her waiting there as soon as I opened the window. Sometimes she would bring me a dead mouse, which I tossed out into the yard. Ginger snuggled with me all night—I liked having her furry body next to me, her light heartbeat—and she woke me every morning around dawn, before my parents got up, as if she knew we'd both be punished if we got caught, and I'd open the window for her to slip out again.

The wild kingdom had always appealed to me more than the human one, but it wasn't until I watched the Adélies feeding their chicks that I saw my family reflected in their behavior. The female Adélie makes her fluffy, charcoal-colored chicks chase her around for food; the chicks tumble over each other to eat, and one invariably goes hungrier than the other—but their mother wants to ensure that the stronger chick, the one most likely to survive and usher in a new generation, will get the most attention, the most food. To my own mother, I was the weaker chick: As soon as she realized I was more interested in grad school than in marriage, she focused her attention on my brother, who settled down with his college sweetheart, Cheryl; he remained in suburban St. Louis, where he played the role of faithful son year-round, no travel required. When I called home to tell my mother I'd gotten accepted to graduate school, she said, "Did you hear Cheryl's pregnant again?" That was all.

I suspect she turned her attention to my brother because he'd replaced my father in so many ways, but he was also her only other chance at family—Mark and Cheryl, the happy couple, their three kids. Mark never bent or broke the rules; he didn't find things he wasn't supposed to, or, if he did, he never spoke of them. I'd been the one to force my mother to acknowledge what she hadn't wanted to see, and I don't think she ever forgave me for that.

It became clear six years ago, the last time I was home for the holidays. Helping my mother prepare Christmas dinner, I watched her put a place card for my father on the dining room table, even though he hadn't been home for Christmas for the past two years. Earlier, she'd sent me out to the liquor store for the Scotch he liked because we were out. And when I scooped chopped onions into the vegetarian stuffing I was making, she let out a gasp, then insisted I take them out. "Your father hates onions, remember?" she said.

I looked down into the mixing bowl; the onions were still on top, and I sighed and began to spoon them out. She stood over my shoulder, watching, then pointed out a few bits of onion that had slipped down the side of the bowl.

"When are you going to stop?" I asked her. "Just because you make everything perfect doesn't mean he's going to magically appear."

She stared at me with her flat gray eyes, then reached over and yanked the bowl away. "I'll do it, then," she said.

"Mom—"

She picked up a knife and began to scrape the rest of the onions from the cutting board into the garbage. "If this is your idea of help, I don't need it," she said and waved the knife in my direction, as if for emphasis. "Go on."

I stood there for a moment, but she ignored me, so I left the kitchen and stepped out the back door, taking comfort in the cold.

Now I look out the library's view window, doubting whether I'm equipped for what's ahead—marriage, parenthood—when my relationship with Keller has so far been as precarious as the lives of the penguins. For us as well as them, everything depends on near-perfect timing, and as I stare at the ring he's given me, as much as I want to bring our lives together, finally, for good, I wonder if such a future is possible for me, the weaker chick.

Booth Island

We've spent the morning on Booth Island, taking tourists on walking tours, and now, as the passengers are fin-ishing their lunches and taking early-afternoon naps on the *Cormorant,* Keller and I are wrapping up some census work for the Adélies. We've split up to cover the entire colony in the three hours we have, and I've lost sight of him as I study the birds in the rocky nests in front of me.

The project's goal this season has been to do an Adélie count during the peak of their egg laying—which Thom and another APP researcher did two months earlier—and again toward the end, which Keller and I will do on our last voyage in another two months, just as the chicks are getting ready to fledge.

Yet now, in the middle of the breeding season, it's not look-ing good—broken eggs are scattered around the colony, and skuas perch on the slopes above, waiting to swoop down upon errant or abandoned chicks.

I pause and stare at an Adélie sitting on an egg, knowing

there's no way the chick inside is going to make it. By the time we're back for the final count, his parents will be heading north, and he won't be old enough to fledge. Unable to fend for himself, he'll die of starvation, or end up prey for skuas. A few yards away, two charcoal-fluffed chicks sit alone on a rock, shivering, squeaking for food. They won't survive much longer if they don't have a parent show up soon.

As a scientist, I'm not supposed to let this break my heart, but it does.

I linger for a moment, watching the chicks, wanting to pick them up and wrap them into the warmth of my parka and take them home.

I go back to the landing site to meet Keller. The beach is deserted, which doesn't make sense; we'd arrived together in one Zodiac, and I hadn't heard its engine start up again. Then again, you can't hear much of anything over the wind and the sounds of the birds.

I feel a sharp beat of panic at the thought of how unimaginable it would be if anything were to happen to Keller. There's been a certain distance between us on this trip, which isn't entirely unusual—on these expeditions, we are little more than fellow crew members; we don't have the luxury of time or space for much else. I often wish we were back at McMurdo, that we could've stayed there forever—gotten jobs in maintenance or in the galley, in the store or in the bar. Just to stay together.

Now, standing alone on the beach wondering where he could be, I'm about to call him on the radio. Then I see a Zodiac approaching—it's him, his sunglasses coated in sea spray.

"About fucking time," I say, trying to cover my relief. "Anyone ever tell you it's not polite to leave a person stranded on an island?"

He only smiles, stopping the Zodiac a few yards from shore. "Get in," he says.

I wade through water nearly up to my knees, feeling the icy chill against my boots. Keller holds out his hand to help me into the boat. He guns the engine as we leave the beach, hugging the shoreline as he swings around a small, snow-capped hill.

"Where are we going?" I ask.

"You'll see."

His back is to me, and I can't tell what he's up to. I watch the movement of his shoulders as he guides the boat, his weathered hands on the tiller. It still amazes me that this lawyer-turned-dishwasher knows nearly as much about these birds and these islands as I do.

The bergs rise tens to hundreds of feet above us, their craggy white tops etched with the deep blue of older ice beneath. Below the surface, the ice fans out, turning the water a Caribbean greenish blue. Ahead, on a small, indigo-steeped iceberg, a chinstrap penguin flaps its wings as if waving at us. Then it flops onto its stomach and slides into the depths below.

As I gaze out at the white face of the largest berg, its rime scratched with forked edges revealing the old, dark-blue ice deep within, I wonder if Keller and I might age together as beautifully, whether we can last in a world in which everything is melting, disappearing.

Keller glides into a precipitous, stony landing spot. Above us, a gentoo colony is nestled into the staggered, snow- and moss-covered hills. Keller jumps out into knee-deep water and yanks the Zodiac farther ashore, then holds out his hand for me.

As we climb over the slate-colored rocks toward the base of the hill, he says, "There's someone I've been wanting you to meet."

He leads me up to the colony, staying clear of the penguin tracks. The penguins let out a chorus of growls as we pass by—the same sound they use to ward off the skuas.

"What have you been doing over here?" I ask.

"Sit down," he says instead of answering, indicating a large, flat piece of granite. When I sit on the edge, he waves me farther back, so I scoot toward the middle. "Good—right there," he says.

"What the hell are you up to, Keller?"

"You'll see." He sits next to me, and I hold my breath for a moment, realizing how completely alone we are, for the first time so far on this journey—away from the ship, the crew, the passengers, with no eyes on us except the penguins'.

But Keller is looking straight ahead, at the gentoos, almost as if I'm not there. From this height, I can see past the iceberg skyline into the gray-green water beyond. The sun begins to poke through the fog, creating a silvery haze, and its blurred reflection appears on the surface of the water, illuminating the smaller chunks of ice that float like stepping-stones toward the icebergs.

"Nice spot," I say. "I don't think I've ever been here."

He smiles and shoves his sunglasses atop his head, as if to get a clearer view. He nods toward the sharp, steel-colored points of the rocks, rising from the hillside like spires. "Like cathedrals, aren't they?"

As the sounds of the penguins fill my ears, I think of the

last time I'd been in a real cathedral, the Cathedral Basilica of St. Louis, during that last Christmas at home. My schedule makes it easy to skip holidays; I'm usually on my way to Antarctica, heading home, or on board. I send cards and gifts for my brother's kids, and I leave a voice mail when I know they're at Midnight Mass. The rest of the year, I stay in touch with each of them, separately, via e-mail and birthday phone calls. We live our own lives, and I spend my winters with those whose behaviors I recognize most—the chinstraps, the gentoos, the Adélies.

And Keller. He and I sit on this rock, quiet, right next to each other. After a few minutes, a lone gentoo, a male, emerges from the colony and begins to meander toward us. I watch his bobbing head—black, with two swirls of white above the eyes, flourishes of pale shadow. The marks meet in a thin band on the top of his head and are sprinkled with flecks of white, like spilled salt. He raises his orange bill in the air.

"Here's the little guy I want you to meet," Keller says.

I laugh. "You two know each other?"

"I call him Admiral Byrd."

"Admiral Bird?" It takes me a second, and then I get it. "Oh. After Richard Byrd."

As the penguin approaches, I remain still. My legs are stretched out in front of me, ankles crossed, and the penguin hops over to the toes of my boots and gives them a few curious pecks.

"I banded him last year," Keller says. "He just came right up to me, climbed onto my shoes, nipped at the equipment."

Byrd turns his head to the side to look at both of us. He begins walking around toward the edge of the rock.

"Sit back," Keller says. "Here, put your legs up." With his hands on my knees, he guides my legs into another position: thighs parallel with the ground, feet flat, knees slightly apart.

As I'm focusing on my legs, Admiral Byrd is hopping up, stone by stone, and, a moment later, he's right next to me. He's about two feet tall, and from where I'm sitting, he looks me in the eye. I notice the metal band at the spot where his left wing meets his body.

"You've got to be kidding," I say.

I drop my hands. Admiral Byrd takes a few more steps, then in one swift and inelegant move, propels his body onto my lap, belly first.

I gasp at the surprising weight of him; in all my years of research, I've never had a penguin sprawled in my lap like this, relaxed as a cat. I grip the rock with my hands to stay balanced, pressing my feet down into the snow.

"He looks a little heavier this year," Keller says. He reaches for my hand and pulls off my glove. He covers the top of my hand with his palm and places it on Admiral Byrd's feathered black coat.

Our usual contact with penguins is nothing like this; we touch them only to put on bands, to weigh them, to do the unpleasant but necessary things to learn about and, we hope, eventually to save them. I hate knowing that every time we come near, it could shorten their lives, that every contact must be pure terror, even if it lasts only a few moments.

Tentatively, I run my hand down the penguin's back, his feathers smooth and soft and firm. I can feel his heartbeat through the thin skin of my waterproof pants.

"One day," Keller says, "I was sitting in the snow making

some notes, and he jumped into my lap. I couldn't believe it. I snuck over here this morning, during breakfast, to see if he was still here. I knew it was him even before I looked at his band."

"What happened? I mean, how'd he become so socialized?"

"I have no idea. I thought it was a one-time thing. When he climbed into my lap that first time, I thought he was sick, or dying. I wasn't sure I'd see him again. And even when I saw him, I didn't know if he'd do this again, until just now."

"He could be a whole new project for you. The penguin who thought he was a lapdog."

A few minutes later, Admiral Byrd raises his head and wiggles forward. Keller moves aside to make room as Byrd clumsily eases his body off my lap and hops down from the rock, as slowly and patiently as he arrived. He wades into the water, as if to gauge the temperature, then dives under.

I turn to Keller. He's watching me, smiling, squinting a little as the sun breaks through. He's still holding my glove and hands it to me. I take it, my hand cold and dirty from the penguin's feathers. I get to my feet, turning to take in the vistas from another angle.

"I like it here. No room for landings. Just us and Admiral Byrd."

"And about a thousand other gentoos."

"You've been holding out on me," I say. "I didn't know you'd been over here."

"I'm not holding out." He looks at me. "I just wanted to surprise you. Me being here at all—it's only possible because of you. I wanted, for once, to show you something you haven't seen yet."

I hold his gaze, remembering the first time we kissed, as

we observed the Adélies; remembering how he'd followed me day in and day out, his curiosity about the birds insatiable. "So you're my teacher now."

I wrap my arms around his neck and settle in there, the way Admiral Byrd had settled in to me. We stand like that a long time, the wind rippling through our hair, against our jackets. I let go first, and I look out at the water, where Admiral Byrd had disappeared a few minutes earlier. When I turn to Keller, he nods toward the Zodiac and says, "We better be getting back."

I'm standing close to him, and we're so very alone, and I try not to think ahead, to when we won't be. When we're apart, I feel a tension run through me, an elastic band stretched too thin, but when we're together, Keller calms me, much the way this landscape does; there's a stillness about him, a quiet peace, that I haven't been able to keep with me when we part. I wish we could stay here, just the two of us, with the penguins, build our own rocky nest and somehow survive.

Keller is looking at me as if he knows what I'm thinking, but he doesn't move; neither of us do, for a long couple of minutes. Then he steps away. "Come on," he says. "It's getting late."

I don't want to leave, and, as if sensing this, Keller stands by, waiting as I take one long, last look around. Finally we begin walking back to the beach. We climb into the Zodiac, and as I sit down on its rubbery edge and he fires up the engine, I say, "I'm glad I met you."

He smiles at me, then turns away, his eyes focused ahead, as we speed away from the island.

TWO DAYS BEFORE SHIPWRECK

Prospect Point
(66°01'S, 65°21'W)

I'm halfway through my jog on the treadmill, at a lower intensity than usual, thinking only of when I can get back to the business center to call Keller. When I'd stopped by earlier, the phone was in use, and so here I am, waiting. I've already gone back once, and the same man was still talking—a business call, from the sound of it.

The walls of the ship's fitness center are all glass, and my eyes fix on an iceberg in the distance as the potential conversation plays over and over in my mind.

I'm pregnant. Or, I should say, we're pregnant. Isn't that what couples always say?

The joy in his voice. *I can't believe it.*

Do you really think we can make it work?

We can make anything work. Do you know if it's a boy or a girl?

I forgot to have Susan check during the last ultrasound.

Laughter. *Sorry. I almost forgot where we are.*

As if we could ever forget where we are.

I tire more quickly than usual. I lay my hand against my abdomen and think of the baby's heartbeat, whether it's picked up as mine has. I set my pace to cooldown mode and check my watch—another fifteen minutes has passed, and I hope that passenger is off the phone by now.

It isn't until I step off the treadmill that I notice Kate Archer, stretched faceup on a yoga mat, her dark hair fanned out around her head. It looks as though she's asleep, and I'm startled when she opens her round, plum-brown eyes and looks right at me.

"I've been reading this book Richard bought," she says, as if we're already in the middle of a conversation. "About Shackleton. Did you know he was in his early forties, just about Richard's age, during that expedition? The famous one?"

"Mmm." I hold the treadmill for support as I stretch my legs. I glance over my shoulder, where I can see the passageway that leads to the business center.

"It makes you think about stuff," she says. "Like how little I've done in life, when I really think about it."

"We can't all be Shackleton," I say. "Besides, he was pretty damn lucky. If things hadn't gone his way, he wouldn't be remembered the same way, trust me."

"I hadn't thought of that." She sits up, pulling her legs to her chest.

"How's Richard doing?" I ask, donning my sweatshirt. "Has he recovered from his fall?"

"It's only his pride that's wounded," she says. "It's funny about Richard—he's always so hard on himself. He's never felt comfortable without a bit of pain in his life. Falling off a cliff puts him back in familiar territory." She looks up at me. "He feels terrible. He apologized to Nigel, and he even asked Glenn to get in touch with the other man who helped."

"That won't be easy," I say.

"I think you're right about the medication—that patch he's using. I've never seen him like this before. But he's so afraid of being seasick he won't take it off."

"In these waters, he'll be fine. You should convince him to give it a try."

She doesn't answer, and her eyes drift toward the horizon. "What about you?" I ask. "How're you doing?"

"I've been thinking," she says. "About how I don't want to be another bystander. One of those people who looks at all this melting ice and says, Oh, well, there's nothing we can do about it anyway. I'm just not sure what it is I should be doing."

"There's plenty," I say. "The little things really add up."

"Like what?"

"Well, don't tell Glenn I said this, but you can ask for more environmentally friendly meals on this ship."

"I assumed they were already."

"That's what they want you to think," I say. "It's ridiculous that they serve seafood on this ship, with thousands of penguins killed by fishing nets every year."

"That's awful."

"But do we mention this in the lectures? No. Do we avoid serving fish? No. Because God forbid anyone should have to forgo five-star dining in the Antarctic."

"I didn't think about that," she says.

"No one does." I remember Keller's rant on our last voyage and stop. "I'm sorry. I've got to get going. Besides, Glenn would have my ass if he heard me right now. I shouldn't be saying any of this."

"I don't know," Kate says. "Maybe you should."

"Well," I say, "if it came from a guest, Glenn might actually listen." I look at my watch, realizing I'm going to be late for the day's landing if I don't head belowdecks right now.

I force a smile. "Ready to walk on a new continent?"

OF THE THOUSANDS of travelers who venture to the Antarctic peninsula every year, fewer than 5 percent actually set foot on the continent. Most of our landings take place on the surrounding islands, not the continent itself—but they don't report this back home; it's always *I went to Antarctica*. And everyone assumes going to Antarctica means the South Pole anyhow, when only a couple hundred ever make it that far.

Even the *Cormorant*'s crew, who will bend over backwards to get tourists' feet on the continent, can't always make it happen. It's not for lack of trying but usually for lack of a place to land. Even Shackleton's party never actually made it to the continent. Antarctica does not lay out its welcome mat very often—for eleven months of the year, sometimes twelve, ice prevents boats from landing on the sliver of exposed continent we're heading for today. The winds are calm, the sun is shining, and clear, relatively ice-free water awaits our arrival.

There is no beach at Prospect Point, so ferrying passengers between the *Cormorant* and this steep outcropping of land is a challenge. The clouds are hanging low, obscuring the sheer white cliffs in front of us. Amy and I take turns piloting the Zodiacs and holding them steady against the rocks, while Thom and Nigel help the tourists up an elevated, scraggy shoulder.

Up the rocky incline, the main attraction is what's left of the hut at Station J—the one Nigel helped take down. It was built in the 1950s by the British Antarctic Survey and was occupied for only two years. The inhabitants left almost everything behind—rusting, unopened cans of food, utensils scattered on rickety shelves, books on a moldy cot, a wall calendar open to 1959. It remained a museum of sorts until it was dismantled in 2004. Now there is nothing left but the foundation and the mummified carcasses of two Weddell seals, their gray skin weathered and dirty like old leather but still intact.

The passengers step gingerly over slick, dark rocks, over patches of moss and tiny frozen pools. Some are finished with the views after twenty minutes; others find rocks and settle down for a while. We have two hours scheduled for this landing, and because the first batch of tourists is ready to return to the *Cormorant* so soon, I take a roundabout way back to the ship. I steer the Zodiac through fields of icebergs, pointing out the Doyle Glacier, showing them a piece that has chipped away: a gigantic, flat-topped tabular iceberg in the distance. Closer to us is a newly flipped berg, its tall, wavy blue underside revealed, slick and deep indigo, as if lit from within. The passengers snap photos, and I wonder whether they feel the same change in temperature among the icebergs that I do, the sudden chill of being so close.

As the Zodiac chugs through the ice fields, I remember being here with Keller, after we found each other again, two years after McMurdo. Today I'm looking at an entirely new skyline—the icebergs have split and shifted, floated and collided and melted—not unlike Keller and me over the past two years. We're all still here, only different.

I give each Zodiac full of passengers its own iceberg tour, glancing occasionally at my watch to see when I might be able to steal a few minutes to call Keller. As anxious as I am to get back to the ship, I'm careful not to rush as the afternoon wanes. The weather holds steady, with light winds and a wispy cloud cover that lets in the occasional glow of sun.

Finally we're ready to get the last passengers on board, and as I'm helping them into Thom's Zodiac, I notice a life preserver on the rocks, unclaimed. I motion for Thom to wait a moment, then take a step toward the hut.

There, sitting on a rock, facing away from the landing site, is Kate.

I turn back toward Thom and wave him on ahead. He understands and motions that he'll come back for us.

I climb the rocks to where Kate is sitting. She seems to be expecting me; she stands, then spins slowly around, turning in a complete circle. "I thought it would feel different," she says. "My seventh continent."

She looks toward the left, where, on the rocks rimming the bay, a small group of Adélies keeps a watchful eye on us. "Richard didn't come," she says. "Not even to step on the con-tinent—a once-in-a-lifetime opportunity. I guess that's why I stayed so long. I kept hoping he'd show up."

"I'm sorry he didn't," I say, "but we need to get down to the landing. Thom will be right back."

Kate keeps her eyes on the birds. "I was sitting here thinking of something you said the other night during dinner. About how the Adélies are in trouble, how the warmer weather has been interrupting their breeding cycles. It's just so sad, you know? They do everything they're supposed to do, and it's still all for nothing."

Then she turns to look at me. "I don't know how I can justify bringing a child into a world that could allow these birds to go extinct."

"I know the feeling," I say without thinking.

"You do?" She's staring at me.

"Sure." I backtrack. "I've studied these birds for years. And you're right, it's depressing as hell. But it's not all bad. The gentoos, for example—they're doing well, adapting a lot better. And satellite imagery recently discovered a huge colony of emperors we didn't even know about. That doubles the number we thought existed."

"That doesn't save the Adélies."

I laugh but stop when I see her expression. "I'm sorry—it's just that you sound so much like me right now."

A tiny smile breaches her lips. "I don't mean to sound so gloomy. I know I should be enjoying every minute."

"Not everyone who comes down here leaves happy," I say.

She frowns. "Why do you say that?"

"It seems like there are two kinds of people who come to Antarctica. Those who have run out of places to go, and those who have run out of places to hide."

"This is my seventh continent, so I guess I've run out of places to go. Which one are you?"

"This is only my third continent. So you figure it out."

"Are you ever going to leave here? I mean, stop coming back?"

"No. It may only be my third, but it's probably my last."

"It never gets old?"

"Never. Everything's changing so quickly down here, I can't know what awaits us from one season to the next."

"How do you keep from getting depressed?"

"I'm actually more depressed when I'm *not* here. I may see the consequences of climate change here, but at least I don't have to watch everyone going about their lives as if it's not actually happening."

"See, I get that," she says. "I really do. Richard can't wait to have a baby, but he doesn't think about changing the world for the better instead of adding to its problems."

Until a few days ago I would've agreed without a second thought. Yet I find myself saying, "But babies themselves aren't inherently problematic, are they?"

"You know what I mean. At the rate we're reproducing, the planet will hit ten billion people by the middle of this century. That's not sustainable."

"No, but unless you're talking about having eleven children, a baby can be a positive thing. Maybe you'll have a kid who grows up to do good in the world."

"That's what Richard keeps saying. Maybe you two are right." She sighs. "I just wish he could see it the way I do—but it's so black and white for him. If else."

"If what?"

"That's one of Richard's sayings," she says. "Computer speak—you know, how in programming, every event is predetermined by the outcome of another? If we do one thing, it leads to the next. He thinks like this—in absolutes. *If* we have a child, we could strengthen our marriage; *else* we could not."

This makes me think of Keller—of him and his ex-wife,

Britt; of him and me. Would having another baby have saved them, or done the opposite? What would it do to us? "It's a big issue for couples, I guess," I say to Kate, trying to keep my voice neutral.

She offers up that same tiny, sad smile. "You're lucky," she says. "To be so free. So unattached."

I shake my head but can't think of anything to say. Then I hear the rumble of an approaching Zodiac, the sound of Thom returning for us. "Ready?" I ask her.

She nods but doesn't move for a long moment. I watch her eyes linger on the Weddell seals and follow her gaze. Looking at their well-preserved bodies, I don't know whether to envy them or pity them, lying there untouched, stuck forever in a landscape that won't allow them to disappear.

The Cormorant

The lounge is crowded and dim, the shades drawn. I'm holding a microphone in one hand, and in the other I use a remote to flip through my penguin photographs, behind me on a large screen: close-ups of Adélies courting, their elongated necks stretching skyward; of chicks putting their whole heads into a parent's mouth for a meal of regurgitated krill; panoramas of rookeries blanketing the sides of islands, barren landscapes transformed into checkerboards of black and white.

"Unfortunately," I say, "we have less than half the number of Adélie colonies that we had thirty years ago, and the birds within those colonies are at only a third of their original numbers."

I continue to the next photos: cracked and abandoned eggs, adult penguins sitting on empty nests. Keller is standing next to me.

After I go through all the slides, I ask the passengers near the portholes to release the shades, let the light in. "We have time for questions," I say.

"Is there any way to keep the penguins from extinction?" someone asks.

"Our research translates to things we should *all* be doing," I answer. "Deal with the climate, which is complicating the weather patterns that affect the penguins' breeding. Stop eating fish, which is like taking food from their mouths."

"I only eat sustainable seafood," a woman says. "Like the Chilean sea bass."

"It's good to be aware of where your food is coming from," I say. "And how it affects everything else in the environment."

What I don't tell her is that there's nothing sustainable about "Chilean sea bass," which is the name some clever public relations team came up with for the Patagonian toothfish. Thanks to its hip new name and subsequent popularity, it's been overfished to the point of being endangered. And I don't tell her that while menus may claim that it's sustainable, most toothfish still comes from illegal fisheries—and, as if that's not enough, they use longlines, which wreak havoc on the birds.

Keller takes the mic from me. "Any other questions?"

"Getting back to the penguins." A self-assured voice in the back. "I'm not sure all the evidence is in regarding global warming."

I swivel my head to see a smirking man dressed head to toe in extreme-weather clothes that look so new I expect to see price tags dangling from them.

Keller looks at him for a long moment. "You're saying you don't believe in human-induced climate change?"

"I'm not yet convinced, no."

"The temperatures here on the peninsula have gone up nearly five degrees in the past fifty years. That makes this region one of the fastest-warming areas on the planet, about ten times faster than the global average. Does that qualify as evidence?"

"It's not *enough* evidence."

"The Antarctic ice sheets are melting at an unprecedented rate," Keller goes on. "I'm talking billions of tons per year. This could mean global sea-level rises of ten, twenty feet."

I step closer, hoping he'll notice me and stop talking. Keller has already been warned by Glenn not to lecture the passengers, after Glenn overheard a dinner conversation in which Keller took a passenger to task for taking supplements made from krill. Yet Keller doesn't see me, or isn't ready to be silenced.

"As Deb was saying, in the years we've been coming down here, we've seen the Adélie counts drop—in some colonies by as much as seventy percent—and it's not just the fact that they can't nest on snow-covered rocks. The depletion of the ozone layer affects the phytoplankton, which in turn affects the krill, which means the penguins are left with less to eat. They need to go farther in search of food, which means they may not make it back in time to relieve their partners, and their chicks will starve or end up abandoned. Is *that* enough evidence? Or do they have to go completely extinct first?"

The man rises to his feet. "I don't appreciate your tone."

"I'm sorry," Keller says. "I guess I find it frustrating when people refuse to see what's right in front of them."

The man looks aghast. "You can't speak to us like that." He gives Keller a hard stare before he turns and walks out the door.

An uncomfortable silence fills the room, and through it Keller continues.

"The truth hurts, I know," he says, "but it hurts the continent a lot more than it hurts any of us. I know you all came down here for the experience of a lifetime—but there's just too many of you."

Subtly, I reach for the mic.

"You don't need a passport to visit Antarctica," he goes on, "and now there's a whole new breed of so-called adventurers who don't care one bit about the continent. They just want to skydive or paraglide or water-ski in the coldest place on earth so they have something to brag about at the next cocktail party."

This time, I wrest the mic from Keller's hand.

"Who are you to tell them they can't?" a voice calls out from the back. "You can't pick and choose who comes here. It's not a country club."

"No," Keller says, his voice naked and raw without the mic, "it's more like a cemetery."

Glenn seems to come out of nowhere—I don't see him until he's right next to me, holding his hand out for the microphone. A high-pitched whine is emitted by the speaker, and Glenn lets the noise die down before he says, in his usual smooth, calm voice, "Ladies and gentlemen, this concludes our program. Thank you."

Silently Keller and I begin unplugging the A/V equipment, and I zip my laptop away in its case. I'm hoping Glenn's busy enough to go back to the bridge, but he hovers, and as soon as the last of the passengers has cleared out, he turns to us. He opens his mouth to speak, then simply shakes his head.

"Sorry, Glenn," Keller says. "I got a little carried away."

"This is getting old, Keller. I'm not warning you again."

Glenn looks as if he's about to say something more, but instead he turns on his heel and leaves the room.

I look at Keller. As if he knows what I'm about to say, he holds up a hand before I can speak. "I don't want to talk about it. I'm going to the gym."

"What about dinner?"

"Fuck dinner."

I sigh and gather the rest of our equipment. By the time I stow it away, dinner has begun, but I'm not in the mood either. I know this won't sit well with Glenn, that Keller is in enough trouble already, and that, although I have no appetite now, I'll probably be hungry later. But the head chef, Eugenio, likes Keller and me and always lets us sneak in after dining hours, while the galley staff is hanging out, cleaning up. Keller rinses dishes and scrubs pots, I grab a mop, and Eugenio fixes us a vegan version of whatever the galley staff had for dinner—always a Filipino dish, noodles or fried tofu or vegetable empanadas.

I change into running clothes and head to the gym, but Keller's not there. I notice the light on in the ship's tiny sauna—a cedar-scented wooden room with a single long bench just wide enough to hold a human body. I take off my clothes and don a towel, and when I open the door, a gust of hot air blows out. Keller's sitting on the bench, back against the wall, legs stretched out. I sit on the opposite end, and I just barely fit. My toes rest against the arches of his feet.

It's our last voyage at the end of a long season, with two stints on Petermann and four shiploads of different passengers. We're both spent. And I worry, at times like this, that Keller isn't cut out for this type of work after all. He's become

an incredible naturalist, yet he doesn't like being around people, especially those who know so little. *You were once just like
them,* I reminded him a couple of weeks ago, when he got
cranky with a passenger who'd stepped on a penguin trail. *I
was never that stubbornly ignorant,* he replied, defensive. And
I said, *Well, you are stubbornly impatient. Give these people
a break.*

Now I shift on the hard wooden bench and say, "I've never
seen Glenn that pissed off."

Keller shrugs. "He'll get over it." He looks at me, then
presses his feet forward, bending my toes slightly back. "I
know what you're thinking," he says. "I'll apologize to Glenn,
once he's cooled off a bit. And he knows you had nothing to
do with it."

"That's not it at all. You know by now what you're risking,
and still you keep doing it."

"Glenn's more bark than bite," he says, closing his eyes.
"Don't worry."

"I do worry. I don't know what I'd do without you on these
trips."

I feel as though Keller and I help each other stay sane
during these journeys; we remind each other that we'll soon
have a couple nights together in Ushuaia, or two weeks alone
among the penguins at Petermann.

We're alike in so many ways, even in the way Keller had
taken the mic from me after the slide show, and how I'd taken
it again from him—both of us trying to save each other from
ourselves and the consequences with Glenn. And with a sudden, sinking feeling, I wonder if what Keller and I have been
doing isn't keeping each other sane but something more like

the opposite—a folie à deux born of our love for the continent, and for each other, that is steering us not closer to but further away from reality. It's the passengers who reflect the real world, its opinions and habits, its denials and truths—and we're more removed from this world all the time, maybe to the point where we're unable to exist within it at all.

With Keller's eyes closed, I take the opportunity to study him unobserved, blinking out a bead of sweat that has trickled into my eye. He looks unconcerned, relaxed, despite what happened earlier, yet I can see that every moment he's spent on the continent is already etched upon his face: skin ruddy from the cold and wind and sun, eyes receding into a growing nest of crow's-feet. What draws me to Keller are things I think few people outside Antarctica—even Glenn, especially Glenn—will ever see. Watching Keller put out a fire in one of the tinder-dry dormitories at McMurdo. Seeing him break up a fistfight between two mechanics in the Southern Exposure. Watching him secure a loose egg back under a penguin's brood pouch when the bird couldn't leave its nest, sustaining a gory bite wound for his trouble. But most of all, what I know about Keller comes from the shared silences of our glacial hikes, from stealing away from the tourists for a few moments alone on the uppermost deck of the ship, from the reunions that feel as though we've never been apart.

I stand and pick up the sauna's large wooden spoon, ladling water over the lava rocks. A great sizzle rises, and the room fills with steam, intensifying the heat. It's getting harder to breathe, and as Keller opens his eyes, as I look at him through the steam, his eyes dark and wet as a seal's, I realize that, though I may know him as well as anyone, he will always be a bit out of reach, even to me. Not listening to Glenn is one thing—not listening to me is something I hadn't expected.

"You've got to get your act together," I tell him. "I know you hate sucking up to Glenn, but if that's what it takes—"

"We work for the APP, not Glenn," he murmurs, his eyes falling shut again.

"As long as Glenn transports us down here, we *do* work for him. The whole program depends on getting a free ride."

"It's not a free ride," Keller says. "There's a huge price to pay."

"Believe me, I know. But it's worth it."

Keller opens his eyes and looks at me. "So you agree with Glenn? You think seafood belongs on the menu?"

"No, of course I don't, but at least I see the reality—that it's impossible to fill a cruise if you don't serve what the passengers want to eat."

"These passengers need to know what a disaster this is."

"I hear you," I say. "I do. But since we're bringing people down here, we have to teach them, show them how important it is, everything they're seeing firsthand. If you had your way, you'd just fence it all off."

"Damn right, I would."

"Well, if that were the case, none of us would be here. Including you."

The heat of the sauna blurs my vision, and I can no longer see him clearly.

"The explorers," Keller says, "were obsessed with firsts. Scott, Amundsen, all of them—it was about doing it first. Now everyone's obsessed with lasts. Checking off their last continent. Seeing it before it's all gone. Soon they'll be brag-ging about who photographed the last living Adélie."

"God, I hope not."

"Brace yourself," he says.

Abruptly Keller gets up, opens the door, and walks out, letting in a blast of cool air. More quickly than I believed possible, I feel the heat leave my body.

ONE DAY BEFORE SHIPWRECK

South of the Antarctic Circle
(66°33'S)

It's not uncommon in Antarctica to see what does not exist—to see the mountains levitate in the distance, to see the rising towers of a city on the horizon. When the sea is colder than the air, a layer forms that creates a polar mirage. The more layers, the more refracted the light: Mountains are born from the sea; cliffs turn into castles. Such mirages usually last only moments, until the air layers mix, and then they disappear.

These illusions can be dangerous—they often caused explorers to miscalculate distances—or simply embarrassing, leading the explorers to identify land that was not actually there. In the middle of the nineteenth century, Captain Sir James Clark Ross discovered a mountain range he named the Parry Mountains, about twenty-five miles from his position east of Ross Island—but there were, in fact, no mountains there at all; what he'd seen was a reflection of another mountain range, more than three hundred miles away.

Such visions have a name—*fata morgana*—and I feel as though I'm seeing a mirage right now: a large, multilayered building rising from the sea, moving along the horizon. I'm on the foredeck, braced against a biting headwind, and I'm hoping that this is only a trick of the eyes. It's normal to see a fata morgana just before a storm or change in the weather.

But this mirage doesn't waver or blur; it doesn't disappear. Heart thudding, I raise my binoculars to confirm what is even more bizarre than a fata morgana, and all too real—the *Australis*, about half a nautical mile away, headed in our direction. Headed south.

I run up to the bridge. Glenn is standing next to Captain Wylander, who's speaking into the radio.

"What the hell is that ship doing down here?" I ask.

"That's what we're trying to figure out."

The captain hands the radio to Glenn, who barks a warning to the ship. "Lack of advance notification is in violation of IAATO protocol."

"They're making a run for the Gullet, aren't they?"

"They won't make it that far."

I leave the bridge and return to the deck, raising my binoculars, as if I might see Keller on board. I look for an orange crew jacket, but it's freezing cold, and hardly anyone's outside—only a scattering of passengers among the *Australis*'s five decks, with no idea what their captain is risking. They are already fading in the mist and the sleet that is beginning to slicken the deck under my boots.

I peer through the fog at the stiffening ice. Just yesterday Glenn had been planning our own run for the Gullet, the scenic but narrow strip of water that cuts between Adelaide

Island and the continent. Few tourist vessels ever make it that far, and given the changing weather and the amount of ice forming, Glenn had decided to turn around. Unlike whoever's at the helm of the *Australis*, Glenn is far too careful to attempt anything tricky unless conditions are just right. And so we are headed north again as the *Australis* is heading south.

The sea is incredibly icy even here, with bergy bits clanging against the hull. Passengers always freak out when they hear the metallic thud of ice—I'll spend most of my day reassuring skittish passengers that the *Cormorant* has a reinforced hull, that it'll take a lot more than a few growlers to sink it. If only I could say the same about the *Australis*, which is not built to navigate the icy conditions she's headed into.

In the hundred years since the *Titanic* sank, ship design and construction have improved drastically; it's not a stretch to assure passengers that today's cruises are safe. Yet the one thing that hasn't changed is human nature—ego and folly and hubris and whatever outcomes these may bring—and every ship is only as safe as her captain and crew and the choices they make.

I listen to the smaller pieces of slushy ice rub against the steel like a wire brush; the familiar, uneven rhythm normally relaxes me. I lean on the railing, eyes still on the *Australis*. I'd like to think I'd have known the ship was this far south, that I'd have felt Keller's proximity somehow. More than ever, I need to talk to him. But as I'm heading up to the communications room, Glenn radios.

"We're doing an ice landing," he tells me. "Be ready to scout in five."

I LOWER THE gangway onto a wide plain of fast ice. The captain has nudged the *Cormorant* into a frozen expanse of ocean, and, despite the cloudy afternoon, the ice burns with white light. Another unforgettable experience for the tourists: a chance to walk on water.

Several inches of fresh powder cover the ice, and Thom, Nigel, and I walk out onto the frozen sea, testing its stability with ski poles, posting flags to mark boundaries the tourists won't be allowed to walk beyond. Within half an hour, we are escorting passengers directly from the boat onto the ice.

Ice landings are my favorite types of excursions—no Zodiacs, no penguins, just three feet of solid ice that, because they're walking on the ocean, the passengers celebrate. A man flops down to make a snow angel. Snowball fights erupt.

I scan the area, and when I glimpse a figure about a hundred yards away, past one of the boundary flags, I think I'm seeing things again. Who would venture past what we've determined to be safe?

I know the answer even before I raise my binoculars to my eyes.

She's several yards past the flag by now, and no one else seems to have noticed. I walk briskly toward her, trying to seem as casual as possible. I'm hoping she's just overlooked the flag and will realize her mistake and turn back. But Kate keeps going.

Once I'm past the flag, I shout her name. If she hears me over the wind, she doesn't respond.

I pick up my pace, and my boots slide on the ice that's just below the thin layer of snow. In front of me, the pearly surface of the ice and the blanched sky meet and blur into one. *Don't fall*, I tell myself. *Don't fall.*

I'm sweating under my parka and all the layers beneath, and I'm breathless from the cold and from calling out to Kate. Finally, about twenty feet away from her, I start to run. I catch up and grab her by the wrist.

She turns, the expression on her face unreadable. I hold fast to her wrist as I try to catch my breath.

"What's with the disappearing act?" I sputter out.

"I just wanted a few minutes away from everyone. I don't like being around people all the time."

"Then you shouldn't have taken a cruise. Let's go."

"I'm not ready yet."

"This is not up to you, Kate. We haven't checked this ice for safety. Come on."

Before I know what's happening, she yanks her arm away and starts running—away from me and the *Cormorant*—and I glance back toward the ship. The naturalists are busy with other passengers, and so I turn and follow Kate. I don't know what sort of suicidal mission she's on, but I do know I can't let her go any farther. She is slipping and stumbling, and when I get close enough to catch her again, I reach out—and this time both of us lose our balance and tumble to the ice.

I break my fall, landing hard on all fours, feeling the searing bend of my wrists, the sharp pain in my knees. My sunglasses fall off, and I turn over and lower myself to the ice, lying there faceup, closing my eyes for a moment against the blinding white of the sky.

When I open them again, Kate is sitting next to me, wincing and brushing snow off her parka.

"What the hell is the matter with you?" I ask her.

I'm surprised to see tears in her eyes when she faces me. "I'm pregnant," she whispers.

I nod but say nothing.

"I've been trying to figure out how I feel about it," she says. "How to be happy, how to be ready. I just can't."

"You will," I assure her.

"How can you say that?"

An enormous pop fills the air around us, and she looks at me in dismay. "What's that?"

"The ice," I say.

"It's breaking?"

"More like breathing," I say. "It makes a lot of noise. Doesn't mean we're falling in just yet. Still, we need to go."

"I'm so sorry," she says, though she's making no move to get up. "I wasn't trying to—" She sighs. "I just needed a little space to think, that's all."

"I know."

"Do you?"

For a moment it almost seems natural to tell her, to have someone to talk to about this. But all I can say is: "Yes. I do."

She shakes her head. "Everyone thinks when you get married, you have kids. There's something wrong with you if you don't want them."

"There's nothing wrong with you."

She gives me a wry smile. "You may think that, but, with all due respect, you're more of a freak of nature than I am. No partner, no kids, living in Antarctica half the year."

I can't help but like her a little bit more. "It doesn't matter what anyone thinks."

I hear agitated garble from my radio, and I pause to listen. It's Glenn, calling us back to the ship.

"Ice conditions are deteriorating," he snaps. "We need to get out of here. Now."

I've hardly noticed that the wind has picked up, that the snow covering this sheet of ice is blowing past us, revealing slick, fickle ice underneath.

I look up and see that, in the distance, the other naturalists are just beyond the boundary flags and spaced evenly apart. I don't see any of the other passengers; Glenn must have called everyone back to the ship.

I scramble to my feet and hold out a hand to Kate. "Come on, let's go," I say, trying to keep my voice even, patient.

As we begin walking forward, toward the flags, I keep my eyes down, looking for fissures, though I know all too well they won't be visible until it's too late. We hear a thundering crack—more vibration than noise—and I grab on to Kate's arm again as I lower myself to my knees, tugging her with me.

A section of rope lands in front of us. I look up and see Nigel and Amy just ahead.

"The ice is no longer stable," I say to Kate, leaning forward to retrieve the rope. "Just to be safe, we'll need to spread out our weight until we get to a better spot."

I tie the rope around Kate's middle, high, just under her breasts. "We have to lie flat and crawl, but Nigel will be tugging you in a bit, too. Lie as flat as you can."

"I'm so sorry," she says. "I didn't mean to cause all this trouble."

"We need to hurry," I tell her, then lie down flat in the snow, to show her how it's done. "Propel yourself forward with your elbows and knees. When Nigel says it's okay, you can stand. I'll be right behind you. Go on."

She flattens her own body on the ice and begins to inch forward, slowly and awkwardly, looking up every so often as if using the naturalists as landmarks.

When she reaches Nigel, he backs himself into safe territory, then helps her to her feet. Amy holds her arm as we walk quickly back to the ship, as if Kate might take off running again.

In the mudroom, Glenn is waiting.

He fixes his eyes on Kate, with an expression that reminds me of the way he'd looked at Keller that day last season, after our disastrous onboard lecture.

"The safety of the passengers on this ship is my first priority," Glenn says.

"I know—" Kate begins.

"I don't believe you do, Ms. Archer," Glenn says. "Your actions today have put yourself and our crew in danger. And I don't need to remind you of the actions of your husband on Deception Island."

Kate's looking downward, and Glenn continues. "Five years ago, a woman who reminds me a lot of you decided she wanted a close-up of a seal sleeping on the fast ice. She walked past the flags, and two crew members went after her. One fell through the ice and nearly drowned. Is this something you want on your conscience?"

Kate raises her head to meet his unsparing gaze. She shakes her head.

"You've risked the lives not only of the crew but of every passenger on this vessel," Glenn tells her. "Ice conditions down here can change in minutes, and our captain needs to be ready to respond. He can't be waiting on rogue passengers who are running around on the ice."

"I understand."

"Good," Glenn says. "Because if you step out of line once more, I'm turning this ship around and taking you back to Argentina. You can be sure your fellow passengers won't be pleased with the change in itinerary."

Kate nods and stares down at her feet. Glenn gives her a withering glare before he walks out, his footsteps echoing back from the passageway.

Kate turns to me, her face flushed deep red, and I can tell she is the sort of person who's never gotten herself into trouble, until now. I also know that Glenn dramatized his story; the crew member had only sprained a wrist.

"He means business," I say to Kate. "Be good, okay? You and Richard both."

She nods again and turns to go. I watch the way she moves—the same way I do these days, protective of the middle of her body. It's only been a few days since everything's changed, since I thought I could avoid the messes of being human, of being a woman, by immersing myself in work.

I press the fingers of my right hand into my left, feeling around for my ring, hidden under my glove. I'd never told Keller the story of the bird it had belonged to, and suddenly I'm glad. So much about the penguins—about his own past—is about loss, and maybe it's better that we don't think about the precariousness of life, the way a piece of metal can be wrapped around a living being in one moment, removed from a body in the next.

FIFTEEN YEARS BEFORE SHIPWRECK

Punta Tombo, Argentina

It amazes me how quickly my first week in Punta Tombo has turned into a month. It's already mid-November, springtime in Argentina, and in three weeks I'll travel home to complete the third year of my Ph.D. program in conservation biology.

In only my second season at Punta Tombo, I feel like a regular as I continue laying down stakes and surveying penguins at the largest Magellanic colony in the world. This time, I've also graduated from the trailer next to the researchers' house to a bunk inside with five other graduate students. Things are otherwise the same—the long journey, the once-a-week showers, the meals of instant soup. While I enjoy being among fellow researchers—late-night talks over glasses of Malbec, shared discoveries in this brand-new world—I also miss the trailer, with the rattle of never-ending wind and the brays of the resident penguin underneath, still waiting for his mate to show up.

Last season, my second year of graduate school and my first visit here, was the first time I'd ever seen a penguin. The *pingüino*, as the locals call him, was on the dirt road near the researchers' building. By then I'd read a lot about the seventeen species of penguins, but nothing compared to seeing the little black-and-white body crossing the road a few yards away. I could see his Magellanic characteristics—black with a white belly, a band of white that starts above each eye and goes all the way around the head, meeting under the chin. Another band of black surrounding the belly in a U shape. A black bill and a bit of pink skin around the eyes. He walked past in the dusk, with a penguin's usual sense of purpose—his head held high and his flippers out—and he paid little attention to us, a carful of jet-lagged scientists, as he disappeared from the road into the drab landscape, amid the tawny dirt and the bushes of myriad shades of green.

Most of the penguins here are accustomed to people and commotion. The land on which this colony resides had been donated by a local family to the province of Chubut for preservation—but also for tourism. In addition to the family's *estancia*—their private ranch—and the researchers' quarters, the penguins live amid a tourist center with a shop and restaurant, as well as public bathrooms and a parking lot.

The researchers' house comes alive shortly after dawn—coffee brewing, doors opening and closing, cereal spoons clinking against the sides of bowls. I wear tan cargo pants and three layers of brown and green shirts; the government requires us to blend in with the colors of the land. I also strap on kneepads because we spend much of our time kneeling, peering into bushes and burrows as we count the birds. I tuck a water bottle and granola bar into my day pack, and I head out with Christina, the postdoc I'm teamed up with. We trek among the penguins, sheep, guanacos, and European hares, their shadows long in the early-morning light.

I'm carrying the *gancho*—a long piece of rebar with a hook at the end—which we guide gently under the penguins' breasts, lifting them slightly off the ground, peeking beneath to see if they're incubating eggs. When we find an active nest with a banded bird, we use the hook to draw him or her out of the nest.

When I discover a banded female in a burrow, I wish we could leave her alone. The penguin is huddled in the nest with her partner, and when they see me peering in, they tilt their heads first one way and then the other, almost all the way around, back and forth in a constant, anxious motion. I lean in far enough to read the numbers on the band, then call out the digits to Christina, who checks the log. As it turns out, it's been five years since we've seen this penguin, so we'll need to check her out. I let Christina draw her from the nest with the *gancho*, then I slide the straps of the handheld scale around the bird and hold the scale up and away from my body. Christina jots down the bird's weight, four kilos, in our notebook, then reaches over and takes the scale from my hands. "I'll lower her down," she says, "if you can hold her?"

I hold the penguin firmly by her neck, gripping her between my knees. With my fingerless gloves I can feel her soft, dense feathers, and I cover her eyes with my half-gloved hand to soothe her as Christina measures the bill's length and width and then the feet, reading aloud the numbers on the caliper as she writes them in her notebook. When she's done, I turn the penguin toward the nest and let her go; she scrambles back into her burrow, and I breathe a quiet sigh of relief.

We continue working the colony under a cloud-studded, teal-blue sky, among the dust and scrubby bushes—the *lycium* and *uña de gato*, the *jume* and *molle*, and the *quilembai*. We pass a penguin pair napping just outside their nest, lying together belly down, the female's bill resting on her mate's back. A mile or so farther on, we see a dead penguin, a male, lying amid small pebbles and short, bright green grass just a few feet from his nest, a burrow under a *quilembai* bush.

I look over toward the burrow. The penguin's mate is sitting at the opening of the nest, her eyes on her mate's body. I don't see any eggs, so they'd just coupled up. Eventually she'll have to leave, returning next season to try again. Magellanics are remarkably loyal to their nest sites—even if a nest is compromised, a bird won't abandon it. We've seen nests trampled by tourists; the penguins rebuild. We've seen burrows collapse after heavy rains; the penguins dig themselves out. We've seen birds scurry toward their nests as tourists crowd around them to take photographs; we've seen them try to cross the road to their nests as cars fly past. Sometimes they make it; sometimes they don't.

And this is what Christina and I encounter when we make our way back to the research and tourist center—a penguin lying in the road, a tour bus just ahead, its driver talking animatedly in Spanish. My Spanish is limited, but it's clear what happened: The penguin was trying to return to her nest, and she got hit. I kneel down next to the bird. I notice the tag on her left wing, and I pull a small pair of pliers from my cargo pants and pry it off. Later, when I look her up, I'll learn that she's fifteen years old, that we've been following her for a decade, that she's raised nine generations of chicks on our watch. I'll make the last recording about this bird in our field notes; I'll write her death certificate.

I look around until I find what I think must be her nest—inside is a single male, lying on two eggs. They may hatch if he doesn't abandon them, but even if they do, the chicks won't survive.

After dinner that night, I head out for a walk. The sun is setting, the evening sky turning violet. A thin, watery stripe of blue brushes the landscape where sky meets water, and the low, rolling hills are bathed in lavender light. I head up a slope from which I can see the ocean, and the brays of the penguins shatter the silence.

In the distance I see the lights of a fishing boat, a boat that no doubt will dump oil-laced ballast and catch penguins in its nets. The colony here has declined nearly 20 percent in the last decade, and we're killing them in big ways and small—by the thousands and one by one—their predators no longer fellow creatures or acts of nature but those at the helms of boats and buses.

Back at the station, I slip into the supply room and find a tent. Gathering my sleeping bag under one arm and using my flashlight to avoid stepping too close to the penguin burrows, I venture past the lights of the house, over a small hill, and down into a hollow, walking until everything ceases to exist but me and the penguins. I fall asleep with the wind shaking the tent, and I wake to the serenade of penguins reuniting nearby—sounds of love and hope and optimism, spoken in a language that science will never be able to decipher, yet one I feel as though I can understand.

ONCE EVERY FEW weeks, a small group makes the two-hour journey to Trelew for supplies, and my turn comes up for the next run. As we traverse the dirt road, I look out the window and think of what I've decided—how, by giving up on my Ph.D., I'm leaving the birds with one fewer scientist to help save them.

Yet I can't ignore the nagging feeling that geographically I've only gotten halfway to where I really want to be. And I know that I can be easily replaced, that I can find work elsewhere, that penguins everywhere need saving.

Months earlier, back home in Seattle, I'd heard about an organization called the Antarctic Penguins Project; only a few years old, it had just gotten some serious funding, and its mission had piqued my interest—the organization collaborates with naturalists from all over the world, with all different backgrounds. Their researchers don't all have doctorates, aren't all affiliated with universities. It seemed like a place that might be a good fit for the rogue scientist I was on the verge of becoming.

Once in town, I arrange to meet the group later, then duck into a *farmacia* to buy a few things and find a phone. I use my credit card to place a call to the States. When a harried female voice barks out, "Antarctic Penguins Project," I introduce myself.

IT'S MY LAST week at Tombo, and as eager as I am to make my way down to the Antarctic, I'm finding it hard to say goodbye to these birds, who have taught me so much.

The day before I leave for Trelew to begin the journey

back, I walk to the tip of the peninsula, out past the research station and tourist center, over sand dunes studded with tufts of pampas grass. I stop at the spot where the point extends into the sea, a bridge of lava and tide pools, light-green water breaking against black rock, penguins floating in whitewash and coming ashore on a curve of black sand.

As I watch where penguins leap from the surf, I think of the bag we have back at the research station—a canvas sack filled with penguin tags sent to us by fishing boats—the tags of all the penguins that died in their nets, or birds they found dead in the water or on shore. I touch the tag in my pocket, the one I took off the bird who was killed on the road, one of so many.

Finally I turn away from the water, from the waves rattling with yet-undiscovered penguin tags, and head toward the station, resisting the urge to look back.

North of the Antarctic Circle
(66°33'S)

B rash, pack, slush, rotten, black, pancake, frazil, grease, fast—there are so many words for the different types of ice conditions in Antarctica, so many ways for a ship to find herself in trouble. And now, as the *Cormorant* continues north through loose brash, I wonder about the conditions farther south, where the *Australis* is. At the first sign of stormy weather, Glenn had gotten us out of there, just as the *Australis* had been venturing in.

It would be less dangerous if the sea farther south were simply impenetrable—but I know that if it looks navigable, a pressured captain trying to please an overzealous cruise director might take a chance. The *Australis* can pass through the harmless frazil and grease ice—the beginnings of the freezing process—and she can sift her way through the pancake ice: the round, flat formations that float close together in the early stage of creating compact sea ice. Yet when the salt begins to seep from the ice into the ocean below, when the wind shoves the pack together, when the hummocks and ridges grow taller and taller, the ice becomes more and more difficult to maneuver. As the ice solidifies and sticks together, the terrain becomes more like ground than like sea, and eventually it becomes impossible to turn back.

Our passengers, thanks to our hasty retreat from the sea ice after the landing, are both fascinated and worried—and full of questions and misperceptions at happy hour in the lounge. One passenger refers to the *Cormorant* as an icebreaker, and I correct him.

"A true icebreaker not only has to have a strengthened hull," I say, "but also has to have the right shape and enough power to drive the bow up onto the ice. What breaks the ice isn't just the hull but the weight of the boat."

"So why don't we use an icebreaker?" the passenger says.

"They're very expensive," I say. "And they don't usually have stabilizers, like we do, so you can imagine how much more seasick you'd be. We'd never take passengers into ice conditions thick enough to require an icebreaker anyway."

I glance at my watch. It's almost time for dinner, so I excuse myself and steal my way to the satellite phone in the business center. When I'm connected to Keller's quarters, I offer up a silent plea for him to be there.

I hear his voice and nearly drop the phone with relief. "Keller, it's me." Before he can say anything else, I blurt out, "There's something I need to tell you. I didn't have time on Deception Island."

"I know," he says. "I didn't mean to pressure you with that ring. I know marriage wasn't ever in your plan, and I—"

"It's not that," I say, talking quickly, aware, as ever, that we never have enough time. "I really didn't want to tell you this on the phone." I take a breath and stutter it out. "I'm—I'm pregnant."

I hear only static, and I wait for a moment, then say, "Keller?"

Nothing.

My stomach turns over. While I've assumed that he'd be happy with the news, maybe I'm wrong.

I think of the *Australis*, heading south—surely she'd have turned around by now, but even so, the sat phone connection could be dicey. I hang up and make the call again. This time, I can't get through at all, and I slam the phone down.

I look at my watch and sigh—I'm supposed to be at dinner by now. I try calling one more time. Reluctantly I give up and head for the dining room, where the only empty seat is next to Kate and Richard. Richard still wears a seasickness patch behind his ear.

"Until this trip, I had no idea there were so many different types of ice," Kate says. "It's like the Eskimos having a hundred different words for snow."

"That's just a myth, Kate," Richard says.

"What?" she says.

"It's an urban myth," he says. His face looks flushed, and he keeps blinking his eyes, as if trying to focus. "Any credible linguist will tell you that the Inuit language may have a number of different ways of referring to snow, but it's basically no different than in English, where we have wet snow, powder, sleet, slush, blizzard, and so on."

Kate only looks at him, and Richard's flush grows deeper, the set of his jaw a little more stubborn. He reaches for the wine bottle in the center of the table and fills Kate's glass. I realize then that Richard doesn't know about the baby, that Kate hasn't decided what to do about her pregnancy.

I try to change the subject. "In May and June," I say, "when the continent is preparing to shut ships like ours out for the winter, you can actually hear the ice crystals forming, if you listen closely enough. It almost sounds like the water is singing."

"Really?" Kate says. "I'd love to be here to see that. Or rather, hear it."

"It's interesting, the way you personify nature," Richard says, looking from me to his wife.

"It beats objectifying nature," Kate retorts.

"And that's what I do?"

Kate presses her lips together, her eyes shooting Richard a look that says, *Not here, not now.*

"We all objectify nature to some extent, don't we?" says a man sitting across the table. "I mean, if we didn't feel some sort of distance, we wouldn't be able to build houses, or put gas in our cars, or turn on the lights. Not to mention food. You can't think of pigs when you eat bacon or you just don't eat."

"Well, according to my wife, we should treat all these animals as humans," Richard says. "Whales and penguins and even krill."

"Kate has a point," I say, in as friendly a way as I can manage. I'm not sure whether my arguing with Richard is better than Kate arguing with him, but it doesn't feel quite as uncomfortable. "Animals are no less valuable to this planet than humans."

"Of course they are. There's a hierarchy involved."

"A hierarchy developed by humans," I say. "Take sharks, for

example. Most people think of sharks as nothing more than props in a horror movie. But they may well be extinct in the next few decades, and they're the ones that have been keeping the marine ecosystem in balance for four hundred million years. Once they're gone, everything changes."

"It sounds like your idea of a perfect world would be free of people altogether." Richard's face is crimson, and his left eye is twitching. He rubs his hands across his eyes.

"That's not such a bad idea." This comes from Kate, murmured so low I almost miss it.

"Why does that not surprise me?" Richard says, his voice tinged with bitterness.

"Stop it, Richard," she says quietly. She pushes her chair back.

Richard grabs her arm. "Wait."

Kate tries to free herself from his grip, but Richard rises to his feet, upending his chair and tipping a couple of full wineglasses as he pulls her up with him. I look again at the medicated patch behind Richard's ear and know something's very wrong. I scan the room, catching Thom's eye. I can't tell what he's seen, but he reads my expression and pushes his chair away from the table, ready to come over if I need him to.

I'm standing up myself when the ship turns hard to port, catching us all by surprise. I grip my chair as plates slide off the table into people's laps and as the servers, barely managing to stay on their feet, try to keep their trays from crashing to the floor. Spilled wine is spreading across the tablecloth like a bloodstain. Glenn runs past us out of the dining room.

I turn back to Kate and Richard—Richard is on the floor, using one of the chairs to stand. Kate isn't helping him.

"What happened?" someone asks. "Have we hit something?"

"No," I say. "We've turned around."

Thom is next to me by now, and when I look at him, he nods, a sickening confirmation that he, too, knows why.

South of the Antarctic Circle
(66°33'S)

According to international maritime law, a passenger ship must be capable of launching all survival craft, fully loaded with passengers and crew, within thirty minutes of the captain's sounding of the abandon-ship signal.

But there's a difference between being theoretically capable of a task and accomplishing it. No matter how many times crew members go through the drills, even if they take into account the possibility of rogue waves and tipped icebergs, they can't predict how long it might take to guide twelve hundred passengers and four hundred crew from a wounded ship in ice-choked waters below the Antarctic Circle, where lifeboats may have nowhere to float.

Nobody can know. It has never happened—until now.

I stand next to Amy among the hastily assembled expedition staff and crew on the bridge, where Glenn is giving us another briefing. As he'd told us earlier, the *Australis* has struck a submerged object, likely ice, in the Gullet and is taking on water. Glenn and Captain Wylander have been coordinating rescue efforts with the Argentinian Coast Guard, the Chilean Navy, and two other cruise ships.

The *Australis* has not yet given the abandon-ship signal, and this gives me hope. The *Cormorant* is the closest ship, and we're ten hours away—ten very critical hours—but the *Australis* still has electrical power, and her captain estimates she'll stay afloat for another twelve hours, depending on weather conditions.

All of us, of course, have received emergency training, in everything from CPR to evacuating the *Cormorant*. But putting together a rescue plan for a sinking ship of sixteen hundred, without knowing what the conditions will be like until we get there, is next to impossible. The *Cormorant*, nearly at capacity, can safely take on no more than two hundred people.

Of course, not every ship that strikes ice is destined to sink; a seaworthy cruise liner is equipped with life preservers of her own: airtight bulkheads, bilge alarms, compartment seals, escape tubes. When all safety measures perform as intended, a debilitated ship may list at an odd angle for days or even weeks without sinking.

Yet the *Australis*, we're learning now, has suffered extensive damage. "Apparently there was a serious malfunction in two of the bulkhead doors," Glenn says. "The failures occurred when they were stuck in fast ice and tried to force their way out. The next closest ship is another eight hours behind us."

Which means that for the next eighteen hours, the *Cormorant* is the *Australis*'s only real hope.

"Any casualties?" Nigel asks.

Glenn says simply, "Yes."

I try to stand still, to breathe evenly. I know that when it comes to the rescue efforts, I don't have the luxury of choosing which life is more important than the next, not when so many are in danger. But I also know that the minute we have the *Australis* in our sights, only one person will matter.

We've already cordoned off a section of the lounge, now a mini–triage center supplied with blankets and first-aid equipment, and it's time to let the passengers in on the news. As we head down the steps to the lounge, Amy leans close and speaks into my ear. "He'll be fine," she says. "If anyone can handle something like this, it's Keller."

The rest of the packed, overheated lounge looks as if it's ready for any regular presentation, with one exception: the silence. The passengers wait, their nervous eyes focused on Glenn as he explains the situation. They remain calm, passive, probably because they're in a bit of shock themselves.

"As a precaution," Glenn concludes, "all guests will be required to wear life jackets from this point forward, around the clock. Guests will no longer be permitted on the bridge, in the fitness room, or on the rear deck, where we will be staging search-and-rescue efforts."

Search and recovery is far more likely; as much as I want to remain optimistic, I've been in these waters and in this weather long enough to know what it can do — to boats as well as to passengers. I picture the listing *Australis* and wonder where Keller had been when it hit. Had he been on the phone with me at the time; was that why we'd lost our connection?

"I know this is not what any of you signed up for," Glenn says, "but I urge you to remain in your cabins as much as possible. I know many of you have medical expertise and other skills we'll need, and we may call on you. But for now, you need to keep yourselves safe and out of the way." He draws in a breath. "Finally, and I know this is another of many inconveniences you'll experience over the next few days, I'm going to request that everyone agree to take on an additional passenger or two, if possible, in your cabin. You can double up with one another or take on someone from the *Australis*."

Glenn signals to the staff, and I get into place as we begin the emergency lifeboat drill, the same one we'd gone through the first night on board, in the Beagle Channel. It seems much longer than a week ago—back then, everyone was laughing and taking photos as they put on their frumpy orange life jackets, excited as they anticipated the Drake and what awaited them beyond. I remember thinking that this would be a long journey, but for entirely different reasons.

Now the passengers are somber as they put on their jackets and assemble at their muster stations. I stand at my station, unable to make eye contact with anyone. Nature and I have always gotten along, or so I'd believed; we've had a good relationship of mutual respect and understanding. But perhaps I've had little to fear from nature because for so long it's always been only me. As the *Cormorant* hurtles south, I feel anxiety knitting closed my throat. As every Antarctic traveler knows, once you begin to fear the ice, the relationship changes forever.

TWENTY YEARS BEFORE SHIPWRECK

The Missouri Ozarks

Deep in the forest, the humidity is oppressive, especially for September. It's too hot to cover up completely, and I've been slapping at mosquitoes all morning. I wear long pants to avoid poison ivy, but I'm in a short-sleeved shirt, drenched in sweat and sticky, acrid bug repellent.

Everything in these woods has a way of enveloping you. As I bend down to pick up my field notebook, I brush my bare arm against a bush that's sprouting poison ivy. I look at the batch of triple leaves, then dump half the contents of my water bottle on the spot where the plant touched my skin.

Pam hears me and looks over. It's only midmorning, but her dark-brown hair is escaping its loose ponytail, and her face is bright red, as I imagine mine must be.

"How're you holding up?" she asks.

"Great."

Pam's twice my age, and this is my second year as her research assistant, but still she's always asking.

"Beastly out here today," she says.

"Better than serving mystery meat at Dobbs." Until I'd begun working for Pam, my work-study job had been food service in the cafeteria near my dorm.

I'd registered for Dr. Pam Harrison's biology class two years earlier, during my first year at the University of Missouri. Even then I knew I wanted to focus on birds; my childhood obsession with them had never waned.

I'd hoped to go to Seattle for college, to the University of Washington, where I could get involved with the Magellanic penguin program I'd heard so much about. But I was too daunted by the size of the loans the UW program would require to consider it. *Stupid*, Pam would later tell me, when she heard how I ended up at Mizzou. *How're you going to get anywhere if you don't take risks?*

The housing lottery assigned me to Jones Hall my freshman year, and I soon learned that the all-women's dorm is a coveted place to live for sorority girls thanks to its proximity to Greek Town. My roommate, Taylor, was a petite, lively blonde from Springfield whose main goal in college was getting into the Tri-Delts. Taylor invited me to all the parties, insisted on doing my makeup—since I usually wore none—and opened up her wardrobe to me. "It's too short," I'd say after squeezing into one of her tiny skirts. "That's the *point*," she'd reply and hand me a tube of lip gloss.

Thanks to Taylor and her makeovers, I felt as though I'd just met a new version of myself, along with scores of other new students, and, for those first months, I relished this glimpse of who I could be, having shed the tomboy of my childhood. Yet as the months passed, I found it hard to bond with this new me, as well as with the other students. I'd be in a crowded fraternity basement, beer flowing, music blasting, and feel a sudden need to push my way out, happier the moment I began walking home alone in the cold night air. I'd find myself wanting to sneak out of a guy's bed so we wouldn't have to try to make conversation as soon as we sobered up. The fun was fleeting, even though, week after week, I'd show up hoping it would be different.

In my second semester, I took my first class with Pam, and my focus shifted—sharply, as if snapped back into its natural place—from parties to science. A tiny, dark-haired woman in her mid-forties, Pam was energetic, blunt, no-nonsense, and her passion for ornithology was palpable and contagious. She could answer any question without hesitation, many answers based on her own research, and I wondered what it would be like to have that sort of knowledge, to know as much about a species or an environment as you did about yourself.

Pam taught several courses in biological sciences and ran the avian ecology lab. That semester, I read everything I could about birds and registered for her avian ecology course in the fall. One day, she took me aside after class. She said she needed a field research assistant, and while she usually hired graduate students, she sensed that I might be interested. The job entailed searching for and monitoring nests, resighting banded birds, and recording field notes.

"I've never done anything like that before," I said.

"Are you in decent shape? There's a lot of hiking involved."

An active runner back then, I logged about fifty miles a week. I nodded.

"How's your hearing?"

"Fine."

"Are you color-blind?"

"No."

"Any problem being out in bad weather?"

I shook my head.

"Poison ivy, bats, snakes—problem?"

"No."

"Then you're hired," she said. "We leave from the Tucker Hall parking lot tomorrow morning, seven sharp," she said. "Don't be late."

I didn't have any idea what I was doing that first morning, but gradually I learned. I learned how to catch a bird in a net, how to weigh and measure and band it. I learned how to listen and how to wait, how to spend hours under a canopy of trees in volatile midwestern weather, how to spot well-hidden nests.

And now, a year later, I'm working with Pam on a long-term study evaluating the response of various species to deforestation and restoration in the Ozarks. We look at breeding patterns, predation, and the birds' rate of return in clear-cut forests.

As we walk among the oaks and junipers, I can see the delineation between old and new growth from the last clear-cut. Ahead of me, Pam stops short, and I crouch down next to her. She's peeking under a low bush, at an empty nest. As usual, she says nothing, waiting for me to see what she sees. And a moment later, I do—shell fragments, so small they're barely perceptible to the naked eye. Unless you're Pam, or have been trained by Pam.

"What do you think?" she says.

I sit back on my heels and look around. I don't see tracks among the fallen leaves, but snakes are the main predators of songbirds around here.

As Pam pages through her field notebook, I know we'll be adding another component to her half decade of research—and this is what I've grown to love: the way each day brings a new discovery, the way species' lives are layered so intricately, the way we begin to ask the questions that will eventually puzzle out all these mysteries. Working with Pam had become, for me, far more intoxicating than the beer bongs and Jell-O shots of Greek Town.

"I'll do some research on snake predation in this region," I say to Pam.

She shuts her notebook and looks at me. "You're always talking about working with penguins," she says. "Where are you thinking about graduate school?"

I have stacks of brochures and applications in my apartment, but, on the other hand, I don't want to leave. I feel as though I need to finish what I've started here with Pam—the problem is that it could take years, even decades.

"I've still got time," I say.

"You need to plan ahead."

"I don't know," I say. "I'm thinking maybe I'll stay here. Keep working on this."

She takes a drink from her water bottle and shakes her head. "Bad idea. You want seabirds, you need to go east or west, north or south. To the sea. In two years you'll be done here."

"You don't want me to stay?"

"*You* don't want to stay," she says. "You want penguins, not songbirds. What is it, a boyfriend?"

I've been sleeping with a guy named Chad I'd met in a photography elective, but I'm not calling him a boyfriend. Not yet.

"No," I assure Pam. "Nothing like that."

"Great," she says. "Then nothing's stopping you."

"What if I like working with you?"

"Get out of your comfort zone. That's the first rule of making it as a researcher."

"And the second?"

"You choose science," she says, "or you choose family. Women don't have the luxury of doing both."

Though she is my mentor, I don't know a lot about Pam's personal life. I know she is single and lives in a small house not far from campus; she bikes to work in almost any type of weather and, like me, usually works weekends and holidays. She doesn't have pets because she travels to Central America to track the migration of the songbirds, and I once heard her refer to her graduate students as "my kids."

We get back to work, and later, when Pam returns to the car, I stay behind for a few minutes on the pretense of taking some more notes. I like the quiet out here, and when I'm all alone and very still, I can sense the ghosts of the Civil War battles; I glimpse deer passing delicately among the low branches, or a turtle sunning on a rock near the river. On campus I often feel lonely, left out. Here in the woods, there's no such thing as loneliness, only quiet, and something like peace.

WE'RE AT A winery in the tiny town of Rocheport—Chad and me, his friends Paul and Heather—less than half an hour from the university. The trees are on fire, bursting in shades of red and orange, and we'd arrived this afternoon, with enough light and warmth in the air to walk through the historic little town and around the vineyard, where we'd settled in to sample the wines.

It was supposed to be an afternoon getaway, but now, having just opened a fourth bottle as the sun sets over the Missouri River in the valley below, I'm wondering when we'll get back to Columbia. And, to my own surprise, I don't really care.

Chad and I have been sleeping together for about a month, and this is the first time we've gone anywhere beyond a mile of campus. Chad is a grad student in the print journalism program, a few years older than I am. We'd met in our photography class a couple months earlier, at the beginning of the semester. I'd registered for the class because it fulfilled an art requirement; he did it to learn enough to photograph his own stories. I was instantly drawn to his unshaven, dog-eared good looks; he doesn't have the polished, preppy look and attitude so many of the undergraduate guys have. He's smart and ambitious, which I like—and, as a budding journalist, he's always picking fights with local politicians about things I care about, like logging in the Ozarks, though I sense for him it's more about getting a good story than actually changing the world. Chad writes for the local newspaper, reporting on everything from city council meetings to local art lectures, and he's been inviting me along to some of the cultural events—film screenings, dance performances, readings by visiting writers. Though I might insist to Pam that I don't have a boyfriend, I've enjoyed the chance to experience a world outside of dirt and birds and sweat.

Before Chad, my sex life had been limited to a boy from Science Club in high school and a few short-lived, drunken flings with fraternity guys. But with Chad, I discovered the liquid-body pleasures of sex, the addictive and all-consuming nature of it. Being desired was, for me, an unfamiliar sensation, an exhilarating one, and it didn't matter that we didn't have much of a relationship outside the bedroom. We'd see each other in class, and we'd go out on the occasional photo shoot together, and all of it led to the same place—the tiny room in his apartment, which he shares with two other grad students who are never around.

And Rocheport, despite being a last-minute plan, feels like a step forward for Chad and me—spending the day with another couple, in a romantic spot. After class that morning, Chad had mentioned it casually, suggesting it might be a good place to get some photos—the river, the vineyard—and it would only take a few hours. I'd looked at him in the autumn morning light, wanting to touch the hair at the back of his neck, to feel the curve of his cheekbone under my fingertip, and within an hour we were climbing into the back of Paul's car.

It wasn't long before I relaxed in a way I rarely allow myself, letting the day unfold, enjoying the unscripted moments. Chad's arm around me as we walked through town. The effects of the wine, which smoothed away my concerns about having skipped a class that afternoon. The sensations of experiencing a part of life that I've never known and that was so remote it felt almost fictional—as if we were playing the roles of ourselves years into the future, grown-ups on a weekend getaway. And as the fourth bottle is opened and poured amid our laughter and slurring voices, I know we won't be going home tonight.

When Chad excuses himself to find the bathroom, I get up, too. Though I've only had a couple of glasses, I rarely drink and find myself wavering, grabbing his arm for support.

"I take it we're not going back tonight?" I say.

"Yeah, no way Paul can drive," he says with a laugh. "We'll stay in town. It's on me."

"So you planned it this way." I squeeze his arm, pleased.

He squeezes back. "It was Paul's idea. Don't tell Heather."

He hadn't thought of me at all. I drop his arm. "I hope he doesn't mind getting up early," I say snappishly. "I have to be at work at six-thirty tomorrow."

He laughs again. "Don't worry so much." He puts his arm around me. "Let's just have some fun."

Back at the table, Chad raises his glass toward mine, as if to make sure all is copacetic between us, and I clink my glass against his. By the time I finish the glass, my head is pleasantly spinning, and it no longer matters that this overnight wasn't Chad's idea; we're here, together, and that's enough.

We make it back to town, where the guys had gotten rooms at an inn that used to be a schoolhouse. In the four-poster bed with Chad, I let go of all lingering thoughts; it's just us and the soft cool sheets beneath our bodies, the slight creak of the bed as I take in the heat of his body and sink deeply into the warmth of my own. We've never spent a whole night together, and I soften into the curve of his arm before falling asleep.

The next morning, I wake with a headache. Chad is sprawled on the other side of the bed, his back to me, and I doubt he'll move for hours. It's almost seven already, and my headache sharpens as I remember. Pam.

There's a phone on a little desk across the room, and I wrap myself in one of the inn's robes as I dial Pam's number, catching her in the office.

"I'm in Rocheport," I say, "but I'll be on my way soon."

"Rocheport?" she repeats, and I can picture her expression as she figures it out—her research assistant, the one who insisted she didn't have a boyfriend, missing work because she's at the region's most popular couples' retreat.

"I'll be there as soon as I can."

"Forget about it," she says. "You're there. Enjoy it."

"I didn't expect to—"

"Take a day off, Deb," she says. "I'll see you tomorrow." And then she hangs up.

I stare at the receiver in my hand for a long moment before putting it down.

Chad has barely stirred. I put on yesterday's clothes and go to the inn's reception desk, thinking I'll take a taxi back to Columbia. But once I'm there, I realize I don't have money for a fifteen-mile cab ride, and even once I get back, I'll have no way to get out to the Ozarks if Pam's already left.

It's barely light outside, and I sit in the empty breakfast room with a cup of coffee. I cling to the mug, letting it warm my hands, staring into my wavy, dark reflection, trying to decipher what Pam said. Her tone was the same as always—brisk, no-nonsense—but somehow I get the feeling I've disappointed her. Pam herself never takes a day off, at least as far as I can tell, and I worry she's thinking what I'm thinking—that I should be out in the field instead of lounging around in a bed-and-breakfast with a man who still hasn't earned the label of boyfriend.

I'm not sure how long I sit there before someone pulls out the chair next to mine. "I was wondering where you'd gone," Chad says.

He still looks half-asleep, with his mussed hair and weighted eyelids. When a waitress walks by, he asks for coffee. I hadn't noticed, but now there's another couple sitting across the room, and yellow light is sluicing through the windows.

"I've missed work," I tell him. "I think my boss is pissed."

"Why didn't you just call in sick?"

I hadn't even thought of that. "I shouldn't have come here. This was a bad idea."

His coffee arrives, and he fills the mug with cream. Watching him, I try to make myself savor this moment, our first morning together, but I can't.

"What's on your mind?" he asks.

I push my mug away and straighten my back. "This has been fun," I say.

"Has been?" he asks, smiling. "Am I past tense now?"

Despite myself, I smile back. "You call yourself a journalist? That's not past tense. It's present perfect."

"Thank God for editors," he says with a laugh. "Okay, remind me—what does present perfect mean?"

"It means a past action that remains an ongoing present action."

"You're saying you'd like us to be ongoing?" he asks.

I'm surprised; I'd been thinking only of preempting the inevitable. "Would you?"

He's still smiling, and as I look at his face, I remember

the night he took me to see the Parsons Dance company, a modern dance troupe with a wildly creative use of light. The dancers had spiraled into darkness, then leapt into a beam of light, fluidly, as if made of water. And then, moments later, the effects of a strobe light held them in place, highlighting them in split-second poses—and as I think of how they moved across the stage, their bodies frozen in midair, it occurs to me that this is Chad and me, inching forward and yet motionless at the same time.

He gets to his feet and says, "Sit tight. I'm going to check us out and then call a cab. Maybe you can salvage at least part of the day."

"Really?"

Now standing behind me, he leans down. "Sure thing," he says in my ear. With his lips, he traces my jawline to my mouth, giving me a kiss that asks for forgiveness, a kiss I return.

As I wait for him, I sip my cold coffee and hear Pam's voice in my head, and I wonder whether love and science are incompatible after all. I'd embraced her philosophy because I've mostly had only work. Now, through Pam, I can see who I might one day become, and I want to prove her wrong, to find a way to have both.

The Gullet
(67°10'S, 67°38'W)

Freshwater freezes at thirty-two degrees Fahrenheit, but seawater has to be colder. Depending on the salinity, it freezes between twenty-four and twenty-eight degrees. At these temperatures, of course, the odds of survival for humans come down to a matter of minutes.

Right now, I wish I didn't know what it feels like to be in that water; I wish I couldn't even imagine it. In all my years in Antarctica, I've fallen through the ice exactly once. It happened seven years ago in the Ross Sea; I'd been with a group of geologists from the U.K. who were planning to drill a hole in the ice for their research on fossils. We traveled in a caravan of snowmobiles but also had to do a lot of hiking on foot, across pressure ridges formed by overlapping pack.

I don't remember falling in—it was so sudden, so unbelievably quick—I recall only the sound of the ice breaking, the heart-stopping rumble and crack, and then I was submerged. The water was violently cold, sucking every bit of heat from my body. When I opened my eyes, gasping for breath, I realized that I was being pulled underneath the ice by the current. I reached up through the opening my body had left and grabbed on to the shelf of ice. Turning my head, I saw one of the geologists holding out a pole for me, standing well back from the edge, lowering his body to the ice so he could crawl toward me. It was dangerous for him to be so close, but he had no other choice. I caught hold, kicking my legs, trying to help him in his efforts as he reached down to haul me out. As he towed me up onto the ice, I saw that behind him another geologist was holding his legs, and yet another was holding hers—a chain of humans flattened out on the ice, desperately moving backward, away from the thin part that had given way.

As soon as we backed onto more solid ice, one of the geologists helped me strip off my clothing, and the one who'd reached in for me was taking off layers of his own, dressing me in his socks, his sweater, his parka, calling out to the others to bring me dry pants, gloves, a hat. My skin was bright red, the blood having rushed to its surface in an attempt to preserve the body within. My limbs felt numb, and my entire body shook convulsively for the next hour—but I was lucky. Many who meet head-on with the waters of the Southern Ocean don't survive long enough to die from acute hypothermia; they suffer cardiac arrest, or they go into what's known as cold shock and drown. Within the first few moments of submersion, the heart rate escalates, the blood pressure increases, and breathing becomes erratic. The muscles cool rapidly, and those closest to the surface of the skin, like the muscles of the hands, quickly become useless. You can't move, can't speak, can't even think. Even at forty degrees Fahrenheit, let alone twenty-eight, it only takes three minutes for hypothermia to set in. Water rescues are rare; recoveries are not.

I PULL OFF the mask from over my eyes, which I'd hoped would help me sleep, and turn my head to the side. Amy is lying in bed on her back, a similar mask over her own eyes. I can't tell if she's asleep or, like me, she's been lying awake all night.

Glenn had encouraged us all to get some rest while we could, and Amy and I had lain in our bunks, speculating about the *Australis*, daring to hope the situation might not be as bad as it seemed. She assured me that Keller would be okay, and we told each other that the damage might, in fact, be minimal—that we could end up encountering a scene of calm and order. Finally we fell into silence.

I get up, throw on extra layers and my crew parka, and look at my watch—nearly five in the morning. We must be getting close.

Amy stirs and sits up. "Did you sleep?" she asks, and I shake my head. "Me neither," she says.

Outside, the water has given way to a dense mix of brash and pack ice. The sea is now a chunky soup of pure white, with a few specks of dark gray where the water peeks through. Amy and I stand together on the foredeck, not speaking, and I strain my eyes while the *Cormorant* creeps along, feeling it shudder as it punches its way forward. There are only a half dozen passengers out here—most are still asleep. When we'd passed through the lounge moments earlier, we'd glimpsed a few people with books in their hands, their eyes focused on the portholes. And here on the deck, several passengers shoot videos of nothing, maybe hoping to be the first to capture footage of the sinking ship, and a few others take selfies.

I have to look away from them. Not far off, crabeater seals doze on icebergs and floes. Some raise their heads briefly and then return to their naps; those who are closer slump toward the water and slide in between the tide cracks, frightened by the rumble of the engine and the thunk of ice hitting the ship's hull.

We're getting close, but thanks to the murky air, I can't see very far ahead. The fog has coalesced into the ice, wrapping the *Cormorant* in a whitish haze. As we push forward, the muffled drumbeat from the hull intensifies in proportion to the ice in our path. I glance up over my right shoulder toward the bridge, half-wanting to be there and half-needing to be away from all that tension.

"We should check in," Amy says, catching my gaze.

I don't want to take my eyes off the ghostly fog, as if I might see Keller emerge from the mist. But Amy's right.

I nod, and just as we turn to go, the air is pierced by a scream. I whip my head toward the sound and see a woman backing away from the rail.

Amy and I rush toward her. "Are you all right?" I call out.

The woman can only point toward the water, and when I see the horror in her face, I know what she must've seen. I want to close my eyes, back up, run inside. But I look past her to the water. Floating below, amid the slush, is a bright blue parka, hugged by an orange life jacket. As the ice parts, I see the legs, the arms, the lifeless body within.

It's begun.

They've seen it on the bridge, too, or maybe they're seeing even worse. The engines whine, dragging the ship to a stop. Amy's got her arm around the weeping passenger, attempting to calm her, and I look up at the bridge and see that most of the crew has disappeared, probably down to the Zodiacs. High above, a flare explodes, bathing us all in a pale-red glow. In this burst of sanguine light, I see that this is not the only body; there are dozens of blue jackets bobbing in the water among chunks of ice, bodies floating facedown in the churning slush.

We're too late. As a second flare fires into the sky, I strain my eyes but still can't see the ship, just gloom and icebergs and penguins scattered about on distant floes. And then, as my eyes adjust—and maybe as my mind adjusts—I realize that those figures on the ice aren't penguins at all. They're humans, passengers, dozens and dozens of them—some crouching on patches of breaking ice, others waving their arms for help.

From the stern, cranes whir, preparing to drop the first of our eight Zodiacs into the ice-packed water. Amy is leading the woman toward the staterooms, and I start heading below-decks. Suddenly I stop, remembering Richard's binoculars. They are far superior to anything we crew members have, and they could make all the difference in helping me locate Keller.

I race up to the lounge, searching frantically for Richard. I don't see him, but Kate is there. We instantly make eye contact, and as I rush across the lounge, she meets me halfway.

"Richard—where is he?"

"I don't know," she says, looking surprised, as if just realizing she hasn't seen him for a while. "I've gotten our room ready for passengers, so I don't think he's—"

"Find him," I tell her. "Tell him we need his binoculars. Give them to a crew member to pass on to me. Okay?"

"Okay." I see her nod her head before I'm off again.

Down below, at the open loading hatch, I look up at Captain Wylander, standing at the controls just outside the bridge, struggling to find an ice sheet large enough and thick enough to hold hundreds of stranded passengers. We need a pathway—a bridge of ice, or even a river of seawater—that we can follow to the *Australis* and its victims. Yet right now I see only large floes and patches of slush lurking everywhere, conditions that are impossible to traverse easily either by foot or by Zodiac. We'll have to manage it somehow.

I think of our ice landing, only days ago—that one had been challenge enough, but at least we'd been able to choose the field of ice; we'd been in control. And the *Cormorant* is by no means an icebreaker—in unstable waters, at the wrong speed or angle, a large berg could pierce even a reinforced hull, and then we'd be in no better shape than the *Australis*. The stabilizing fins that soften our ride through waters like the Drake are vulnerable to the ice, and the *Cormorant* has no defense in place to safeguard the propellers. Our ship is prepared to rub shoulders with icebergs, but she's in no position to push them around.

And I know that if the ice gets too thick or the winds too extreme, our captain will not risk damage to the ship; we'll have to retreat. With the temperature dropping and the winds shoving ice floes roughly into one another, I need to find Keller as quickly as possible. We might have only one chance.

I'm sure Keller is still on board. He'll put the passengers first, even if it means going down with the ship. And, given the options, on board may well be the safest place—though it's clear that no one ended up in the water, on the ice, by choice. It already looks as though things are a lot worse than we've prepared for.

Wylander is now maneuvering the *Cormorant* into a large expanse of white, stretching unbroken for at least a hundred yards, and as the cracking of ice stops and the ship comes to a halt, I look up to see his signal. It's time.

We lower the gangplank, and I step down to a relatively stable section of ice; as one of the lighter crew members, I'd volunteered to be first, though I'm sure everyone knows I have other reasons. About fifty yards in the distance, a dozen passengers are gathered together on the ice, but the *Australis* herself is still only a dim glow of lights in the fog beyond. Those who are on this patch of ice should be able to make their way over. Some are already hurrying toward us. I hear Glenn's voice on the PA system, telling the *Australis* passengers who we are, urging calm, exhorting them to follow our instructions.

But they are exhausted and panicked, and still coming forward—to keep them safe, we need to slow them down, spread them out. As I step forward carefully on the ice—poking it with a sharp trekking pole, hoping the pole won't meet with slush or weak ice, keeping my ears on alert for that dreadful splintering noise—I wonder whether the other naturalists are as calm as they look. Despite our training, and despite the knowledge, in the deepest parts of our minds, that something like this could happen, I don't think we ever really believed it would.

The ice under my feet holds up well, and I signal to the others behind me to follow; at the same time, I hold up a hand to stop the passengers coming toward us. As distressed as they must be, they obey.

I turn around and see Thom heading down the gangway. The plan, hastily assembled once Glenn and Wylander assessed the ice and weather conditions, is for Thom and me to scout out a trail for the passengers to follow to the *Cormorant*, and once we find a safe passage, we'll leave marker flags along the way. Nigel and Amy will then lead the rest of the expedition team along the trail to make sure the passengers remain spaced evenly apart, so they don't create more pressure than the ice can bear. It's obvious, from the bodies floating past, that some have made that fatal mistake already—and our plan is only as good as the weather allows.

I try not to look down, not wanting to see an orange naturalist's jacket floating past, or Keller's signature bandanna.

Focus, I tell myself. I need to take one moment at a time, one tenuous step at a time. As I begin to make my way across the ice, I realize that we'll have to revise our plan sooner than we expected. The group of passengers ahead is stranded on a forty-foot-wide patch of ice with about thirty feet of slush between them and us. They hadn't stopped in response to Glenn's or my signal; they stopped because they had nowhere else to go.

"Ease up," I call over my shoulder. As Thom joins me near the edge of the ice floe, the passengers on the other side advance to the edge of theirs.

"Move back!" Thom shouts. "Spread yourselves out!" He splays his arms wide. "Stay near the middle of the ice, as far apart as you can," he calls to them. "We'll get you. Just hold on."

"We'll need a Zodiac," I say, and Thom nods. We'll have to carry the Zodiac over the ice to this small stretch of water, then use it as a ferry. Despite their rubber construction, these Zodiacs aren't exactly lightweight; they're nineteen feet long, and transporting them over land requires at least two or three strong crew members. Even if the ice holds, once we get the boat in the water, boarding anxious passengers safely from a fragile rim of ice is yet another challenge.

Another flare bursts above, and as it fizzles in the sky, Thom turns to me. "If you want to keep going," he says, "I'll take care of these folks."

"You'll need help with the Zodiac," I say.

"I'll get Nigel. Go on. Be careful."

I turn toward the flickering light of the flare and begin walking gingerly in its direction, the ice here still sturdy and unbroken for as far as I can see. Yet appearances are often deceiving—the pack ice that surrounds us, formerly attached to the continent, has been blown around the sea all winter by ocean currents and winds, broken apart and thrust together again, and now that it's covered with a layer of snow, it's impossible to tell where weak spots are until you're right on top of them. Worse, the winds are picking up again, which means that, no matter how stable the ice may look, conditions could change in an instant.

Up ahead I see another group of passengers moving toward me in a blur of blue. "Stop!" I shout at them. "Stay where you are!"

But they can't hear me; I need to get closer, to tell them

to wait for Thom. I stab at the ice as I move forward. Then I hear a sharp, cleaving echo and freeze.

The sound is not beneath me but up ahead, and I look up in time to see one of the blue jackets disappear. The other tourists stop in their tracks, one of them screaming. I force myself to proceed slowly, testing the ice as I move forward. After a few more steps, the tip of my trekking pole sinks into slush.

It's not much of a hole, but it's wide enough for a human body. I back up, then flatten myself on the ice and shove my right arm into the water. Most of the passengers are wearing life jackets, so I extend my arm laterally across the ice ceiling, less than two feet below, hoping that underneath the current isn't as strong as the wind indicates.

My hand makes contact with something, and though my arm is quickly growing numb, I grab on and pull, seeing a flash of blue as I drag the body toward me. When it's closer, I plunge both arms into the water and pull as hard as I can, using my legs to propel myself backward, away from the hole. I'm gripping an arm, and I quickly find my way to the jacket's collar so I can pull the body out facefirst. I catch a glimpse of the man's face, gray and frozen in shock, and I continue to pull, heaving the body up as I inch backward, the ice chipping away at the edge of the hole.

I get the man's shoulders above water, but I can't get him out. I turn and call out for Thom, for Nigel, for Amy, hoping one of them will hear me. Then I hang on, waiting. The man seems to have stopped breathing, but between the current and the violent shaking of my arms, it's hard to tell.

At first I think no one's going to come, but then I feel a body edging close to mine. "I've got him."

It's Nigel. I slip backward and let him pull the man farther out of the water. When the torso emerges, Nigel gets to his knees and drags the man all the way out. He turns the man onto his back and kneels over him, feeling for a pulse as he simultaneously pinches the man's nostrils shut and bends down to force air into his lungs. With a sputtering cough, the man's lungs empty of seawater, and his eyes flutter open.

The man is shivering uncontrollably, and just because he's now breathing doesn't mean he's out of danger. Nigel radios for help.

I myself am shaking, and I wrap my arms around my body to steady myself. The other passengers are still huddled close together on the ice, very near to where the man had fallen in. "Back away," I call to them, though I know their instincts and fear and the cold are drawing them together. "You'll have to stand apart from one another—three feet, at least."

I watch them separate—slowly, reluctantly, dubiously.

Nigel's talking to the man who'd fallen in, asking him his name, age, where he's from, anything to keep him conscious. But it's not looking good; the man is incoherent, sputtering fragmented words, his teeth drumming violently together.

In my mind I'm assembling a chain of events: the *Australis* trapped in ice, desperate efforts to push its way out, ripped hull, ice floes crashing together, people jumping, fog, chaos, death.

Amy arrives, responding to Nigel's call, and the two quickly strip off the man's jacket, sweater, and shirt and wrap him in a fleece blanket, which will have to do until someone else arrives to help Amy take him back to the ship. Already we are too few rescuers, with too few resources, too late to the scene.

I turn to Nigel, who waves me ahead, and for a moment I hesitate. The sleeves of my jacket are soaked through. My arms are still numb, and water courses from my sleeves down the front of my chest. The fabric against my skin is wet and cold. Yet I start out again, clenching my jaw tightly shut to keep my teeth from chattering—as much from nerves as from cold—and I move my arms up and down as I walk, to keep the blood flowing.

A shadowy ridge of icebergs rises like giant incisors in the distance. I continue slowly, cautiously, watching for signs of movement in case any of them, like ancient trees, decide to tip over and crack the ice I'm standing on. Despite the thickening fog, I can tell I'm getting closer to the *Australis*; I hear the sounds of tortured, twisting steel and muffled human voices. As I navigate the ice, I place flags marking my route, the places that are safe to walk—for now, anyhow.

And then I see her.

Still shrouded in mist, about a hundred yards straight ahead, is the *Australis*, listing heavily to port. I pick up my pace.

Everywhere I look, I see lifeboats and passengers in the cruise company's bright blue jackets: some in Zodiacs, some on the ice. I scan the jackets for a glimpse of orange, a flash of red.

My throat swells with despair, and I swallow it away and try to breathe. As I study the scene in front of me, I do a rapid triage in my head. The *Australis*'s lifeboats may be able to navigate out of this maze of ice with the wind thrashing the floes together, assuming they're manned by crew members; at any rate, those inside are safe for now. Zodiacs are more maneuverable and easier to pilot, though they're also smaller and more prone to tipping; passengers might be able to get to safety as long as they don't get stuck in pack ice, which is becoming increasingly likely.

Those who are stranded on the ice need help, and fast—but there are so many of them, and though I know Nigel and the other naturalists and crew members will be following close behind, for now I'm the only one here. I look at the groups of passengers, clustered together like penguins at a nesting site, and realize the agony of the choices ahead, weighing lives against the thickness of ice, weighing my safety against theirs, weighing the fact that there is only one of these victims who really matters to me and I don't know where he is, and, as much as I'd rather look for him, these people in immediate danger can't be ignored.

The *Cormorant* is now at least a quarter mile behind me, and I radio Glenn and give him my position, tell him what the situation is. I don't see anyone I recognize as *Australis* crew; they're likely still on board, trying to get more passengers to safety, and this gives me hope.

As I get closer to the ship, pockets of water widen, opened up by her shifting and sinking, causing ice floes to split and drift. As the water continues to separate the floes—some the size of a dining room table, others the length of a city block—I have to slow down more and more to stay on the same sheet of ice.

Then I find myself at a dead end. Between me and the ship, a mix of brash and bergy bits stretches for twenty, thirty feet. Beyond that is a stretch of ice about the size of ten parking spaces; standing on it are twelve passengers, and there is no direct path to them. My only option is to retrace my steps and take a wide route to the left or right, devouring vital moments while I may or may not get myself any closer. But I have no choice.

I motion with my hands for everyone to stay put, to spread out. And they understand, doing as I instruct while I make my way around. I find a path, but the wind is growing relentlessly, and when I finally reach them, I look back at the trail I've marked.

Already the ice has begun to break up in the wind, and through the rolling fog I see that my markers are now in different places than where I'd left them—which means I've lost the only way to get these survivors to safety. The ice is too broken to traverse on foot, too tight to come in by Zodiac. The frightened passengers have begun to bombard me with questions, and I hold up my hand to silence them as I grab my radio to call Glenn again.

"We can't come in any farther," he says. "The winds are gusting to thirty knots and the ice is at eight-tenths. We'll need to push back—soon."

"I've got a dozen people here," I say, "and I don't have a solid path back."

"Just hold on. We'll get a couple of Zodiacs over there."

But I don't see how Glenn will spare two more crew members to haul even one Zodiac over the quarter mile I've just traversed. We may be stuck here for hours—if the ice holds out that long.

I try to take in a breath, but my lungs freeze, refusing the intake of air, and then my head begins swimming through waves of black. I lean over, hands on my knees, and take short, hiccuping breaths until I feel my chest expand at last.

Finally I straighten up, trying to put on a mask of composure. The wind drives sleet into my face as I look around me. I'm hoping for a glimpse of Keller, but all I see are scared, unfamiliar faces.

There's a movement to my left, and I turn in time to see a towering iceberg in the distance swaying in the rough surf.

As I watch, it begins to tip.

All unstable icebergs will flip eventually, and when bergs of this size tip and roll, the waves they spawn can be monumental: large enough to wreak havoc on ships, and certainly large enough to be fatal to anyone standing on nearby ice.

"Lie down, lie down!" I yell at the passengers; then I collapse, spread-eagle, on the ice. "Like this," I shout, raising my head, straining to make myself heard over the cracking ice. "Spread out your arms and legs!"

The passengers follow my lead. I turn my head, my cheek against the ice, to watch the iceberg as it rolls—gracefully, gently, though I know what's about to come will be anything but.

A moment later comes the rise of the water, the wave moving toward us as if in slow motion. I shut my eyes, digging my fingers into the ice sheet under me, whispering *please hold, please hold*, my breath warm against the ice—and when I feel the floe lift and sway, rolling us as if we're on a giant water bed, I visualize us all moving with it, as one, staying put, staying together.

Then I hear the screams of passengers, and I open my eyes. We're still moving, the ice curving and bending below us, but so far we're okay. A few people keep screaming, panicking, but we're all still here. We're going to make it.

Then, a tremendous crack—the ice begins to split and crumble. I feel a splintering, and, my body acting faster than my mind, I roll away just as a fissure opens up beneath me, a yawning mouth of water where I lay just a moment before. When I hear a shriek, I look over to see a woman slipping into another cleft in the ice. A passenger grabs her arms and manages to hold her there, in the water up to her thighs, until two more passengers crawl over and help pull her out.

As the waves reverberate under the tender ice, we all lie still. I close my eyes for a moment, not sure I ever want to move again. I'm safe here, for now. The baby is safe. And, until I learn otherwise, Keller is safe. The minute I open my eyes, I'll need to stand up, to pretend I know what I'm doing, and to keep moving ahead, toward what I'm more and more certain I don't want to see.

I hear a few more creaks, normal sounds given the weight and motion of the ice, and when I'm sure that nothing else is splitting apart, I stand up, looking first toward the *Australis*. She's nearly shrouded in fog again, the wave having pushed us farther away. Near the hull, lifeless bodies drift in the water.

I turn away, and in front of me is the first bit of good news: The wave has pushed us hard against a large ice field, which means we might have a temporary bridge to the *Cormorant*. And there's no time to waste.

I try to shake off the mounting stress and quickly move forward, testing the ice. Within moments, I'm radioing Glenn, barking instructions to the stranded passengers, and leading them to sturdier ice, step by excruciating step. I find my first marker flag, and then I find another. The ice is still shifting, and making our way back will be a slow and dangerous process, taking time I don't want to spare without knowing where Keller is. I look back over my shoulder, at the fading ship, at the wide-eyed passengers who are trusting me to save them.

I'M HALFWAY BACK to the *Cormorant* when I see Thom and two more crew members dragging a Zodiac across the ice. When they reach us, Thom and I leave the two crew members to continue leading the *Australis* passengers, while we forge ahead toward the open water that will take us to the ship. My arms feel as though they'll snap off with the cold and the weight of the inflatable, but I'm grateful for the heat my body has to generate to get it done.

As we approach the water's edge and nudge the boat into the sea, we both pause to take a breath. Thom looks past me, and his eyes sharpen. "Shit," he says, then hops into the Zodiac and holds out his hand. "Get in. Hurry."

I take his arm and step into the Zodiac, barely staying on my feet as he guns the engine and spins us around. "What happened?"

"Someone just went in," he says. I follow his eyes and see a bobbing figure in a blue parka, arms in the ice-fogged air but already slowing with the cold.

Thom pulls up as gently as he can, while I reach out and grab the blue jacket with all the strength I have left—but it's not enough. The man is heavy with the weight of water and panic, and I struggle to hold on to him as he flails against me. Thom cuts the engine and leans over to help; together we manage to haul the man into the Zodiac. I pull a blanket out of the hutch and wrap it around the man's head and shoulders. He's red-faced and shivering, his mouth working though he's unable to talk. He wasn't in very long, and he should be okay—if he gets warmed up, and fast.

"We need to get him back," I say, and Thom nods. This guy isn't stable enough to make it back alone, and he's probably too big for me to handle—which leaves us with only one real option.

I see that Thom's thinking the same thing. "Get us back over to the ice," he says. "I'll find someone to bring him in. Then we'll go."

"It'll take too long," I say. "No one's even been over to the *Australis* yet. If you can take him in, I'll keep going and report back."

He doesn't say anything as I pull up alongside the ice. He gets out, and I help the man to his feet. We get him out of the Zodiac, and then Thom looks at me. "Be careful," he says.

"I'll let you know how things look when I get closer."

He nods, then steps away. He pulls one of the man's arms over his shoulder, and they begin the walk back to the *Cormorant*. I watch them for a moment, making sure the ice is stable, that it'll hold. We are surrounded by a seemingly endless number of survivors—and these are the lucky ones, the ones who are close to safety. We still have no idea what is happening farther away, on the ship.

I turn the Zodiac around. The ice is thickening quickly, as is the fog, and I can find no direct route to the *Australis*. The Zodiac can handle open water and not much more than a little slush, so I have to traverse around the jagged floes at a maddeningly slow pace, moving almost parallel to the ice field I've just left, making very little forward progress.

I'm maneuvering through small lakes of water, gray as ash, when I see someone standing a few yards in the distance, alone, turning around in a circle—it's a crew member, in a bright orange parka, but with the hood up I can't yet see who it is. My heart kicks up with a wild, sudden hope, and I'm about to shout over there when the figure slips and falls hard onto the ice, getting up a moment later only to fall again— this time below the ice, into the water.

I make my way there as quickly as I can without punc- turing the outer tube of the Zodiac on the rough ice. I can see where the ice is thinning and am surprised that whoever had fallen in hadn't seen it, too. No crew member should be walking anywhere near ice that thin—unless maybe it was to help someone in danger, but I don't see anyone else around. Maybe this means it's not Keller—I doubt he'd make such a mistake. Unless, of course, he was exhausted and freezing and out of his mind, which by now all members of the *Australis* crew must be.

I catch a glimpse of orange in the water and stop the boat. Bracing my legs against the deck of the Zodiac, I reach over and grab the parka by the collar, hauling the body toward me. I'm getting a little help—the body below me is kicking, moving forward and upward—and I manage to get the head and shoulders draped over the rubber side of the Zodiac. I take a second to breathe and see that it's a man, and that he's not wearing a life jacket, but I can't see his face.

"Come on, dammit," I say. "Help me out."

I brace my legs against the inside of the Zodiac and pull.

A few more kicks, a little muscle from both of us, and he's halfway in. I lean over, cringing as I feel the pressure on my belly, and drag his legs into the boat, swinging them over the side. He lands hard on the deck, then looks up.

I can't believe what I'm seeing. "Richard? How the hell did you get out here?"

"You wanted my binoculars," he says, teeth chattering.

"I told Kate to give them to one of us. You have no business being out here. And why are you dressed like this?"

"I borrowed a jacket."

I look around for the quickest route back to the *Cormorant*, dismayed that I have to take yet another detour, and furious with Richard, who is babbling about something and stealing away crucial moments when all I can think about is finding Keller.

"Once I had—the jacket on—with the hood—no one knew." Richard's teeth are clattering so hard he can hardly talk. But he continues.

"I went out—onto the ice—in a different direction. Saw two people—stranded—on a piece of ice." He begins to cough, then recovers. "Tiny piece of ice. I threw them—the rope—and pulled them over. They jumped across—made it. I sent them back to—the boat—and then—looked for more. People—who need saving."

I look over at Richard and see that he is so detached from reality he has no idea, despite his body's convulsive shaking, how close he'd come to being a victim himself.

"I saved them," he breathes. "Two people."

"And you almost got yourself killed, Richard. You could've gotten me killed."

"But I didn't." Then he looks at me, and suddenly he appears completely lucid. "What about the other one?"

"What other one?"

He rubs his eyes, his brief moment of clarity gone. "Wait," he says, then he has to pause to breathe. "There was someone on the ice. Back there." He tries to stand. His strength is surprising given he'd plunged into the water, and his manic energy alarms me.

"Sit down," I snap. But I look over my shoulder, briefly, to where we'd been. I don't see anyone.

Richard struggles to his knees, pointing. "He was over there."

I look at him. "Are you sure?"

He nods, his body shaking.

"Fuck." I'm not sure I believe him but can't take the chance on leaving anyone behind—especially when this person could be Keller. I turn the Zodiac around, returning to the spot where I'd hauled Richard out. I don't see anyone, or even the trace of someone having gone under, and when I look at Richard, he seems equally confused.

"He was right around here," he says, swiveling his head.

"Was he passenger or crew?"

"He was right here."

"What happened? Did you see him fall in?"

"No," Richard says. "He was—lying—on the ice."

Whether it's the cold, an adverse reaction to the medication, or his own delusions, Richard isn't making any sense. "You probably saw a seal. That's all." I turn the boat around yet again.

"No, no, it was a man—a blue jacket—"

I remember the binoculars and look at Richard, my eyes searching for a strap around his neck. "Where are your binoculars? Let's have a look."

His hand goes to his chest, as if he expects them to be there. "I—I don't know."

"For fuck's sake."

"I saw him," Richard insists.

"Well, I haven't seen anyone but you out here. I've got to get you back to the *Cormorant*."

"I have to get out," Richard says and moves toward the side. "I have to look."

"No," I say, pushing him back down. I place my rubber boot on his chest to keep him there while I pilot the Zodiac. Ice scrapes against the sides as we cut through the slush, sometimes lifting us entirely as we crest on more slush than water.

"How'd—you find me?" he asks.

"I saw you fall in."

"But I was—under—for so long."

"No," I say, looking at him. "It was only a few seconds."

He shakes his head. "It was at least ten minutes," he says.

I want to tell him he'd be dead if that were the case, but there's no point. He babbles on. "The water—so green and clear," he says. "Stalactites underwater. I saw birds flying—thought I was in the sky—so heavy down there. So heavy."

"Try to relax, Richard," I tell him, as gently as I can. "You're in shock. Just sit tight. We're almost there."

"I saved two people," he says.

"Okay," I tell him. "Okay."

As we head back to the *Cormorant*, I cast another glance behind me, at the devastation I'm leaving behind. I prod the

Zodiac through the ice, thinking about my last conversation with Keller, how we'd been disconnected. I wonder when the phone had cut out, whether he'd heard me tell him I'm pregnant. I wish I'd been able to call him back to make sure he knew. And now, I hope I'll get a second chance.

Columbia, Missouri

A few blocks away from my dorm I meet the volunteer, right where she said she'd be. Before we come into view of the clinic, I hear the voices of the protestors, and as we approach, I keep my eyes downward, avoiding their signs, the photos of fetuses, the huge letters spelling their outrage over what I'm about to do. The volunteer guides me past them, talking softly the whole time, helping me shut out their voices.

Inside, I complete the paperwork, and when I get on the scale on my way to an exam room, I'm surprised to learn I've lost eight pounds, the opposite of what I'd expected. They give me a pregnancy test, and when they do the ultrasound they ask if I want to see it. I say no.

They explain the procedure in more detail than I need or want, and then I put my clothes in a locker and change into a gown. They can't give me anything other than local anesthesia and ibuprofen because I don't have a ride home. I haven't told anyone.

I put my feet in the stirrups and close my eyes. Even when

I feel the pressure, the cramping, I tell myself it's no different than a pelvic exam, a regular checkup, only this one will last a bit longer. I try not to think of the signs I've seen on Interstate 70: SMILE—YOUR MOTHER CHOSE LIFE and ABORTION CAUSES CANCER. I try to clear my head, but I end up thinking of Pam, of how, if I'd taken my job more seriously, devoted myself more fully to the work, maybe I wouldn't be here at all.

After returning from Rocheport, I'd planted myself in her office, apologized, and sworn I'd never miss another day of fieldwork again. She'd waved it off, but I still felt guilty, as though I'd let her down. After that, I showed up early for class and fieldwork and submitted everything she needed ahead of the due dates, as if to make it up to her. I'm not sure she noticed, or cared, but it made me feel better.

As I lie on the exam room table, unable to avoid the sounds—the movements of the physician and her assistant, the clanking of their instruments against the metal table, the suction of the aspiration machine—I try to pinpoint exactly when it happened, when this cluster of cells being removed from my body first started growing. It had to be right before Chad and I ended, if not our very last time together, and this feels like the cruelest part of all.

I think it was the night we were in the darkroom, developing film and printing photos for our next assignment: a portrait. It was late on a Saturday night, and we were alone, just the two of us under the crimson light, amid the sound of water trickling.

It wasn't long after Rocheport that I sensed Chad withdrawing from me—he was always busy with classes and reporting, and he no longer invited me to events. I began to mirror his behavior, to convince myself we were on the same page. We still saw each other in class, still ended up in bed at his apartment from time to time, and we began fitting each other into our schedules rather than the other way around. Once, I'd tried to talk to him about it, lightly: *I thought we were going to be ongoing. Present perfect, remember?* He'd looked at me and said, *Present tense and future tense aren't the same thing.*

As Chad slipped a print into the developer, I glanced over at him and realized it had been a couple of weeks since we'd been together. Under the warm red wash of the safelight, I felt a sudden pull, the familiar, weak-kneed feeling I got around Chad. I waited until I couldn't stand it a second more.

I moved closer, behind him, reaching around to his chest, his stomach, which tightened under my hands, and then I reached lower, and he abandoned his photo in the developer and turned around. He pressed me back into one of the enlarger booths, lifting me up so that I was propped against the counter, and I could hear the enlarger, heavy as it was, rattling behind me as we banged against it.

It wasn't until just after that I realized I hadn't even thought about a condom, and neither had he. But we were careful most of the time, and I shrugged it off even though I knew too much biology to have been so careless, so cavalier. We were breathing as though we'd just run ten miles, flushed and sated as we found and handed each other the items of clothing we'd strewn across the painted black floor.

Chad returned to the tray of developer, where his photo had turned black. He tossed it out and started again. My portrait already done, I hovered around in a sort of afterglow; I had nowhere else to be.

Chad had spent the day out at Eagle Bluffs, a conservation

area of mostly forest and wetland that, because this was Missouri, was better known for its fishing and hunting than for birding and wildlife. His portrait was of a weathered old fisherman, and it was exquisite. Chad had captured the man's features, his concentration; he'd caught the history of the man's face in perfect light, shadow, and depth.

It was because I'd recommitted to my work with Pam that I'd chosen her for my portrait. She was among a minority of women on the science faculty at Mizzou, and I thought it would make a nice piece for my portfolio. I'd photographed her in the lab, whipping out my camera with the sole intention of getting the task done, not thinking about the light, the angle, or of taking a variety of shots. When the image first emerged in the developer, I liked what I saw—Dr. Pam Harrison in her white lab coat, bent over a microscope, a wisp of dark hair falling from behind her ear, eye wide open at the eyepiece. But later, when I saw Chad's portrait, I glanced over at mine, already hung to dry, and saw that it looked flat, emotionless, static. Most of all, it seemed to be a symbol of everything I had in store for myself: a dull, colorless life of feathers and data and little else.

I looked away from the image of Pam's face and, trying to distract myself, leaned over the sink as Chad agitated a new piece of photo paper. I watched the image of a bird emerge, a wood duck he must've seen at Eagle Bluffs while he was shooting the portrait.

"Wow," I murmured. "She's beautiful." The image was black and white but captured the gray scale of the female of the species perfectly: her smooth-feathered face, her white-shadowed black eyes, her salt-speckled breast.

And then I noticed that the image was a little blurry, that Chad was agitating the photo more vigorously than he needed to, as if to hurry up the process—and that his lens hadn't been focused on the wood duck in the foreground but on a woman, long-haired and smiling, stretched out seductively on a blanket.

I released my prints from their clothespins and stuffed them into my folder. I mumbled that I had to go, and Chad, still busy with his photo, paused and looked at me.

"It's just a photo," he said, in a weary, halfhearted way, as if we'd had this discussion a hundred times before and he couldn't decide whether to try to convince me to stay.

I flung the door open as I left, flipping on the overhead light, exposing his print. I heard his muffled curses as I walked down the long hallway.

Breaking up, such as it was, happened as naturally and unceremoniously as getting together had, as if it was meant to be all along. He never knew about the pregnancy.

BEFORE I LEAVE the clinic, they give me a brochure on birth control, as if I hadn't known better, as if this had been a mistake of ignorance rather than impulsiveness.

The weeks leading to my appointment had been excruciating. I felt that everyone who looked at me must've been able to tell; I worried that Chad would find out somehow, even though there was no way he could possibly know. And my choice seemed inevitable no matter how I looked at it, no matter how many ways I tried to imagine another outcome.

As I walk slowly back to campus, I think of Chad's photograph, the wood duck, how lovely it was. It feels hypocritical that I wouldn't dream of eating an animal but that I hadn't thought twice about ending a pregnancy. Maybe I've begun to live too closely by the rules of the animal kingdom, where sacrifice makes sense, where it's necessary and just and often more humane.

THIS YEAR I'M dreading my visit home more than usual. Alec's family has just moved to Kansas City, so he's spending the holidays there. My cat, Ginger, is gone—she'd disappeared after I left for college. The first time I came home to find her missing, I put up signs and checked the shelter, to no avail. I feel her absence most acutely at night, alone in my childhood bed, and I can only hope that she's found a new family, one that welcomes her more than mine did.

My father's empty seat at the table is filled by Mark's new son, Christopher, the first grandchild. I'm watching the baby examine a soft plush rattle, holding it up to his face, when my mother suddenly says to me, "Deborah, are you all right?"

I swing my head toward her, not realizing until that moment how intensely I'd been staring at Christopher. "I'm fine."

"You don't look well," she says. "You look like death warmed over."

"I'm fine," I repeat, and a few moments later I get up and lock myself in the bathroom. A glance in the mirror tells me she's right—my face is pale, eyes sinking into dark hollows—

and I prepare myself to tell them, if they ask again, that it's because of work, because of finals. But it isn't.

I turn my back on my reflection and lean against the sink, taking deep breaths. I always feel most alone when I'm here at home, but this year the feeling is sharper than ever, and I can't help but think it's because I've made a dreadful mistake.

The next night is a repeat of every other—it's all about the baby—and for a moment I wonder what it might've been like to have come home pregnant. Though my mother hopes I will one day have a big family, at this stage of my life it would've been scandalous—but it also would've made me less invisible.

When I run this notion by Alec over the phone, he convinces me otherwise. "You don't want that sort of attention, believe me," he says. "You did the right thing."

Still, the emptiness I feel goes beyond the solitude I'm used to and often enjoy. It's that something was there, a chance at something, and then it wasn't—I'd had it and given it up, destroyed it, and would never get it back. I'm on the bus heading back to Columbia when I finally figure out what I've lost: the chance to have another person in the world I could relate to, someone who might turn out to be a little bit like me, someone I could love, who would love me back.

The Gullet
(67°10'S, 67°38'W)

The code *Mayday*, always repeated three times, signals that a ship is in urgent, life-threatening danger. There are no degrees of Mayday—just the one word—and because we haven't received any further information from the bridge, for me, right now, this leaves room for interpretation, for doubt and hope.

Both these emotions mingle in my mind as I gingerly move across the ice. After stepping on board the *Cormorant* long enough to change into a dry sweater, find a dry parka, and tell Kate to keep her idiot husband on board, I rushed back out—only to find that my Zodiac had been appropriated by another crew member, leaving me to find my way to the wreck of the *Australis* on foot, over the ice.

I make it only about ten yards before I begin to pass survivors on the ice, wet and shaking in the freezing rain and sharp wind. I help guide them to the *Cormorant* and ask if they know Keller, but his name doesn't register—these people are barely capable of responding to even the most basic of questions. The state in which we're finding the survivors—and the fact that we haven't heard anything from the *Australis* in the past three hours—means that something more than an ice collision has happened on that ship. There's no leadership, no order, and the result is turning an already grave situation into a tragic one.

I continue to describe Keller to one passenger after another, but no one knows him. Despite the slickening of the ice under my feet, I begin to make tangible progress toward the *Australis*, and a fifty-yard stretch with no stranded passengers allows me to hope that things may not be as bad as they seem.

Then, ahead in the mist, I encounter a group of twenty survivors, immobile on a large swath of ice. I find a secure trail to them and begin leading them back toward our ship, a shivering procession of cold bodies and warm breath, of fear and blind faith.

And then I realize that while I've been following a slightly different path back, I should have seen the *Cormorant* by now, or someone should've seen me; I'd radioed that I was bringing in more passengers. I strain my eyes ahead, but through the mist I don't see even the shadow of our ship. This could mean only one thing—that with the winds at thirty knots, Glenn had to pull back, and this means that we're stranded.

I radio Glenn again but get no reply. I look back at the passengers, who form a long, evenly spaced train of cold, frightened souls.

I try again. "*Cormorant*, this is Deb, do you copy? Request position. Over."

When I look down, I see that the light on my radio is out.

Either the charge is gone, or it's been destroyed by water or by impact or by a combination of the two. I stare at the device, then shake it a couple times, as if to wake it up. But nothing changes.

I hear a rumbling in the distance and glance up. A few seconds later, two Zodiacs emerge from the fog, with Thom in the lead boat. He weaves among the floes with a preternatural skill, giving the other driver a clear wake in which to follow him, and a moment later he pulls up alongside the ice. I want to hug him with relief.

"Where'd Glenn run off to?" I ask.

"He's landing passengers at Detaille. I doubt he'll be back; the ship got banged up pretty bad trying to get out. Messed up at least one of the propellers."

I do a quick calculation in my head. Detaille, a small island to the north, is probably an hour away by Zodiac, depending on ice and weather, and if the *Cormorant* is there, the rescue will continue by Zodiac only, with at least five hours before more help arrives.

"Any sign of Keller?"

I shake my head.

Just then we hear it—seven short blasts of the *Australis*'s horn, followed by one long one. The order to abandon ship.

Thom steps out of the Zodiac, planting one foot on the ice. "I'll get Nigel to request backup, and we can—"

I shake my head. "There's no time."

"Do you need a Zodiac?"

"The ice has gotten too thick over there. I'm better off on foot."

"Okay," Thom says. "I'll catch up with you as soon as we take this group back."

"Thanks," I say, meeting his eyes. "See you soon."

"See you."

Our promise to meet later feels, like *Mayday*, like a code of sorts. Something that means *good luck*. That means *be careful*. We aren't going to say those words; we aren't going to admit that we're now in the middle of something far more serious than we'd imagined. But we both understand.

I turn back in to the haze and begin walking carefully along the ice. As soon as I'm out of sight of the passengers, I pick up my pace. Though the ice feels solid, I know it's risky, but I don't want to waste any more time. I'm rushing toward the *Australis*, completely hidden in the fog, when I stop short.

I haven't replaced my inoperable radio. I look around, hoping to wave down Thom, hoping someone is still there, but they've all disappeared.

ORCAS HAVE EARNED the name killer whales neither because they hunt humans—they don't—nor because they are whales—they aren't. This is something I often find myself explaining to passengers: that orcas are dolphins, highly skilled hunters of seals, whales, and other dolphins. They're fast—they can swim up to thirty miles an hour—but, more important, they're creative. They hunt in packs of five to fifty, and if they come upon a group of seals lounging on the ice, they circle in formation, slapping their tails on the water, creating waves that break up the ice or roll the berg. If that doesn't work, they lift the ice with their noses.

About four years ago in the Gerlache Strait—on the peninsula, between the continent and Anvers and Brabant Islands—I saw a pod of orcas knock a leopard seal off a berg. Then, like cats playing with a mouse, they let the seal climb back up again. There were two pups among the pod: The orcas were training their young to hunt, the leopard seal their unwitting assistant.

Nature can be cruel, and down here its mercy depends upon which side of the ice you're on. I am, for the moment, on the right side, watching the glassy black fins glide in lazy circles just beyond the ice I'm standing on. About two hundred feet farther is what's left of the *Australis*.

The ship has listed considerably since I first saw her—though it's been no more than two hours—and at some point she'd gotten jammed up against the ice. Now visible is the faded blue from the deep end of the empty swimming pool on the top deck, and a green playing field circled by a running track. The detritus of sixteen hundred desperate passengers and crew litters the ice floes—backpacks, purses, life jackets, hats, cameras. And there are bodies, some floating, some on the ice.

It's these bodies, I suspect, that are attracting the orcas. Orcas aren't dangerous to humans, unless they've gone mad in captivity; the few known attacks on humans in the wild have occurred when orcas have mistaken people for prey. Right now, from under the ice, these bodies look a lot like seals.

The ship moans, her metal straining under the weight of the water inside, the ice outside. Crew members are still loading passengers into lifeboats and Zodiacs, but they're boarding from the ice. The *Australis* has been abandoned.

I scan the jackets and faces for Keller. Then, reluctantly, I scan the bodies, looking through the floating graveyard for his dark hair, an orange jacket. The fact that I don't see him offers only temporary relief.

I shout out to a few crew members, describing Keller, asking if they've seen him. No one has—not surprising, given the size of this floating city, given the pandemonium.

The ice in front of me looks weak, but I find a firm stretch a few yards away and use it to loop back toward the ship. The narrow inlets of water are choked with Zodiacs, not all of them manned by crew members. As I help stranded passengers step from the ice into the boats, I describe Keller to them. When I find crew members to pilot them to Detaille, I ask if they've seen him—but if anyone has, they're too traumatized, too preoccupied, to remember; I get mostly blank stares in response.

I stretch my neck backward to look up at the ship. The expected order of evacuation in a maritime emergency is passengers, crew, captain—but it doesn't always happen this way. Given the chaos here, I'm not sure anyone knows whether the *Australis* has been fully evacuated. On big ships like these, most of the crew are not experienced mariners but waiters and bartenders and entertainers; they may not have had the training they need to deal with circumstances like this. And not every captain has the integrity to go down with the ship.

I know that before I can give up on Keller, I need to consider boarding the ship. My biggest fear is that he'd have stayed on board and is trapped. When a ship goes down this fast, it's all too easy to get trapped in a passageway or pinned beneath shifting furniture. And so I begin scanning the length of the ship, looking for points of entry.

The lowest part of the bow is wedged against the fast ice. The port-side balconies, normally forty feet above the ship's waterline, are within reach, but barely. I test the ice in front of the lowest balcony; then I take a running leap, grabbing the lowest rung of the balcony's railing. I catch it, but my grip is more tenuous than I'd like, and my strength is waning, and if I were to fall, the force of gravity could send me straight through the ice. I struggle to pull myself up, flustered by how little energy I have left.

The ship groans and shifts, and I hang on desperately, swinging back and forth. Then, arms burning, I lift my body enough to swing my legs up; I wrap them around a lower rung, temporarily relieving my arms, then use my legs to push myself upward and over the side.

Collapsing on the deck, I lie there for a few seconds, gathering strength. I shouldn't allow myself this luxury—there's not a moment to spare—but suddenly a part of me is afraid to continue. You get used to death in Antarctica—from reading the explorers' tales to witnessing the inevitable losses of wildlife—but human casualties are rare, even in this harsh landscape, and I'm not at all prepared to encounter Keller if he's not alive.

Then I feel my body slip, aided by my wet clothes, and I raise my head. The ship's deck is at a thirty-degree angle and tilting farther. I need to move.

I stand and try the glass door—locked. I swing my body over to the adjacent balcony; this door slides open. Now in a private cabin, I quickly exit to the passageway. A crew member flees past, ignoring me, using the bulkhead railings to keep from stumbling. I hear a scream from somewhere deep inside the ship, but I can't tell where. So there are still people on board—but how many, and whether they're passengers or crew, I don't know. I blindly begin to run, using the rails to keep myself upright.

Emergency lights are flashing, and an automated message repeats the order to abandon ship in multiple languages. The ship's enormity strikes me yet again as I lean into the endless passageways, straining to see amid the strobes. I begin to feel hopelessly lost. I call Keller's name, again and again, until my voice breaks.

I try to think: If he's still on the ship, where could he be? He'd probably be wherever there are people to evacuate—or maybe, by now, he'd be wherever he can find his own way out. This would most likely be the muster stations, though at this point protocol is moot, and those still on board are probably getting off the ship any way they can.

I keep moving, sliding along the bulkheads, and soon I enter a large banquet hall. The ship is listing so heavily that it forces me to my knees, and I have to climb my way to the other side of the room. I stop at the higher end and call out again, hoping my voice might echo far enough to reach someone. Then suddenly the ship heaves; the floor drops beneath me, and, as I struggle to fight the downward momentum, I see that there's nothing to break my fall except a jumble of tables and chairs below.

I HEAR A waterfall in the distance, a peaceful sound that evokes mountains and meadows, but when I open my eyes

I see only the garish gold of an oversize chandelier. I realize in a panic that I'd gotten knocked out in the fall, and I don't know for how long. The *Australis* is now on her side, let loose from the ice, and sinking fast.

My head aches, and when I reach up to my temple to find the source of the pain, I feel a rising bump, and my glove comes back bloody. I try to stand but collapse as my left leg fails me. At first I think it has fallen asleep, but then I reach down and feel that my foot is swelling rapidly, painfully, against my boot, and as I try to stand again, my ankle can't support my weight. I loosen my bootlaces and straighten up again, putting a hand to my stomach. No pain there, no cramping—it seems my ankle, and perhaps my head, now throbbing, took the brunt of my slide down the tilting ballroom floor.

I fight off the blackness that nudges at my consciousness; I call out again, as loudly as I can, for Keller, for help. No one answers. I crawl a few feet to a doorway and tumble into a passageway. The ship's power is gone, and, despite the light from the portholes and from the emergency lighting, it's hard to see; my vision's blurred, wobbly. I have no idea whether I'm getting closer to an exit or simply going deeper into the ship.

I OPEN MY eyes in a darkened, slanted passageway. The glow of the emergency exit signs turns everything a muted red. I can't remember passing out and can't tell how long I was unconscious. When I raise my head, I see water pooling below me, lapping at my feet, rising past my ankles. As I try to sit up, the pain in my ankle explodes, shooting upward; at least the water has numbed it a bit. I twist my head to look up the sloping floor, toward light.

At the end of the passageway, I see something red on the ground. I pull myself upright, ignoring the pain this time, and start crawling toward it. Using my arms and my one good leg, I move slowly, crab-like, toward the spot of color.

When I get closer, I see that it's only a scarf, a red scarf. It's absurd to think I could find Keller in this mess — and now I'm not even sure I'll be able to make my own way out.

I wrap the scarf around my ankle, yanking it tight, gritting my teeth against the pain. Then I sit up straight and draw a deep breath into my lungs. I shout as loudly as I can, calling for Keller, for help, hoping that there's still someone, anyone, on board who can hear me.

But there is no one here.

With a burst of renewed energy, I get to my feet, pain searing through my ankle, though at least it's stable now. At the rate the *Australis* is sinking, I'll have to climb quickly, against gravity, and somehow make it out to the starboard side — the only side still above water.

Using the handrail, I begin to drag myself up first one companionway, then another. Eventually I reach a long passageway that leads to a narrow deck. I struggle to haul myself up the steep incline, using the side railing for support as the ship wavers, rapidly filling.

Finally I manage to crawl out onto the deck, where I observe, with an odd sort of detachment, that I'm almost completely trapped. The ice immediately surrounding the ship is broken and churning, and the nearest floe is five, ten feet away. If I were able-bodied, the distance might be swimmable, but right now it looks like the English Channel. In order to do what I know I have to do, I can't allow myself to think—about Keller, about the baby, about the black water below, about anything.

I drag myself to the edge of the railing, and I lower myself over the side, where I hang for a long, dreadful moment. The ship suddenly shifts with an enormous sigh, and I let go, tumbling twenty feet down along the side of the vessel and into the sea.

The cold rips the air from my lungs, and immediately I force myself to move. I paddle toward the ice floe, my life preserver keeping me afloat. I focus on moving steadily; I don't let myself flail, don't let myself waste energy on unnecessary movement. I have mere moments to make it to that ice, and every second counts.

It amazes me how time slows during moments like this. I think of Keller, of the look on his face when I left McMurdo, the sound of his voice when we last spoke. Of our argument last season, how I should've been kinder, more understanding—and how I only seem to realize such things when it's far too late to take anything back.

My limbs are quickly numbing—and by the time I reach the ice, I can only grasp and hold on. The floe is large and solid, but the edge I'm gripping is slick, and I don't know how I'll drag myself out of the water.

Scanning the ice, I glimpse a small hummock rising a few feet away from where I'm holding on. Hand over hand, I slide across the floe and take hold of the ridge of ice, which gives me the leverage to heave myself up.

I lie there a moment, shivering, then turn my head toward the *Australis*. All I can see is the underside of her hull, dark and curved like a whale floating on the water. Bubbles run alongside as she exhales her last breaths.

I see no signs of life. Floating past are empty parkas and life jackets, gloves and earmuffs—the hollow shells of passengers who once inhabited them. I smell diesel fuel and smoke. I curve into the fetal position, to save what body heat I still have, to try to protect this baby, who may be all I have left of Keller.

I don't have much time before the shaking stops, before hypothermia sets in, before my limbs cease to respond to my brain's commands. I think I hear the sound of a motor, and I lift my head. But I don't see anything resembling a Zodiac, and there's no movement in the water except the gurgling of the sinking ship and the flow of debris and bodies.

I catch a glimpse of color and prop myself onto my elbow for a better view. I scrabble to the edge of the floe before I realize it's nothing but an empty hat. My eyes trace the ice, the water, everything, for the sight of something more—but there's nothing.

I try to claw my way back to the center, to sturdy ice, but my strength's gone, my body useless. And that's when I realize that I can no longer feel my hands.

Detaille Island
(66°52'S, 66°47'W)

I've long thought of Antarctica as a living being, like Gaia: the deep breaths of her storms, the changing expressions of her ice-sculpted face, the veins of algae and flora that survive under her snow-covered skin. Now more than ever, the continent seems far more person than place, with a temperament that's unpredictable, resourceful, and wild.

On the other side of the porthole, Detaille Island stares back at me with haunted eyes. For the first time I can relate to the words Robert Scott scrawled in his journal: "Great God! this is an awful place."

I'd woken alone in a cabin on the *Cormorant*—I remember a wavy feeling, like being on the water, the sensation of a body next to mine. I'd felt a strong sense of Keller, and when I opened my eyes, I lay there for a long while hoping it was still possible that he was alive somewhere. Then, reality hit—a jolt of panic as I realized we still hadn't found him—and I tried to stand, to get up and return to the search. But my legs buckled, the pain in my ankle seething under my weight. I noticed then that my ankle had been wrapped, the wound on my head cleaned and bandaged. My hands were red, and they stung like fury, as did my ears and face. I pressed my prickling hands against my middle. I felt a subtle ache, and it wasn't long before the feeling spread through my entire body, fueled by images of Keller on the ice, under the ice. I managed to get out of the bunk and prop myself near the porthole, and I've been unable to tear my eyes away, despite the devastation ashore.

Passengers gather on the uneven terrain. Beyond them, the black hills, marbled with snow, frame a threatening sky. Huddled in blankets and moving mostly in pairs, the survivors remind me of penguins braving a strong wind; their figures mirror the Adélies a few hundred yards away. Circling, shoulders bent toward the ground, they're looking for spouses, children, friends; they call to one another, hoping for reunions. Some sit alone, like birds on empty nests.

I feel my own body closing in on itself, hunched toward the porthole. *I just wish I had more time,* Kate had told me on Deception Island, and I hear her words echo in my head. If only we could, somehow, have more time—the other ships would be here by now, more passengers could have been saved, perhaps even the *Australis* herself could have been salvaged. And we could have found Keller.

We never had enough time, Keller and I—he didn't get the chance to learn he would be a father, and I had only begun to embrace the idea of having a family. My throat closes up, making it hard to breathe. I rest my forehead against the glass and start to weep.

The cabin door opens, but I don't turn around, not even when I feel a hand gently touch my shoulder. I don't want to see anyone.

Then a voice—a deep, familiar voice, though hoarse—says my name, and soon I'm looking into the moss-strewn eyes I thought I'd never see again.

"Oh my God." I try to catch my breath. "Are you real?" I smack my burning palm against Keller's chest—he's solid, all warmth and fleece, and under that, as I press my hand as close as I can bear through the prickly pain, I feel his heartbeat. He's real. He's alive.

"You don't remember?" he asks.

"Remember—what?"

Keller brushes his fingers across my face, still wet. "How we found you. On the ice."

So it wasn't a dream but a memory, and still hazy. "Tell me."

He eases me back into the narrow berth and sits beside me. Though it hurts my still-warming hands, I can't stop touching him, afraid he might vanish.

"I was stranded on the ice," he says, "and saw a Zodiac weaving around—really erratic. I thought some *Australis* passenger had commandeered it, but it was crew, someone in an orange parka. I tried flagging him down. He ignored me at first—it seemed he was looking for someone—then finally came over."

Keller's voice is raspy but strong. "Turned out the guy wasn't a crew member at all—he was a passenger. From here."

"Richard," I manage to say. How the hell had he gotten back out on the water?

"How'd you know that?"

"He nearly killed himself—and me—earlier. He's crazy on seasick meds."

"That may be, but he's a hero in my book," Keller says. "He picked me up, and it's thanks to his delusion about someone else being out there that we found you. He wouldn't give up the helm, was going in circles, and I was just about to take him down and tie him up in the Zodiac when he spotted you." Keller grins. "He seemed disappointed it was you, not who he was looking for, whoever that was—he wouldn't say. But if we hadn't found you just then—"

"I was out looking for you."

"I know."

There's so much to ask, and so much to say—and even as I begin to repeat what I'd told him on the phone, he's smiling, his hands coming to rest softly on my belly, and I stop. "So you did hear me. You didn't hang up on me."

There are more wrinkles around his eyes than I remember, or maybe it's because he's smiling in a way I've never seen before. "No, I didn't hang up on you. Communications went down."

"Am I okay?"

"You've fractured at least one bone in your ankle and have four stitches in that thick head of yours. But Susan says there's no evidence anything's wrong with the baby. Nothing she can see. She's eager to get you to a hospital, though."

"I'm glad you two have talked this over. Apparently you're both assuming it's yours?"

He laughs, and I squeeze his hand, tightly, despite the pain that shoots up my arm. Now that we're sitting here together, it all feels more real. "You're okay with this? You really do want this baby?"

"Don't you?" he says.

"Yes, of course, but—how do we manage it? Between our work, and coming down here, and—" I'm rambling, thinking aloud.

He puts a finger to my lips. "Later, Deb. There's plenty of time to figure it all out. Now's not the time."

"Why not now?" I ask. "It's not as if we're going anywhere."

I stagger to my feet and limp to the porthole again. Over on the island, a long and narrow hut built by the British Antarctic Survey is serving as a temporary refuge for rescued passengers. I've been inside enough times to remember its weathered gray walls, its cold bareness but for a few remnants: the tins of Scotch oats, rusted cans of sardines, shelves of books, long underwear and socks still strung above the stove to dry—and I try to picture this small snapshot of history crowded with twenty-first-century survivors.

As I watch, another Zodiac full of passengers lands on the beach, and the porthole becomes a panorama of Detaille's past: the ghosts of the British researchers, the skeleton of their shelter, the tracks of nearby Adélies in the snow—and now, this scene from the island's gruesome new history as a temporary home for survivors.

"What a nightmare," I murmur, and I feel Keller behind me, his arms gently sheathing my shoulders.

"You need to rest," he says. "Another cruise ship just arrived, and more boats are on the way. We'll be heading north soon."

I ease myself back down on the bed, with Keller's help,

but this time he doesn't join me. I look up at him. "Aren't you staying?"

"I'll be back soon," he says. "They need extra hands—"

I sit up straight. "Are you kidding? You almost died out there."

"I'll be careful. I always am."

I struggle to stand again, galvanized by fear, by hormones, determined not to let him go.

"Don't worry," he says. He kisses my forehead, his lips lingering there, and then he's turning to leave.

I grab his arm, holding fast through the sting. "No, Keller. Don't even think about it."

As I get to my feet, I tighten my grip, fiery pain screaming through my fingers, and when I look down at his ungloved hand, through a blur of sudden tears I see jagged penguin-bite scars in the web of flesh between his thumb and forefinger.

"Come on, Deb," he says gently. "You would do the same thing."

"I fucking *did*, Keller—I was out there looking for you. I almost died, remember? By some miracle, we both made it—and now you want to go back?"

"Yes, we made it," he says. "That's my point. Don't you think those who are still out there deserve a chance, too?"

I'm still holding tightly on to his wrist. "I won't let you. Not without me."

"You can't even walk."

"That's my final offer—stay here, or take me with you."

He sighs, his whole body pausing, and he leans his forehead against mine. While I don't relax my grip, I let myself savor this shred of time, the impossible fact that he's here. I'm barely breathing, not wanting to break the spell, to turn this moment into a memory—we have so few as it is.

He's still and silent for so long that I think maybe I've convinced him. Then I feel his hand on mine, trying to loosen my fingers. I'm losing strength but clamp my hand down as firmly as I can.

He raises our hands. "Your ring held up," he says.

I look down at my hand, flushed and swelling with frostnip, the ring more snug on my finger than ever.

"It's tough, like you," he says. "Like us."

"Everything has a breaking point." I turn away from him and look out the porthole. "Don't you know how lucky you are?" I say, more to my reflection in the glass than to Keller. "You're not even supposed to be here."

I hear him behind me, his breathing slow and steady, as if he's waiting patiently for my permission, which I'm not about to give. I jerk backward as a wave leaps up and slaps the glass.

"Remember Blackborow?" Keller says.

The stowaway on Shackleton's journey.

"He wasn't supposed to be there either," Keller says. "And he worked longer days than anyone."

"Yeah, and didn't he lose all his toes to gangrene?"

"But he made it," Keller says. "They all did—because that's what it takes. It takes everyone."

"What about *us*? Would it kill you to stay behind for once?"

"I'll be fine," he says, his arms around my shoulders again, his cheek against mine. "I'm impervious to ice, remember?"

I know he's trying to make me smile, but I can't. "It's not just me you need to come back for."

"I know that," he says. "And there are still parents and children out there who need help. You know why I have to do this."

I do, just as he knows I'd be out there, too, if I could. And I know he won't leave without my blessing, and that not giving it to him would change everything that we are.

I turn around and let my forehead fall to his chest. I feel his hands in my hair, and I shift my head to the side. Through the fleece I can hear his heart beating, reminding me of the rhythm of Admiral Byrd's heartbeat as he'd sprawled in my lap.

I look up at Keller. There's so much I want to tell him—how helpless I'd felt, being unable to locate him; how lost, thinking he was gone—but my thoughts are nothing more than a mental mirror of the bay outside, a mix of brash, of hope and fear floating and cresting and crashing until they'll either merge or melt away, and I don't know which.

ALONE IN THE stateroom, I stare at the ceiling, unable to sleep, even to close my eyes. I turn my head and look around. Unlike our utilitarian crew's quarters, this is like a hotel room, painted a warm, soothing green. Photographs of whales and albatross adorn the walls.

I sit up and swing my legs over the side of the bed. I test out my ankle, which hurts, but not as much as before. I stand up, feeling dizzy, and wait for it to pass. Once I feel steadier, I look around for my jacket. I don't see my naturalist's jacket—in fact, I'm not wearing any of my own clothes—but when I open the closet door I find a red cruise-issued parka, and I put it on. It's big on me, a man's size, and it makes me wonder whose room I'm in and why the guy isn't wearing it himself.

As I make my way up to the main deck, I peek into the lounge. I recognize many of the *Cormorant* passengers who are now helping Susan care for the injured, or comforting the distraught, offering blankets and cups of coffee and tea. I glimpse Kate applying a bandage to a woman's scraped and bleeding hand. I walk past to the port deck, where I can see the island and watch the crew unload Zodiacs down below. I know at this point they are doing more recovering than rescuing.

I see Keller in a Zodiac near the beach at Detaille — at least I think it's him. I reach for my binoculars before realizing they're gone — lost to the sea, probably. I can't bear to think about how much detritus from the ship, from its passengers, is going to end up at the bottom of this ocean — and, worse, floating on its surface, and later in the bellies of penguins and seals and whales. The victims we're seeing now are only the very first of what eventually will be too many to count.

I hobble my way up one more level to the crew deck, the one Keller and I sneak off to for moments free from tourists, questions, demands. It offers a better vantage point, and from here I continue to look for him. The Zodiac I'd thought he was in has disappeared.

I try to breathe slowly through the tangle of anxiety in my chest. When my ankle begins to throb I lean heavily on the rail with my forearms. My hands, in dry gloves, are still burning, and my face is unprotected from the cold and wind. I shouldn't be outside in this condition, but I don't know how else to be.

I'M STANDING AT the porthole in the stateroom when the nausea hits. I stumble to the cabin's tiny bathroom just in time. Afterwards I sit there on the floor for a few moments to catch my breath.

I hear a knock on the cabin door. I get to my feet just as Kate enters.

"How're you doing?" she asks. "I heard you broke your ankle."

"Just a fracture." I turn away from her and stumble toward the porthole, swallowing hard against another wave of nausea, my hands hovering around my middle. "I hate being stuck on board like this."

"I know the feeling," she says.

"Your husband does, too," I say, turning around. "Did you hear? About how he found Keller and they found me?"

She nods, then wraps her arms around herself. "I'm glad. I mean, I know he screwed up the first time—"

"Don't worry about that. We're all grateful he snuck out again, as stupid as it was. I should thank him. Where is he?"

"Up in the lounge, I think," she says. "I asked him not to come down here because you need to rest."

"This is your cabin?"

"I wanted you to have a quiet place to recuperate. Richard and I aren't going to get any sleep anyway."

"You didn't have to do that."

She smiles. "And you'll be happy to know he's taken off that patch, finally."

"Good."

Kate takes a step closer, studying me. "Are you okay? You look really pale."

"I'm just a little queasy, that's all."

She glances at the bandage on my forehead. "That doesn't sound good. I should go find Susan."

"No," I say. "Not necessary."

"But if you hit your head—"

"It's not that," I say. "I'm pregnant."

Kate smiles, then turns to the little coffee bar all the staterooms are equipped with. "Peppermint tea," she says over her shoulder. "I've been drinking it like water. It helps a lot."

After handing me the mug of tea, Kate sits down on the bed across from mine and asks me how far along I am. I repeat what Susan had told me, with a little difficulty, my stomach beginning to churn again. I take a few sips of tea but can't handle more and put the mug on the top of the storage compartment between the beds.

Kate takes a blanket from the closet and lays it over me. The gesture is so kind that I don't have the heart to tell her I'm already too warm. Sitting cross-legged on the other bed, she tells me she's planning to tell Richard about her own pregnancy as soon as they're off the boat, maybe over a nice dinner in Ushuaia or Santiago, when they're back on land and everything is feeling more normal.

Maybe it's the sound of her voice that soothes me, or the exhaustion catching up with me, or the fact that the nausea is finally abating—I let my eyes shut, and the next thing I know, I'm waking up with a shudder.

Kate is gone, but when I raise my head I see Susan across the room. She's got her back to me, rummaging in her medical bag.

"How long have I been asleep?" I ask. "Where's Kate?"

She doesn't answer but comes over with a glass of water. "How're you feeling?" she asks.

"Not bad. A little sick earlier. Better now." Yet when I sit up, my head spins, and I feel a bolt of pain shoot through my temple.

Disoriented, I lie back down and try to look out the porthole, but all I can glimpse is a faint glow of light. The ship's not moving, but I don't otherwise have a sense of where or when. There's no clock down here, and my diver's watch is gone. "What time is it?"

"About four."

"In the afternoon?" It feels as though I'd slept for more than a couple of hours.

"No, morning," she says. "You slept through the night. You really needed it."

"All night?" I'd slept for more than twelve hours. The *Australis* would be underwater by now, her fuel leaking. Finding any more survivors would be more than we could hope for.

I struggle again to sit up. "How's the rescue going?"

Susan looks as though she hasn't slept at all, her eyes puffy and barely open, her mouth taut with tension.

"We're still at Detaille," she says. "There's a flotilla of ships out there now."

"So why aren't we heading north?"

She pauses. "They're still looking for two people."

This could only mean one thing. "You mean two of our people."

She nods.

"Who?"

But she doesn't say anything.

"Who, Susan?"

"One is Richard Archer."

I'm not surprised by this, but I feel a pang of sympathy for Kate. I wait for Susan to speak again, and when she doesn't, I ask, "Who's the other one?"

"Why don't you rest a bit more?" she says.

"Susan, just tell me." When she doesn't, I answer my own question. "It's Keller, isn't it?"

She nods.

I feel something inside me sink and drown.

"They're looking for him now, Deb. Everyone is, crew from all the ships." She pauses. "They'll find him."

I reach out and clutch her hand. "You've got to get me out there. Wrap up this leg and shoot me full of whatever you have to. I need to be out there looking."

"Deb," she says. "You can barely walk."

"He saved me," I say. "You can't just let me sit here and do nothing."

Susan's eyes begin to water.

I try to breathe, try to stay calm. But I know the odds.

I turn away from Susan and shut my eyes. I hear the rumble of Zodiacs outside, the occasional petrel cry. Then I feel the ship tremble, hear the engines come alive. This means they're preparing to leave, with or without Keller, with or without Richard. I can tell by the vibrations that they haven't fixed that damaged propeller. The ship feels shaky, unwhole.

A PHYSICAL PAIN envelops me so fully I can hardly tell where it's coming from. Susan offers me acetaminophen, but I shake her off. Even something stronger wouldn't help—even if I had no body at all, I'd feel the shock and tremble of all that we've lost. At least without medication, I can focus on something: every ache, every twinge, every throb.

Kate makes us tea, and we wait together, taking turns looking helplessly out the porthole. The *Cormorant's* engines are running, but we're still at anchor. Rescuers have already pulled hundreds of bodies from the water, and the decks of the British and Russian icebreakers that have arrived to help are lined with corpses. And when Glenn and Nigel appear at the cabin door, their expressions grave and focused on Kate, I know instantly that Richard is now among them.

I watch Kate's face lose its color. Though it's hard for me to walk, I insist on accompanying her as she follows Glenn and Nigel to a Zodiac. She takes my arm, as if to help me, but I can feel her shaking. Glenn tells us that a Russian team found a Zodiac grounded on a sheet of ice, with two frightened *Australis* passengers inside. Not far away, the Russian crew discovered a body, buoyed by his life preserver.

When we board the icebreaker, they take us into a room. Richard's body lies stretched on a makeshift table. He wears a life jacket stamped with the tour company's logo. His face is a whitish blue, his skin slick and waxy. Kate reaches out to touch his face. "At last," she murmurs to me, "he looks almost relaxed."

In the Zodiac on the way back to the *Cormorant*, she asks Glenn the question I'm not able to ask myself: "What about Keller?"

"Nothing yet," Glenn says.

"But you'll keep looking?"

"We need to head back soon," Glenn says, his eyes meeting mine. "But the others are going to keep looking, yes." For the first time, I hear Glenn's voice waver, on the edge of breaking.

"Then I'm staying, too," I hear myself say. Glenn doesn't answer, but I feel his hand on my shoulder, and he keeps it there until we return to the *Cormorant*.

Back on board, Kate brings me a bowl of soup, which I can't eat. Amy comes by to see me, but I can't talk. I press my face to the glass of the porthole, where I continue to stare out at the water—dirty with brash ice and with debris from the wreck, from the rescue operations—and think of all it has taken.

Nigel, Amy, and a few crew members will remain with the other rescue teams—more bodies need recovering; the *Australis* is leaking fuel. The recovery work has only just begun.

I look over at a nearby ice floe. An Adélie has just leapt onto it and turned his head to the side, considering the ship. I want to call out to him, warn him to get away—that soon he will be covered in oil; he will lose his body heat, his ability to swim and mate and feed his chicks. But Adélies are territorial. They don't know how to leave.

THE PAIN AND nausea get worse, and it's only when I notice the bleeding that I realize I've neglected what's happening inside my own body, where a part of Keller is still alive.

Susan doesn't have the equipment on board to offer the reassurances I need, but she instructs me to stay in bed. "The body will take care of itself," she tells me, and this is an odd source of comfort, this reminder that we're all just bodies in the end, like all other animals.

I sleep fitfully, waking from nightmares of broken eggs, of skuas scavenging dead penguins, of baby chicks drowning in meltwater. I think of the penguins I've observed over the years, those who've lost their young to predators or bad weather or bad timing. They move on, I remind myself; they can't afford to stop.

But this doesn't mean they don't mourn. When I close my eyes, I can see the Magellanic penguin watching over her mate's lifeless body at Punta Tombo. I see Adélies wander their colonies, searching for mates that never return; I see chinstraps sitting dejected on empty nests. And, perhaps most clearly of all, I see the grieving of the emperors. The female returns, searching, her head poised for the ecstatic cry. When her calls go unanswered, she lowers her beak to the icy ground. When she locates her chick, frozen in death, she assumes the hunched posture of sorrow as she wanders across the ice. And then, when it's time, she'll let the sea take her far away, as I'm doing now.

The Drake Passage
(58°22'S, 61°05'W)

One thing the animal kingdom had not yet taught me is that hope is more punishing than grief.

We don't know much about animals' capacity for hope. We do know that they grieve, that they are joyful and playful and mischievous and clever. We've seen animals work together toward a common goal, and we've seen them use tools to get what they want. Despite what many believe, they are not so different from us.

Yet we can't know their hearts and minds; we can only watch their behaviors. One winter, I watched an Adélie penguin minding her nest during an unexpected snowstorm. Soon covered with snow herself, she didn't move. Her eggs would never hatch, and even if they did, her newborn chicks would freeze, or drown—but still she didn't leave them. Was this instinct? Or was it hope? Did she wish, as I'm wishing now, for something that by all accounts would be nothing short of miraculous?

During the journey home, I remain confined to my bunk. I don't sleep, though I need the rest, and with every sway and dip through the Drake, I cling to the sturdy wooden slats of the bunk and dare to hope—even as part of me wonders whether hope is only a blind instinct as well.

And, with nothing but time to think, I try to piece together what happened to Keller.

Richard must have still had medication in his system, and he was apparently suffering from some mad, misplaced belief that he was helping the rescuers—whatever the reason, he decided to go back into the water to search for that elusive person he'd been obsessed with rescuing. Kate said he seemed desperate to assist, to prove he could do something good, perhaps to make up for his rock-climbing stunt on Deception Island, which he still felt bad about.

She'd seen Richard getting into a Zodiac with Keller, and she'd shouted after him, but they were too far away to hear. She saw Keller and Richard arguing, Keller pointing back toward the *Cormorant* several times, then finally tossing up his hands, as if he realized he couldn't argue with Richard anymore. Then they took off in the Zodiac. That was the last Kate saw of them.

They must've been heading for the *Australis*, looking for more victims, dodging the pack ice, their path steadily growing narrower. From what Glenn told us, the ice had closed in after the *Cormorant* retreated to Detaille, making rescue efforts nearly impossible. At that point, only one other small cruise ship had arrived to help.

Keller would have been constantly stopping and backing up, turning around to try to find a good route. I can see him clearly in my mind—the weight of each passing moment on his tensing shoulders, the reluctance to let even one opportunity to find more survivors slip by. When one route dead-ended in a sheet of ice, he would try another, and then another.

At some point, Keller took off his life jacket and gave it to Richard.

This I know because Kate said when Richard got into the Zodiac, he wasn't wearing a life jacket, but Keller was. Richard's body was found only because he was buoyed by a life preserver, and the fact that Keller has not been found is likely because he wasn't.

Keller, still determined, would aim their rubber boat into the narrow channels of ice, firing forward at full force, the ice tearing at the sides, scraping as it broke away beneath them. He would know that the Zodiac's multiple compartments allowed for some damage, and that, at a time like this, saving lives was more important than salvaging a rubber boat. He would push ahead, and gradually the ice would begin to loosen its grip as the river widened. They would emerge into a broad lake of liquid that allowed them to turn back in the direction of the *Australis*.

Keller would have been too focused on the ice ahead to pay much attention to Richard. And Richard, unable to think clearly, would have been focused only on finding that survivor he thought he'd left behind. Was it possible he'd seen something that wasn't there? I remember Keller's words: *It's thanks to his delusion about someone else being out there that we found you.*

Is it possible to hate Richard for finding me, and losing Keller?

During the course of the rescue, I heard crew members

say they'd glimpse a body writhing on the ice and approach it through the fog and snow only to find, once they got closer, that it wasn't a human but a seal. Or they'd see a jacket floating by, only to fish it out and discover it empty.

I don't know what could have gotten Keller out of the safety of the Zodiac without a life jacket unless it was to help someone. Someone who was there, or someone who Richard thought was there.

Keller would kill the engine, bring the Zodiac up hard against the side of the ice—and this is where I'm at a loss.

I can only surmise that Richard believed he saw something, and that Keller believed him, too. I envision Keller on the ice, looking around.

Perhaps he did see someone. Or Richard insisted someone was there. Maybe he pointed, and Keller ventured forward, walking gingerly, peering into the water from a safe distance away.

But why had Richard left him behind?

As crazed as he was, I doubt Richard would deliberately leave Keller stranded on the ice—his intentions were good, and, according to Kate, his biggest enemy had always been himself. And maybe that was it—maybe he was still, at that moment, trying to prove himself a hero. To redeem himself for everything he thought he'd done wrong on this trip, to make up for every argument he'd had with his wife.

We know that two *Australis* passengers were found alone in a Zodiac—*We were stranded on the ice; we would've been goners. But after he got us in the boat, he wouldn't take us to shore. Said he had to keep looking for someone*—and this is when I think things took a turn.

Richard had heard them somehow—two women, calling for help. At first he shook it off, knowing he had to wait for Keller, or thinking it was just the wind, the sounds of birds overhead—but soon he realized that they were human voices, and he turned to see their small figures through the fog, waving their arms, shouting at him.

Richard would yell out to Keller, who by then was too far away to hear—and, having heard the desperation in their voices, would decide to save the women, then return for Keller.

He would start up the Zodiac, but it would prove far more difficult to pilot than he'd anticipated. It changes direction easily, and he would have trouble keeping his arm steady. With each bump into a wedge of ice, he would lose his balance, each time taking another precious few seconds to regain it.

He would look up to see if he was making progress. He wasn't. He was driving and driving, and yet these two women didn't seem any closer. Turning around, he could still see Keller against the white of the ice. *Be right back*, he would promise. Richard would wish, suddenly, that he hadn't left him there.

But the two women stranded on the ice would be closer now, closer to him than Keller, and he would see that their floe was teetering dangerously in the wind. He had no choice but to save them first, and then return to Keller.

This we learned from the women: Richard approached the ice floe, slamming into it and struggling to keep the boat adjacent to the edge of the floe. The women managed to scramble into the Zodiac just as the ice began to tumble and crack beneath them. They were cold, shivering uncontrollably. They'd been in a damaged lifeboat that had capsized amid the crushing ice, and they'd been fortunate to have clambered onto ice instead of falling into the water. They'd been separated from the other eight passengers with them. Two, they knew, had managed to climb onto another wedge of ice, but they'd been soaked through and had likely succumbed to hypothermia. The others, they suspected, had probably drowned.

Do you have any blankets? one of them asked.

Richard shook his head, turning the boat around and heading back to where he came from, back to Keller.

Thank God you saw us, the woman said. *I don't know how much more time we had on that ice. Where are you taking us?*

I don't know, Richard said, peering into the mist.

The woman looked around, confused. *Where are we going, then?*

I have to pick up someone.

Where?

He's just over there.

But by then Richard could no longer see Keller—the women both said no one was there. Richard seemed to panic; he had a hard time catching his breath. They said he kept trying to get closer, skirting around the edge of the ice as if this person might appear by magic.

One of the women asked: *Are you sure there's someone out here?*

I saw you, didn't I? Richard barked.

Okay, okay, she said. She opened a storage hutch in the Zodiac and found a blanket, which the women spread across their shoulders. They huddled close together, becoming more and more worried about Richard's increasingly freakish behavior.

Who are you looking for? the other woman asked, watching Richard strain to see across the ice ahead. Again Richard didn't answer, and a few moments later he began to shake, the spastic movements of his hand on the steering post causing the Zodiac to lurch and hiccup in the water.

Hello! Richard screamed out into the fog. *Hello!*

There was no answer.

He never said Keller's name.

Help me, Richard said, but when one of the women stood and tried to take over the steering post, Richard shook her off, losing control of the Zodiac again. He stumbled as they hit a large sheet of ice, tumbling out of the boat and falling hard onto the ice.

The women screamed, and one of them leaned over the side, reaching for Richard, while the other tried desperately to control the Zodiac, to keep it against the ice.

But Richard didn't want to get back into the boat. *Be right back,* he told them, pointing ahead. *He's just over there.*

It's hard to imagine what happened next—Richard and Keller both stranded on the ice, too far apart to find each other, and eventually too lost in fog for the women to help them. No radios—and, for Keller, no life jacket.

I force myself to consider Richard, what he must have felt, how he must have suffered—it's the only way I'll be able to understand, and to forgive.

I imagine him stumbling across the ice, paranoid and irrational. The wind would've been brisk, pushing down the clouds, darkening the sky. At some point he must have slipped, ice must've cracked beneath his feet, or a wave knocked him down—somehow, he ended up underwater, choking on salt water, lungs burning.

Something similar would likely have happened to Keller, but for Richard, the life vest would have tugged him upward. Due to a large abrasion on the top of Richard's head, Kate was told that he'd likely been sucked under a sheet of ice so that when he rose up he met a cold glass ceiling, solid and unyielding.

He'd have clawed his way across the ice from below, the tips of his fingers raw, until he'd eventually reached open air. By then, he was exhausted, depleted. He attempted to heave himself out of the water but didn't have the strength, his hands too tattered and numb even to hold on, and so he could only float, his life preserver wedged up against his ears, his cheeks, as the weight of his body pulled him downward.

This is where I stop.

I can't envision what more happened to Richard because I can't allow myself to think of Keller's last moments.

What I do try to imagine about Keller is that some part of it was peaceful—that he didn't suffer when he was plunged into the ocean, that he was visited by the curious penguins he loved, that he drifted away gently, that his last thoughts of life, of me, of us, were hopeful, even happy. That he felt, finally, at home.

FIVE YEARS AFTER SHIPWRECK

Portland, Oregon

I hear my flight number called over the loudspeaker—Santiago via Los Angeles, then onward from Santiago to Ushuaia. My daughter's hand clings to mine, but not as tightly as the year before—and next year, it will be looser still.

Neither of us likes to be apart, but she loves getting calls from "the bottom of the world"; she loves the South American toys I bring her when I return. While Nick is the only father she's known, she's got Keller's and my wanderlust in her blood; she's learned about the brush-tailed Antarctic penguins and is eagerly awaiting the day I take her with me.

After the *Cormorant* had limped back to Ushuaia, much heavier than when she left, I was transported to Buenos Aires, where I was hospitalized for a week. When I returned to the States, I remained on bed rest for most of my pregnancy. Kelly was born three weeks early, small but healthy, and when I brought her home a week later, Nick opened his door across the garden so he could hear her cry, and he didn't shut it again until we'd both moved in with him.

My mother flew out six months later to meet Kelly, and my father made promises to do the same. He died of a heart attack, on a flight during a business trip, before he could. Starting on Kelly's second birthday, my mother has made an annual visit, which has been good for all of us. She doesn't speak of my father often, but when she does it's with more fondness than tension, as if his absence, finally, makes sense to her. In the spring, Nick and I are planning to visit St. Louis as well as Chicago, where his family's from, so Kelly can meet her relatives. And then we'll fly to Boston, so she can meet her Aunt Colleen, Keller's sister. It amazes me how this small child, all of forty pounds, has connected—and, in my case, reconnected—our families.

Even though Nick and I share a bed, I believe it was Kelly he loved first. He was often the one who heard her in the middle of the night; he'd bring her to me, and she'd fall asleep between us. He'd never been a parent before, but he slipped seamlessly into the role, as if the part had been waiting for him all along. And, watching him with Kelly, the way he'd hold her and feed her and sing her to sleep, I knew I'd found the right mate—that I would never come home to an empty nest, and, for the first time, I didn't want to leave home.

But, three years ago, I finally returned to the continent; Nick urged me to go. I've been twice since. I hate leaving Nick and Kelly, so I don't go for more than one voyage a season, and I can't hike as far as I used to without feeling a twinge in my ankle, where the fractured bone never healed.

There is nothing in the landscape that doesn't remind me of Keller.

The first time I returned, his absence was everywhere: in

my new research partner, in the bodies of the oil-covered penguins, in the shimmering meltwater dripping from icebergs. I returned home not sure I could ever go back again. But then I did, because it's where I feel closest to him. Where I can remember.

After the *Australis* disaster, my research had taken a new turn. It's no longer enough to study the effects of tourism and climate change on the penguin colonies in Antarctica. Now we have a whole new field of study—the effects of the shipwreck: the birds dead and injured by the fuel spill, the amount of plastic and other refuse they've ingested, how all of this affects their survival and reproduction.

A videographer on board the *Australis* produced a documentary about a year after the accident, capturing events I'd witnessed only in the aftermath. He had been filming on the bridge the moment the ship hit the iceberg that tore through its hull. He captured images of calm, blue glacial ice; the crew's easy chatter; the nervous jokes about uncharted waters. Then came the moment they knew they were going to hit ice, the captain yelling, *Hard to starboard*, in a desperate attempt to clear it.

And they nearly did. But this particular iceberg offered up a sharp underside that sliced a hundred-foot gash at the waterline.

The film's viewers will see the moment the ship hit—the flicker and shake of the camera, followed by utter silence on the bridge. Even after those first long, eerie moments, when the camera turned and fixed on the captain's face, he remained silent, his face so still it was nearly devoid of expression. He was not among the survivors.

We know that things got bad quickly—that the engine room flooded, that the malfunctions in the bulkhead doors caused four compartments to fill with icy water, that the electrical system and generators failed. The videographer filmed the passengers' terrified faces, many of them covered with blood and bruises after the impact had knocked them down or into furniture. He filmed the lifeboats being dropped, and he continued filming after a crew member stuck an angry hand into his lens. He captured the severe pitching of the boat as it tilted into the sea, the abandon-ship signal and the haunting silence that followed, punctuated by the cries of passengers and explosions from somewhere deep inside the ship. He captured the passengers rushing for lifeboats through air choked with smoke and fog, and the capsizing of those lifeboats in the wake of a calving glacier that roiled the sea around them. And, among the last to evacuate, he captured what were many passengers' last moments: sheets of fast ice shattered by the wave, flares drenching the sky and ice in a blaze of scarlet light, the creaks and groans inside the sinking ship.

I would not ever have watched the film unless Kate Archer had convinced me that it wasn't a *Titanic*-like disaster film but an environmental manifesto. As the one who financed the documentary, she made sure it captured all that is good about Antarctica, all that is precious and beautiful: the penguins, the whales, the eternal sunsets. When people ask me about the *Australis,* I tell them to watch the film.

Richard had left Kate wealthy. After her own daughter was born, she moved to Seattle, where a donation in excess of $4 million earned her a seat on the board of the Antarctic Penguins Project and allowed the organization to expand its small full-time staff, which now includes me. Kate visits Eugene frequently, often staying for weeks in my former cottage, and our daughters are growing up together. When I go to Seattle, Kelly and I stay with her, for as long as we can. When I'm asked to speak or teach, I try to bring Nick and Kelly with me. I want Kelly to be a good traveler, since I plan to take her south one day—and I want to do it before everything changes, before the ice melts, before we begin seeing the last of the Adélies.

In the airport, I hug her tight, until Nick touches my shoulder. "Final boarding call," he says. I'm always the last one on the plane.

I let Kelly go and straighten up, watching Nick palm the top of her head with his hand, which is swallowed up by brown curls. I kiss them both one last time, then turn and hand over my boarding pass. I walk backward toward the gate, waving at them until I have to turn the corner.

While we've made a family, Kelly and Nick and Gatsby and me, I don't think I'll ever stop looking for Keller. When I'm on the peninsula, I tell myself I'm here to rescue the penguins, yet I know that, each time, it's the penguins who rescue me. When the cruises visit Booth Island, I steal away in a Zodiac. I go to a desolate beach and climb up to a remote gentoo colony. There, I sit and I wait. Every time, I feel a moment of dread, wondering if this will be the season he does not appear. And then, I see him.

Admiral Byrd waddles over, turning his head sideways, showing me a round dark eye. I arrange my legs just so. When he is settled, I remove my gloves and stroke his smooth, dirty feathers.

mes, when I feel the weight of Admiral Byrd in my
'hat Keller is here with us. I think about the day
ɪ ɪɪ sit here with Kelly, instructing her to sit, still and quiet,
as her father had once instructed me—and I picture the look
on her face, in those green-flecked eyes that are all Keller,
when Admiral Byrd makes his appearance, then lets himself
tumble into her lap.

Because Keller's body now belongs to the Southern Ocean,
I like to believe we'll see him one day—that we'll experience
a fata morgana and glimpse him standing up amid a cluster
of penguins, his red bandanna around his throat, squinting
as the sun's reflection off the ice bounces into his eyes. That
he'll see us and smile. That he'll say, as he used to, *Fin del
mundo*, and we'll respond, *principio del todo*.

The end of the world, the beginning of everything.

ACKNOWLEDGMENTS

While the places in this novel—the islands of the Antarctic peninsula, the research stations—are real, I've taken a few fictional liberties, among them creating the Garrard penguin colony near McMurdo Station, which is loosely based on a real colony and actual circumstances but is otherwise fictional. The gentoo penguin Admiral Byrd is also fictional and was inspired by an overly friendly Magellanic penguin in the Punta Tombo colony in Argentina, named Turbo, who is beloved by the researchers and volunteers who have had the extraordinary experience of meeting him. (Visit www .penguinstudies.org to learn about the Center for Penguins as Ocean Sentinels and to follow Turbo on Twitter.) The Antarctic Penguin Project is a fictional organization inspired by the nonprofit Oceanites (www.oceanites.org), a nongovernmental, publicly supported organization whose scientific research in Antarctica helps foster education and conservation. Any inaccuracies throughout the novel, made inadvertently or for the sake of fiction, are my own.

I am grateful to all who made the existence of this book possible. Among them: Dr. Dee Boersma, who taught me about penguins from Antarctica to Argentina and whose research with the Center for Penguins as Ocean Sentinels is doing wonders for the conservation of these incredible animals.

Molly Friedrich, whose overall brilliance, keen insights, and tough editorial love helped get this novel ready for the world. A million thanks as well to Nichole LeFebvre, Lucy Carson, and Alix Kaye for being incredible readers and offering enthusiasm and support.

Liese Mayer, who is not only an amazing editor but an absolute joy to know and to work with. Great thanks, too, to the fantastic team at Scribner for such terrific work in every aspect of bookmaking.

Thanks to the Helen Riaboff Whiteley Center, which gave me the gift of time and space to write, and without which this book would still be a work in progress.

Thanks to the *Ontario Review*, which first published my short story "The Ecstatic Cry," from which *My Last Continent* eventually emerged.

Thanks to my family, for love and support. Most of all: John Yunker, for being there for every step of the journey, both on and off the page.

MY LAST
CONTINENT

MIDGE
RAYMOND

This reading group guide for My Last Continent *includes an introduction, discussion questions, and ideas for enhancing your book club. The suggested questions are intended to help your reading group find new and interesting angles and topics for your discussion. We hope that these ideas will enrich your conversation and increase your enjoyment of the book.*

INTRODUCTION

In this "original and entirely authentic love story" (Graeme Simsion, author of *The Rosie Project*), debut novelist Midge Raymond constructs the tenuous and complex relationship between two researchers, Deb Gardner and Keller Sullivan, as set against the imperiled Antarctic landscape.

For a few weeks each year, Deb and Keller escape their personal burdens and disappointments to be with each other, serving as expedition ship tour guides while they conduct research on the habits of the emperor and Adélie penguins that populate Antarctica. However, at the start of the latest season, Deb discovers that not only is Keller not a member of the expedition ship's staff, he is on a nearby cruise liner that has hit troubled water and is sinking fast.

Interweaving the genesis of Deb and Keller's relationship with its imperiled present, *My Last Continent* is a powerful voyage into love, loss, and the mysteries of the human heart.

1. In the first pages of *My Last Continent*, Deb offers the following analysis of why the *Australis* and Air New Zealand Flight 901 both crashed in Antarctica: "Each was felled by what its crew knew existed but was unable to see, or chose not to see" (pages 1–2). Do you think this is a self-aware comment on Deb's personal history or on Keller's final moments? Why do we feel the need to castigate others when analyzing tragedies in hindsight?

2. Consider your first impression of Deb and Keller's relationship coupled with Deb's belief that "we have fallen in love with each other as much as with Antarctica, and we have yet to separate ourselves, and what we are, from this place" (page 14). How did your opinion of their relationship change as you learned more about their history? Do you think Deb's assessment rings true throughout their relationship?

3. One of the major thematic points of Keller's story line is the concept of being changed by a journey. What were Keller's touchstones in his evolution from grief-stricken

lawyer to Antarctic researcher? Do you think it is possible to point to specific moments in his journey, or was it a more gradual development? What role, if any, did Deb have in all of this?

4. According to Keller, whereas previously he lived in blissful ignorance and was then caught unaware, in Antarctica "you know the risks—the hazards are tangible" (page 72). Was Keller truly always aware of the risks in Antarctica? Which way of living do you prefer?

5. Discuss the paradox of Antarctica as Midge Raymond presents it: a place that is attractive to tour groups due to its unique climate and wildlife, yet is faced with a constantly changing landscape due in part to those same tourists. What do you make of the give-and-take nature of environments like Antarctica that are both preserved and harmed by tourism?

6. Kate and Richard are presented as foils and mirrors for Deb and Keller. What similarities do you find between the two couples? Did you like one more than the other? Compare how the two couples relate to each other and their difficult relationships with the truth.

7. Icebergs and what is hidden are a dominant theme in the book. Discuss how the chronological structure and the way previously unknown facts and events were presented influenced your understanding of the characters and their motivation.

8. According to Deb, in Adélie penguin colonies, mothers focus on the chick that is most likely to continue the next generation (pages 162–163), a characterization she sees reflected in her own family dynamics. Would you consider Deb a reliable narrator in this instance? What sort of events may have shaded her understanding of her relationship with her mother?

9. Deb says to Kate, "It seems like there are two kinds of people who come to Antarctica. Those who have run out of places to go, and those who have run out of places to hide" (page 179). Do you think Deb really believes this? In which camp would you place Deb and Keller? Why do you think Deb doesn't talk to Kate about her love for the penguins and the natural landscape?

10. Keller's initial denunciation of tourism in Antarctica seems at odds with his later employment on the *Australis*, a cruise ship, only a year later. Why do you think he changed his mind? Is he rejecting his ideals in order to return to the continent?

11. How do you feel about Richard?

12. Consider the book's title, *My Last Continent*, and Keller's observation that explorers were obsessed with firsts and now society is obsessed with lasts (page 190). In what ways is Antarctica a "last continent" for those who visit? Why do you think the author chose this title?

ENHANCE YOUR BOOK CLUB

1. In the book, Keller describes his feelings toward Antarctica as *fernweh*, i.e., the German term for longing for somewhere you've never been (page 100). Discuss what places you feel *fernweh* toward and why you have never visited.

2. "Sometimes I wonder how long this alien invasion — the ships, the humans — can continue before the continent strikes back" (page 113). As a group, research what conservation measures are being undertaken to preserve Antarctica and the penguin colonies by groups such as the Oceanites (www.oceanites.org), Penguin Sentinels (www.penguinstudies.org), the Antarctic Ocean Alliance (www.antarcticocean.org), and the Antarctic and Southern Ocean Coalition (www.asoc.org) for more.

3. Penguin Watch offers ways to support Antarctic penguin colonies. Consider participating by observing and marking penguins, nests, eggs, and their neighbors in research images. For more information, visit www.penguinwatch.org.

4. To learn more about author Midge Raymond visit her website: www.MidgeRaymond.com.

A CONVERSATION
BETWEEN GRAEME SIMSION
AND MIDGE RAYMOND

What inspired *My Last Continent*?

When I visited Antarctica more than a decade ago, two things in particular stuck with me. One was the concern of the shipboard naturalists about the larger cruise ships that were beginning to visit the region. We were on a small expedition ship of around one hundred passengers; ships carrying thousands of passengers were venturing farther and farther south, which was troubling to them because if something were to happen to one of those ships, rescuers could be days away—and, given the extreme weather conditions and the distance from hospitals, this is an incredible risk. So I began to wonder what a catastrophic shipwreck in this region would look like.

The other thing that stuck with me was seeing a fellow passenger fall on the ice near a penguin colony. He was fine, fortunately, but seeing this happen reinforced the notion that, at the bottom of the world, you are at the mercy of the conditions and of the few people who are with you.

And of course, Antarctica is inspiring in and of itself—there is absolutely nothing else like it on the planet: whitewashed, freezing, uninhabited by humans, and filled with creatures that can't be found anywhere else.

For me, one of the strengths of the book is the way you juxtapose the harshness of Antarctica with the comfort and warmth that Deb and Keller find with each other. How did this love story come together? Did you always know how it would end, or did you discover it as you wrote?

I did have a vague idea of how the novel would end, but I discovered the details through the writing process. The love story came together when I knew Deb could only end up with someone who loved the continent as much as she did. For her, the work and the penguins always came first—and Keller came to feel the same way. Both of them had been unlucky in love in the past, and I liked the idea of them finding home not only in Antarctica but in each other.

Isolation is a recurrent theme in *My Last Continent*: the personal isolation that Deb and Keller experience, the isolation of penguins, Deb's hope to isolate the human footprint on the continent. . . . Is this a topic that's important to you?

I'm fascinated with the idea of isolation, particularly in these days of constant connectivity. I think it's important for we humans to isolate ourselves occasionally—to have time to recharge, to be quiet and still—for me, being in nature is the most invigorating way to disengage. I've also discovered, in recent years, that I need to get away from my phone and especially my Internet connection in order to write. I usually leave my house—sometimes just for a few hours, other times for days or weeks—and when I'm writing, I always take lots of walks outside to clear my brain and to hear myself think.

And, as much as I enjoy exploring natural places, I also believe it's especially important for wildlife to have territory that is free of human influence. Tourism isn't nearly as disruptive as commercial enterprises—for example, whales are still illegally hunted in the Southern Ocean, and krill, which both penguins and whales depend on for survival, are being taken by the hundreds of thousands of tons a year. So we desperately need marine protected areas in the Antarctic in order to keep the ecosystem in balance.

You write about two places you've visited/lived in real life: Antarctica and Oregon. How does place/landscape inform your fiction?

For me, place is essential to character, and in fact, Antarctica became a character of sorts in the writing of this novel. For me, every setting, whether an American city or an icy continent, has a personality, and where a character is from—and where he or she lives now—is so vital to me in understanding that character. That Deb is from the Midwest says as much about her as the fact that she settled on the West Coast and spends as much time as she can at the bottom of the world.

How did your work as a penguin researcher inform the novel?

On a personal level, being part of a penguin census at the Punta Tombo colony deepened my respect for working scientists—the work they do is so important, and also so challenging. The scientists who have made penguin research their life's work spend years, even decades, doing what I did for only a couple of weeks—crawling around looking into penguin burrows from dawn until sunset, weighing and measuring birds, taking showers only once a week with trucked-in water, and so much more: crunching data, publishing results, raising funds to continue everything they do.

It was also interesting for me to see all this from my decidedly nonscientific background; the researchers I met care deeply about the penguins, but they are more emotionally detached than I am, in a normal way that I think is necessary to do good science. They're used to seeing dead penguins, broken eggs, and other things that are par for the course in a day in the field but that I found unbearably sad. And this informed Deb's character quite a bit. She is unlike most scientists in that she cares for the birds on a level that probably isn't healthy; she anthropomorphizes them to an extent, and she is caught up in their fate not only scientifically but emotionally as well.

You've written about a continent that is undergoing rapid change—if you were to write a follow-up to *MLC* set ten years in the future, would Antarctica look the same?

I hope so. But I'm not sure. Right now scientists are forecasting that Antarctic ice melt could raise sea levels by three to ten feet by the end of this century—which could happen more slowly, or more rapidly, than predicted—and this would not only change Antarctica but the map of the entire world.

It would certainly affect the penguins, seals, whales, krill, and myriad other creatures who depend on sea ice.

Tourism is also increasing, and I hope it's managed well so that it doesn't one day look like the Caribbean, with boats everywhere you look. Fortunately, organizations such as IAATO are working at managing tourism to protect the environment and the animals.

If we as a society can make some serious global changes to combat climate change, if we create marine protected areas, and if we can limit tourism to small, educational expeditions, it's my hope that Antarctica could look very much the same in ten years. And perhaps even beyond.

Is there anything you particularly want readers to take away from the book?

Most important, I hope readers enjoy the journey. But I also hope that they fall in love with Antarctica and its creatures, as I have. It may be hard for some readers to fall in love with a cold, icy place. Yet I love that, through this novel, I can introduce several species of penguins and show how incredible they are, which in turn may inspire people to take great care of our planet, since the birds' future depends on it.

My Last Continent is about rescuers—not only in terms of the shipwreck but because Deb and Keller's work aims to save the penguins from the challenges they face. And we all have a role to play in saving the planet and its many vulnerable species.